DINAH MCCALL

STORM
WARNING

MIRA®

F
McC

0840.2176

ISBN 0-7394-1748-7

STORM WARNING

Printed in U.S.A.

As we are born, we learn to listen for the sound
of our mother's voice because we know it
to be the source of our pleasure and comfort—
that she will satisfy our hunger and take away our pain.

It is our first lesson in learning to love.

For some babies the sounds are not loving and kind.
The stroke of the mother's hand becomes
that which we associate with hunger and pain.
The depths of her despair are echoed in the shrill,
unanswered cries of her child.

It is the first lesson in learning to fear.

Then there are the babies whose mother's voice
is forever missing. They have no one to bond to,
no nourishment is shared. There is no soft voice
in the dark to take away their fears.

It is their first and last lesson that nobody cares.

* * *

I dedicate this book to the people who spend
their lives in the service of caring for children.
Whether you are a mother, another family member
or a social worker, or simply the good neighbor on the
block, you are forever blessed in the eyes of God
for caring for those who cannot care for themselves.

ACKNOWLEDGMENT

First, before I mention anything else, I want my readers to know that this is a work of fiction, and while there are many strides being made in the name of healing through hypnosis, the situation I have created in my story is purely fictional. I live with the hope that one day such a thing will be true, but for now the ability to heal completely through hypnosis is only a dream.

And now I must thank John Lehman, Quaker minister, licensed hypnotherapist and family counselor, for his generosity in helping me with certain aspects of this book. Any mistakes that are made in this book are mine, and the places where I chose to stretch the truth of the hypnotist's power were purely for the entertainment of the readers.

_____ Prologue _____

Upstate New York, 1979

Edward Fontaine stood at the doorway, watching the children on the playground while keeping an eye on the weather. As headmaster of Montgomery Academy, a small private school, it was his duty to oversee every aspect of the daily routine, including the welfare of the children.

Granted, his teachers were doing their part as they stood duty out on the playground, but Edward had a bird's eye view from the top of the steps. As he watched, he felt a shift in the wind and glanced up at the sky. The light, fluffy clumps of clouds that had been there earlier were now massing into something large and dark. Although the play period was not over, he didn't want to take a chance on one of the children being struck by lightning, so he hurried into his office and rang the bell. It echoed throughout the building and out on the grounds, and even though he was still inside, he could hear the collective shouts of the children's dismay.

As he reached the top steps, the first rumble of thunder shook the windows. The children's reluctance to end their play was replaced with frantic haste as the teachers began herding them inside.

"Hurry! Hurry!" Edward shouted, calling to the youngest children at the very farthest end of the grounds. "It's going to storm. You must come inside!"

Virginia Shapiro and her best friend, Georgia, had been at the top of the slide when the first bell rang. At six years old, their dilemma now became one of climbing back down the steps or sliding down and risking the wrath of having "played" when they were supposed to be going inside. When the second ripple of thunder shattered the sky above them, Virginia began to cry. Georgia took her by the hand, uncertain what to do.

Edward could tell the children were in trouble and bolted down the steps. As he ran, it occurred to him that he should be in better shape, but the thought disappeared with the first drops of rain upon his face.

"Come, children, come," he urged, standing at the foot of the slide. "It's all right. Just slide to me. We'll go inside together."

Georgia tugged at Virginia's hand, giving her a brave little smile.

"Come on, Ginny...we'll go together, like always."

Ginny sniffled and nodded, and moments later they went flying down the slick, metal surface and right into Mr. Fontaine's arms.

"That's my good girls," he said, quickly taking each one by the hand. "Now let's run. I'll bet I can beat you."

The girls squealed and pulled loose from his grasp as they tore off across the yard. He sighed with relief and then started after them at a jog, knowing full well he was going to be wet before he got back.

They were nowhere in sight as he entered the building. But as his eyes adjusted to the dimmer light, he saw them at the far end of the hall, scurrying toward the last room on the left.

He'd almost forgotten. Today was Thursday. The Gifted and Talented Class met on Thursdays. The niggle of doubt that crossed his mind was not the first he'd had as he watched the door close behind them. It wasn't as if he was allowing anyone to harm them. Quite the opposite. Those particular seven little girls had one thing in common that had garnered them access to the class. And the money he'd received as a "special endowment" for allowing the class to proceed was not something he could overlook. The fact that the parents didn't realize the true nature of the class often disturbed him, but he knew the children were not being harmed. Besides, it was already done, and that was that.

A strong gust of wind blew a curtain of rain against the backs of his legs. Turning his mind to more pertinent affairs, he quickly shut the doors of the main entrance and went to his office. There was always paperwork to be done.

Inside the last room on the left, seven little girls sat quietly in their respective chairs, watching for the teacher to begin. The glass in the windows rattled as thunder continued to rumble. They didn't hear the rain peppering against the windows or see the lightning as it began to flash. Their eyes were on the teacher, their minds focused on the sound of his voice.

That night, long after the children had gone home, the storm still raged. Wind-whipped trees bent low to the ground, their branches bowing in supplication to the greater strength of the storm.

Just before midnight, a great shaft of lightning came down from the sky, shattering wood and shingles alike as it pierced the roof of the school. Before anyone noticed, the school was completely engulfed in flames. By morning, there was nothing left but an exterior wall and a huge pile of smoldering timbers.

Edward Fontaine stood on the outskirts of the playground, looking at what was left of his school in disbelief. He didn't have the resources to start all over again, and going back into the classroom as a teacher didn't seem possible, either. His dream was finished. His heart had been broken.

Within the week, all the students had transferred, some to private schools, others moved into the public school system. The seven who'd been chosen for the gifted class were mainstreamed into first-grade classes in three different districts, and life went on. They learned. They grew. And every night their parents put them to bed, unaware of the time bomb that ticked in their heads.

1

Present Day, Seattle, Washington

"Mommy, Mommy. I hungry. Pwease a cracker."
Twenty-seven-year-old Emily Jackson looked up
from her computer and then glanced at the clock. She
rolled her eyes in dismay as she bolted up from her
chair to attend to her two-year-old son. Of course he
was hungry. It was thirty minutes after twelve. Being
a stay-at-home mommy and still keeping her job as
an accountant hadn't been as easy as she'd first imagined, although using a computer to interface with her
clients had been a godsend.

"Just a minute, sweetie," she called, handing him
an animal cracker and giving him a kiss as she hurried
to the fridge. There were plenty of leftovers, and he
was eating just about everything now. It wouldn't take
but a minute to heat something up in the microwave.

She had three covered bowls and his bottle sitting
on the cabinet and was reaching inside the fridge for
the fourth bowl when the phone began to ring.

"It never fails," she muttered, as she reached for the phone instead. "Jackson residence. Yes...this is Emily. Who's calling please?"

There was a brief moment of silence on the other end of the line, and then she heard the distant sound of thunder and a series of bells—like the chimes of an elaborate doorbell. At the sound, her mind went blank. She turned her face to the wall with the receiver still held to her ear. Cold air from the open refrigerator door wafted against the backs of her legs, but she didn't feel it. In her mind, she was already gone.

Moments later, she laid the phone down on the counter, picked up the box of animal crackers and a bottle of milk for the baby, and then lifted him in her arms. Silently, she carried him to his bed, handed him the box of crackers and his bottle, and walked away without looking back.

The unusual treat was enough to satisfy the hungry child's cries. As he was eating his cookies, Emily was getting into her car and then backing out of the drive. A neighbor across the street waved, but Emily didn't seem to see her. The neighbor thought nothing of it and had started to go about her business when she noticed the front door to Emily's house was ajar.

"Oh my," she said, and then hastened across the street to do her neighborly duty.

When she reached the porch, a spurt of nosiness

reared its ugly head. Instead of just closing the door, she thought of looking inside. What would it hurt? Just a little peek.

With one guilty glance over her shoulder, she stepped inside and then closed the door behind her. She stood for a moment, admiring the color scheme and the plump, overstuffed furniture in the living room to her right. Taking a couple more steps toward the center of the house, she stopped to admire the view through the patio doors beyond. As she did, she heard a noise coming from the bedrooms. How stupid of her. Just because Emily left, that didn't mean the house was empty. Her husband, Joe, who was an air traffic controller, must have the day off.

"Joe! Joe! It's me, Helen. Emily accidentally left the front door open and I came over to shut it."

No one answered, yet she could still hear the underlying sound of chatter.

"Joe? It's me. Helen. Are you decent?"

A shrill squeal startled her. It was then she thought of the baby. She'd just assumed that he'd been in the car with Emily, because she rarely went anywhere without him. She started toward the hallway, fearful that at any moment her neighbor would come flying out of some room and wanting to know what the hell she was about. But the farther she walked, the more certain she became that Joe was not there.

When she stepped into the baby's room, she gasped in shock. He was sitting in the middle of his bed with a box of animal crackers in one hand and his bottle in the other.

"Cookie?" he asked, and offered her the box.

"Oh my God," she muttered, and picked him up from his crib. Surely this wasn't what it seemed? She would have bet her life that Emily Jackson wasn't the kind of mother who would go off and leave an unattended baby behind.

With the baby on her hip, she began hurrying through the rooms. By the time she got to the kitchen, she knew something was terribly wrong. Food was sitting out on the cabinet. The phone was off the hook, and the refrigerator door was standing open. She started to put the room to rights when something told her not to touch a thing. Instead, she grabbed a handful of the baby's diapers and took him with her as she left.

By the time Helen reached her own home with the intention of calling Joe at work, Emily Jackson was on a collision course with destiny.

Emily drove through the Seattle traffic with no thought for care or safety, running red lights and taking corners on two wheels. By the time she reached the Narrows Bridge, the entourage of cop cars behind her equaled, if not surpassed, the attention the L.A. police had given to O.J.'s infamous run. The police didn't know it yet, but she had reached her destination. A cordon of police cars was at the other end of the bridge, a roadblock firmly in place, with traffic behind them backed up for blocks.

But Emily didn't make it to the other side of the bridge. About halfway across, she suddenly pulled to a stop and put the car in Park. She was out and walking to the side of the bridge before the first cop car behind her could pull to a standstill. And by the time that officer was running and shouting for her to halt, she had climbed over the edge. After that, everything started to happen in slow motion.

People were shouting at her not to jump, making promises they could never keep, but it was nothing but a roar in Emily's ears. She lifted her arms to the side as if she were a bird about to take flight, turned her face up to heaven and then fell.

End over end, tumbling quietly, with nothing but the wind whistling around her ears—doing as she'd been told.

The shock of her death reverberated throughout Seattle for all of three days before it was replaced by another equally tragic story. She left behind a puzzled and grieving husband, and a little boy who cried for a mother who would never come home.

One week later, Amarillo, Texas

Josephine Henley, Jo-Jo to the customers of Haley's Bar, was dodging hands and slinging drinks when Raleigh, the bartender, yelled at her across the room.

"Hey, Jo-Jo, you got a phone call."

She waved to him, indicating that she'd heard, as she pocketed her tips from a couple of drunk truckers who kept begging for a kiss.

"Come on, Jo-Jo, just one for the road," Henry said.

"Not only no, but hell no," Jo-Jo said. "You're married."

"Yeah, but I'm also lonely."

"You're not lonely, you're horny, and I'm not about to oblige."

"Then give me back my five dollars," he said teasingly.

"Oh no, I earned that. Besides, it would cost you a hell of a lot more than five bucks to get me on my back."

"How much?" he asked, his interest suddenly reviving.

"You don't have enough money to buy me, mister. Now back off. I've got a phone call."

She evaded his grasp and made her way across the floor to the phone.

"A bourbon and water," she said, turning in a new drink order, then turned to the phone on the wall, picked up the dangling receiver and put it to her ear.

"Hello? Hello?"

She couldn't hear a thing for all the noise and put

her hand over the mouthpiece as she turned toward the room.

"Hold it down a little!" she yelled. "I can't hear myself think."

She tried again. "Hello. Yes, this is Josephine Henley."

As she waited, she thought she heard thunder and turned abruptly, trying to remember if she'd rolled the windows up on her car. Then another sound followed, and as it did, the frown between her eyebrows faded and her chin dropped toward her chest, almost as if she'd gone to sleep. She stood without speaking, her eyes closed, her shoulders slumped. Raleigh noticed and frowned. It wasn't like Jo-Jo to be this still. He touched her on the shoulder.

"Hey, kid, is anything wrong?"

She didn't respond, other than to suddenly drop the phone and try to get past him.

"Here's your bourbon and water," he said, handing her the tray with her new order, but she pushed him aside, and as she did, the tray fell to the floor with a clatter.

"Hey, was that my drink?" someone yelled.

"Shut the hell up," Raleigh countered, and grabbed Jo-Jo by the arm. "What's wrong with you? Didn't you hear what I said?"

Then he saw her face, and the look in her eyes stopped his heart. Later he would say it was like looking into a room, only no one was there.

Jo-Jo was moving toward the exit when Raleigh panicked and yelled at one of the men to stop her, but the order got lost in the noise and confusion.

"Hey, Jo-Jo! Is something wrong? Come back!" he yelled, and then came out from behind the bar and started after her before the men in the room realized anything was wrong.

By the time Raleigh got to the door, more than half of them were following.

He stopped outside the doorway, scanning the crowded lot for a sign of where she'd gone. Her car was still parked against the north side of the building, so wherever she was, she'd gone on foot. He started moving through the cars and trucks, shouting out her name.

"Jo-Jo! Jo-Jo! Come on back inside, honey. If you're feeling bad, I'll have one of the boys run you on home."

She didn't answer, and he couldn't see her. By now, more than half a dozen men were running amok between the parked vehicles, calling out her name. Raleigh was about to chalk it up to some sort of womanly fit when he heard someone scream her name. The fear in the voice made his blood run cold. He started to run, past a line of cars and a one-ton dually truck, then between two eighteen-wheelers, emerging on the other side facing the highway before he saw her.

She was running in the fast lane of the highway with her arms out at her side, like a child pretending to fly. And the faster she ran, the closer she came to the headlights of an oncoming truck.

"Jesus God!" he groaned, and started to run, although he knew he would be too late.

The scent of burning rubber filled the air as the trucker hit his brakes, but she'd come out of nowhere, far too late for him to stop. The screeching sound of locking brakes overwhelmed the thump her body made as it slammed against the truck. And then she was flying through the air like a broken doll, coming to rest in the center median with a solid thud.

The men stared in disbelief. Raleigh turned to the one nearest him.

"Go call 911!" he yelled, and then began flagging down cars so they could cross.

The homicide detective who worked the case wrote it up as a suicide. Case closed.

Except for a bartender named Raleigh, who kept swearing she'd been just fine until she'd taken that call.

Two days later, Chicago, Illinois

Twenty-eight-year-old Lynn Goldberg had reached a benchmark in her career as a criminal defense attorney. All her life she'd been told she was too pretty to ever be taken seriously as a lawyer, but she'd ignored the naysayers and followed her heart. Today she'd proven that she wasn't just another pretty face.

She'd won her first murder case, and it felt damned good. What was even better was that she was convinced the man she'd gotten off was actually innocent, which, in her chosen line of work, wasn't always going to be the case.

She tossed some files that she wanted to review before morning into her briefcase, then slammed it shut. She had thirty-six minutes to get across town and meet her husband, Jonathan, for dinner and drinks. He didn't know it yet, but tonight she was paying. She could hardly wait to see his face when she told him that she'd won.

With one last look around her office, she picked up the phone and called a cab. By the time she got down from the fifteenth floor of the office building where the law firm was located, the cab should be waiting. Smoothing her hands down the front of her dark, pinstriped suit, she draped her raincoat over her arm and was reaching for her briefcase when the phone began to ring.

"No way. My day is over," she muttered and started toward the door.

But the ringing persisted, and it occurred to her that it might be Jonathan. It would be awful if she went across town only to find out he'd had to cancel. With that in mind, she hurried back to her desk and picked up the phone.

"Hello? Yes, this is Lynn Goldberg."

There was a moment of silence, and then the far-off sound of distant thunder. She shivered and glanced toward the windows, thankful she'd thought to bring her raincoat. And then another sound was overlaid upon the thunder—the distinct sound of chimes being struck in slow succession. Within the same breath of identifying the sounds her eyelids drooped and her chin dropped toward her chest. Her shoulders slumped forward as she listened.

The light began to flash on her phone, indicating another incoming call, but she didn't see it, and if she had, would have been incapable of making the decision to answer. Instead, she quietly laid down the phone and walked out of the office toward the elevator.

Gregory Mitchell, a fellow attorney, looked up as she passed by his desk.

"Hey, Lynn, I didn't know you were still here. Congratulations on the win."

She acted as if she hadn't heard him. Puzzled by her behavior, he watched her walk out of the office. He thought little of it until he realized she'd left her briefcase and raincoat on the floor by the doorway. Knowing she would have to come fifteen flights back up to get them, he started after her on the run, thinking he would catch her at the elevator. They would have a good laugh, and then she'd be back on her way.

But when he reached the elevator, it was going up rather than down, which made no sense. The top floor of the building had been vacated and was under reconstruction.

"Damn it, Lynn, where's your head at?" he muttered, waiting for the car to come back and expecting her to get out with a silly grin on her face. But when the car came back, it was empty.

Ignoring a quick spurt of anxiety, he got into the car and went up, telling himself all the while that there had to be a rational explanation for what she'd done. But when the doors opened and he exited into the hallway, all he could hear was the wind whistling through plastic-bound openings where the dark tinted windows had yet to be installed.

"Lynn? Lynn? Where are you? It's me. Greg!"

There was a rustling sound coming from the far end of the hallway, and he started toward it, still expecting her to come fumbling out from around the scaffolding while trying to talk her way out of her faux pas.

Instead, he walked into a large corner office, only to find it empty. Frustrated, he started to turn back when, out of the corner of his eye, he thought he saw movement. He started toward the plastic-shrouded corner where a bank of windows would be, and as he did, he suddenly realized someone was on the scaffolding outside the plastic.

"It can't be," he muttered, but he started to run, his gut telling him there was no one else it could be.

He tore back the plastic, then grunted in disbelief. Lynn was standing on an I-beam sixteen floors above the city. Wind gusting around the corners was pulling at the hem of her jacket, billowing up beneath it and then plastering it to her body.

"My God, Lynn! What do you think you're doing? Get back in this minute before you fall."

Again she seemed deaf to his voice. To his horror, she suddenly lifted her arms out from her sides, like a conductor telling his orchestra to wait. Greg panicked. This was a situation that was out of control. He reached into his pocket for his cell phone, only to realize it was lying on his desk. As scared as he'd ever been in his life, he still couldn't stand there and do nothing. He started to crawl out the window, talking as calmly as he could, when he really wanted to scream.

"Lynn, look at me. Don't look down, okay? You're going to take my hand, and we're going to come back inside. You don't want to—"

In the middle of his sentence, she suddenly looked up at the sky and then walked into thin air. Greg would remember later that she had smiled as she fell—her arms open wide. He didn't see her hit the pavement. He was on his knees throwing up.

The incident barely made the papers. In a city the size of Chicago, a jumper was old news.

The next night, near Denver, Colorado

Frances Waverly was convinced, as she had been off and on for the last five years, that her marriage to

Charlie had been a huge mistake. It didn't matter what she did, in his eyes it was wrong. He spent all day yelling and griping, and then, the minute the sun went down, wanted to crawl in her pants. He couldn't understand why she didn't want him to touch her and was convinced she was having an affair.

"Affair!" Frankie screamed. "Right now I'm so sick of men I wouldn't even have Donald Trump and all his millions, not that he'd be interested in someone like me. You've made me old before my time, with all your whining and griping, and I've had enough! Do you hear me? I've had enough!"

Charlie grabbed her by the arm. It wasn't anything he hadn't heard before, and he was tired and wanted to go to bed.

"Oh, shut the hell up, Frankie. You ain't got nothin' to cry about. You got a nice house and a nearly new car. You don't want for nothin'. All's I ask for is my husbandly due. You're my wife. I got a right to make love to you."

Frankie's laugh was a wild, angry shriek. "Love? You don't know the first thing about love. All you do is take and take. You couldn't give if your life depended on it."

"That ain't so!" Charlie yelled. "Why, I gave you—"

In the middle of a shout, the phone began to ring. Frankie snatched the receiver from the cradle, willing to talk to anybody, even one of those stupid telemarketers, rather than listen to another syllable of Charlie Waverly's words.

"Waverly residence," she snapped, and when Charlie would have snatched the phone out of her hand, she slapped him away and turned her back. "Yes, this is Frances Waverly."

"Damn it, Frankie, hang up. We're in the middle of somethin' important here. Tell whoever it is to call back."

But Frankie didn't respond. Instead, she suddenly leaned against the wall and went limp. For a moment Charlie thought she was going to faint, and then her eyes closed and her chin dropped.

"What?" he snapped, trying to get her attention, imagining every kind of disaster had suddenly befallen one of their family. "Who is it? Is it Mom? Is Daddy all right?"

Frankie didn't respond, and his panic increased. As he watched, he saw a tear roll down her face. Suddenly he was sorry. Sorry for the fight and for making her mad.

"Look, honey, whatever it is, it'll be all right," he said. "I'm here."

He slid a hand beneath her hair and gave her neck a squeeze. Instead of a forgiving smile, she laid the phone down on the table and walked past him as if he'd become invisible. When she picked up her car keys and opened the door, he began to panic in earnest.

"Frankie! Wait! Where are you going? I'll go with you."

She walked off the porch into the night. He reached for the phone.

"Hello? Hello? Who is this? What the hell did you just say to my wife?"

He got nothing but a dial tone for his trouble. Dropping the receiver back on the cradle, he followed Frankie outside. But to his surprise, she was already in her car and backing out of the drive.

"Frances! Goddamn it! I told you to wait!" he yelled, but she was already gone. Grabbing his own car keys out of his pocket, he jumped into his truck and began to follow.

One mile passed, and he kept right on her bumper, honking and blinking his headlights in an effort to make her stop. She didn't act as if she even knew he was there. Another mile came and went, and he was beginning to get scared. This had to be really bad news for her to behave in this way. When he realized they were approaching the railroad crossing, he began to breathe a little easier. The warning lights were already flashing, and the arms had come down, blocking off the traffic at the crossing until the train could pass. Thank God, he thought. He'd talk to her there.

Accelerating a little, he started down the hill at a good pace, his confidence returning. It wasn't until he was at the foot of the hill that he realized Frankie's brake lights weren't on. In fact, she was driving even faster than before. Then, in the glow from his headlights, he suddenly saw one of her arms reach out the window, and he realized she didn't have her hands on the wheel! What in hell was she trying to prove!

He began to mutter in a singsong chant. "Stop, Frances, stop!"

He was wasting his breath.

In disbelief, he watched as she drove through the warning arm and into the side of the passing train. The car exploded, sending burning metal flying into the air. Charlie slammed on his brakes as a part of the fender suddenly hit the windshield of his truck. It was then that he started to scream.

They buried what was left of her three days later. They would have done it sooner, but the day after the accident, they were still picking up the pieces of her body. No one in the family could shed any light on the phone call, but Charlie was convinced it was the reason she was dead. It had to be. Otherwise, he would have to accept his behavior as the reason for her suicide, and he couldn't live with the guilt of that on his conscience.

One week later, Oklahoma City, Oklahoma

Marsha Butler slid into the passenger side of her best friend's car and gave her a friendly smile.

"Gosh, Allison, I really appreciate you coming by to pick me up. My car's been in the shop all week. Thank goodness it's finally ready."

Allison Turner grinned. "No problem, sweetie. Besides, I've got to deposit my paycheck at the bank. Don't want any of those bills I just mailed to start bouncing."

Marsha grinned back. "Don't I know it."

Allison came to a stop, then took a right turn onto Air Depot Drive, ever careful of the Saturday traffic.

"Now, which garage did you tell me it's at?" she asked.

"Hugley's, just before the corner of Reno and Air Depot."

"Oh yes, I know the one you mean. Did they find out what was wrong, or just give you the runaround and charge you an arm and a leg?"

Marsha sighed. "Who knows? You know how women are treated at places like this. This is one of those times when I wish I was still married." Then she grinned. "But not bad enough to wish I had Terry back. The louse."

They laughed in unison, and the moment passed. A couple of minutes later, Marsha pointed.

"There it is," she said. "Take the first turn on your right."

"Got it," Allison said, and began signaling a lane change. As she did, the cell phone in the seat beside her started to ring.

"Get that for me, will you?" she asked.

Marsha quickly obliged.

"Hello? No...this isn't Allison. She's behind the wheel at the moment. Will you please wait?"

"Thanks," Allison said, as she turned into the station.

"Just let me off anywhere here," Marsha said.

"I'll wait until you make sure it's ready."

"Oh, the garage already called me, or I wouldn't have dared risk the trip."

"Just the same, I'll wait," Allison said.

"Thanks, I owe you," Marsha said, and got out of the car.

As soon as her friend left, Allison locked the doors behind her and answered the phone.

"Hello, this is Allison, thank you for waiting. Hello? Hello?"

Her eyes widened as she took a quick breath; then, just as suddenly, they began to close. Her head dropped down as if she'd dozed off, but the phone was still pressed to her ear.

Marsha was paying for her car when she noticed that Allison was still in the lot. She smiled, thinking to herself what good friends they'd become. Moments later, she was in her car and driving toward the street. She paused beside Allison's car and honked to get her attention, but Allison didn't move.

Marsha frowned and started to get out, then noticed Allison was still on the phone. She hesitated, afraid it was personal, and started to leave. But there was something about the way Allison was sitting that made her nervous. That limp, almost lifeless posture could mean she'd just gotten bad news.

On impulse, she got out of the car and knocked on the window.

"Allison! It's me. Are you all right?" She tried to open the door, but it was locked. "Allison! Allison!"

Allison didn't respond. Didn't move. Marsha was starting to get scared when Allison suddenly lifted her head. Laying the phone in the seat beside her, she put the car into gear and accelerated. It was only because Marsha jumped back in time that she wasn't run over. Marsha stared in disbelief as Allison's car shot out across two lanes of traffic, barely missing being broadsided twice.

She screamed. "Allison! Watch out!" But the warning went unheeded. Marsha watched in shock as Allison Turner drove straight beneath the underbelly of a gasoline tanker. Cars began sliding sideways in an effort to miss the oncoming pileup, while drivers who had already stopped were out of their cars and running, aware of what was about to happen. Marsha had one moment of clear vision just before the impact, and she would have sworn Allison's arms were stretched horizontal to her body, as if trying to embrace impending death.

The impact of the cars, metal to metal, rocked the

air where Marsha stood, and then the blast, which came a half second later, blew her backward against the hood of her car. She was still screaming when the ambulances started to arrive.

2

One week later, Sacred Heart Convent—
upstate New York

Five years ago, Georgia Dudley's life had come to rest. After four separate jobs in two years and struggling to find her place in the world, the certainty of where she should be had come to her in a dream. Her family had been in shock—her boyfriend of the moment in grief over her sudden decision. But for Georgia, it had been a true moment of grace.

She was going to become a nun.

For a woman who'd partied and tasted a lot of the pleasures of the flesh at an early age, it was an about-face that no one believed. But she'd come through the fire of her salvation, cleansed in heart and soul and truly happy for the first time in her life. Now, as Sister Mary Teresa, residing at Sacred Heart Convent in upstate New York, she was in her element.

Still feisty, but with God always in mind, she tore through life with verve and joy. She was a favorite among the Sisters. Even Mother Superior had a twinkle in her eye when Sister Mary was around. And now, just coming back from her first sabbatical, Sister Mary Teresa was full of herself and of God, and ready to reinvent the world.

Mother Superior looked up from her desk, breaking into a rare smile of welcome as the young nun entered the main office.

"So...you've come home," the Mother Superior said.

Sister Mary laughed and opened her arms out wide.

"Yes...yes...and it's a blessing to be here, I can assure you. Oh, Mother Superior, it was grand! I saw the Pope. I kissed his ring! And the glory of Rome! It was like something out of a movie. Why, I had no idea that everything was so...so..."

Mother Superior smiled. "It's the antiquity of it all that gets to you, isn't that right?"

Sister Mary clapped her hands. "Yes! That's it! It's the antiquity. You stand on those streets and think of the centuries that the city has endured and the countless millions of people who've stood on the very places where you are walking, and you feel so small and humbled."

"Exactly how one should feel."

Sister Mary smiled. "Yes, I know. I'm still too full of myself. It's a burden I bear. But I do it with a glad heart."

Mother Superior gave the young nun another rare

grin. "And that heart is appreciated by us all," she said softly. "But on to other matters. You have mail. It's on Father Joseph's desk in the other room. Why don't you retrieve it before he comes back? That way he won't be interrupted later."

"Yes, Mother. Thank you, Mother," Sister Mary said, and bolted toward the door to the connecting office.

"Walk, Sister, walk," the Mother cautioned.

Sister Mary skipped once and giggled, then slowed her run to long strides as she went inside to get her mail.

"I've taken my bags to my room," she called back over her shoulder. "As soon as I unpack, I'll get to my duties."

Mother Superior smiled and then shook her head. "It's almost three. There's really no need to worry about duties until tomorrow. Go unpack your things. Enjoy your mail and get yourself acclimatized to the time change by going to bed early. We'll start off fresh in the morning."

Sister Mary giggled again. "Yes, Mother, and thank you, thank you. Oh...it's just so good to be back."

She flew out of the room as fast as she'd come in, her veil and her habit flying out behind her like a sail at full mast.

Mother Superior shook her head and then went back to her work. The child was spirited, that was all, and there was nothing wrong with good spirit. They could use more women like her in God's service.

Sister Mary plopped onto her bed, oblivious to the spartan atmosphere of her room as she dug through her mail.

"Oh, marvelous! A letter from Mother as well as one from Tommy."

Tommy was the brother closest to herself in age. She'd followed his every footstep as a child, forcing herself on him and his friends until they'd had to accept her as the royal pain that she was, and yet part of the lot. Excited about news from home, she ripped into his letter first, expecting to read stories of her newest nephew's escapades. Her hopes were soon dashed as she started to read.

Sis...I seem to remember you were in school for a short time with Josephine Henley, right? The reason I know is I hung out with her older brother Sammy until they moved. Anyway, I got some bad news from him the other day. It seems Jo-Jo, who had been living in Amarillo, committed suicide. Just walked out into the path of an oncoming truck. It's all so sad. The family can't believe it. Says she was happy and doing well, but who knows, right? Anyway, I've enclosed a clipping of the newspaper article that Sammy sent me. Sorry to be the bearer of bad news, but I thought you'd want to know.

She scanned the clipping in disbelief, then dropped the letter onto her lap. Her heart was aching for the family and for the little girl she remembered so well. Making a mental note to say prayers for both Jo-Jo and her family, she picked up her mother's letter, confident it would contain better news.

She was wrong.

Georgia, darling...oh, sorry, I suppose you don't go by that name anymore. I'm happy for your life, but I can't bring myself to call you Sister Mary, so forgive me, sweetheart, if I digress.

Anyway, I've been busy. Volunteering a couple of days a week at the hospital. You should see those "pink lady" outfits they expect us to wear. They're too tight across the hips and too big in the bust for me. Or maybe it's me that's out of whack. Who knows? Oh, Aaron Spaulding said the next time I saw you to tell you hello. You know, he's vice-president of the bank where he works now. He would have made a good husband. It's too bad you broke up with him while he was still a teller. Oh...did I mention he's still a bachelor? Although I suppose that's of no interest to you anymore.

Sister Mary grinned. Her mother, ever the Protestant, was still in shock that her only daughter had not

only become Catholic, but had taken on the veil. She
went back to the letter with interest.

*Another bit of news that I thought you might not
know. Remember little Emily Patterson? She
married that Jackson boy and they moved to Seattle? Well...her mother still lives down the
block, so that's how I know. Anyway, it was the
saddest thing. Emily is dead. I'm so sorry to give
you this news, because I remember you used to
play together out on the sidewalk in front of our
house after school.*

*Anyway, you wouldn't believe! Maybe you
should say a prayer for her soul, considering
what she's done and all. But they say she committed suicide. Yes! Jumped off some bridge right
into the water without a thought for her baby or
husband. Frankly, it's hard to believe, but you
never know what children are going to grow up
to be. After all, I would never have imagined I'd
raise a child...my only daughter...who would
turn herself into a nun. Not that it's bad. But it
wasn't expected. I'm enclosing a clipping from
the Seattle paper about the incident. You can
read for yourself. Call me sometime if they'll let
you. I always think of you behind those stone
walls as if you were in prison, although I'm sure
it's not so. Is it? You do get to call when you
want to, don't you?*

Sister Mary's hands had started to shake. This was more than she could handle. Without finishing the rest of the letter, she dropped to her knees by the side of her bed and began to pray in earnest, sick at heart for the loss of her friends and the families they'd left behind.

Night had finally come to Sacred Heart. Vespers were over and Sister Mary Teresa had retired to her room with the rest of her mail as yet unopened.

She sat down on her bed and then opened the drawer to the small, bedside table, silently dropping the letters from her mother and brother inside. As she closed the drawer, she couldn't help but feel as if she'd symbolically buried two old friends. Glancing down at the stack of letters yet to be opened, she felt an odd sense of dread. Impulsively, she started to slip her thumb beneath the flap of the top envelope and then changed her mind and set all the mail aside. Her heart was heavy, her spirit exceedingly low. There was no room for anything else inside her tonight. But as her spirits dropped, she knew right where to go for revival. She reached for her Bible and, with a heartfelt sigh, whispered a quick prayer and then opened it, seeking comfort between the lines of the ancient text.

Time passed—time in which an acceptance of the news had settled within her—and then a knock sounded on the door.

"Come in," she said softly.

The door swung inward. Mother Superior stood silhouetted against the shadows of the hall beyond.

"I saw your light," she said. "Are you ill?"

Sister Mary sighed. "At heart," she said, quietly closing the Bible she'd been reading and laying it next to her bed.

"Can I help?"

"Pray for the lost," Sister Mary answered, thinking of the souls of two friends who would forever be lost to the Lord.

"Go to bed, child. Tomorrow is another day."

Sister Mary nodded.

The door closed behind the old nun. Sister Mary stared at the doorknob until her eyes began to burn; then she stood and began to get ready for bed. Mother Superior was right. Tomorrow *was* another day.

The same night, St. Louis, Missouri

Virginia Shapiro turned off the water and stepped out of the shower, reaching for a bath towel as she turned toward the full-length mirror on the back of the bathroom door. Steam from her bath had fogged the surface and was beginning to run in small rivulets down the glass. She thought about cleaning it off but was in too big a hurry. Wrapping her wet hair in the towel, she quickly reached for another with which to dry. A few quick swipes of the towel against her body and she was out of the bathroom and heading toward her closet, ignoring the lingering dampness of her long, lanky limbs. The DNA she'd been allotted in life had not allowed for excess in any form, and while many women would willingly have traded her for her tall, svelte figure, it was a great source of disgust to Ginny that she could easily go without a bra and no one would notice. The only bounce to Ginny Shapiro was in her step. Jiggling was a part of femininity that had passed her by, and she had yet to forgive her mother for marrying a man whose inseam was almost double his waist size.

A small clock in the hallway suddenly chimed. She spun, a dress in one hand and a pair of shoes in the other, as she glanced at the time.

Oh no! Quarter to five. Joe would be there any minute.

With jerky movements, she flung the clothes on her bed and began digging underwear from the dresser. Within the space of five minutes, she was back in the bathroom, peering through the drying streaks she'd made on the mirror as she hastily applied her makeup.

Flinging a lipstick down on the counter, she grabbed a hair dryer, turning it on full blast. Her straight, shoulder-length hair was a mass of still-damp tangles when she heard the doorbell chime. With one last look at herself in the mirror, she finger-combed her hair into a semblance of order, blew herself a kiss in the mirror and made a run for the door.

Just before she turned the doorknob, she took a

deep breath, rolled her eyes at the absurdity of making such a fuss over a dinner date with someone who would never be more than a friend, and then flung the door wide.

"I hope you're hungry. I'm starved, and I would hate to eat more than you," she said.

Joe Mallory grinned. "You always eat more than me."

Ginny arched an eyebrow as she shouldered her purse.

"That will cost you dessert," she claimed, and slammed the door shut behind her.

Moments later they were in the elevator and on their way down to the street where Joe had parked. Sounds of their laughter echoed up the elevator shaft as they emerged arm in arm. They were too far away to hear the sudden strident ringing of Ginny's phone and then the message on her answering machine as the call was picked up.

This is Virginia Shapiro. Leave a message after the beep.

The beep sounded, but no message was forthcoming. Long moments of silence passed before the connection was broken. It didn't matter. The call would be made again. There was still time.

The next morning, Sister Mary Teresa's hands were shaking as she reached for the receiver to make her call. The letters in her lap and the one e-mail she'd received from a distant cousin were a truth she couldn't ignore. Five women from her first-grade class had committed suicide, all within the space of a couple of months.

And there was an odd twist to the incidents that she hadn't realized until she'd made her condolence calls to the five women's families. To the last one, they'd supposedly been fine until receiving a simple telephone call. But what horrible news could they possibly have received that would drive them to such destruction? It didn't make sense. Added to that was the fact that those names all rang another bell in her memory, and she knew who to call for answers.

She took a deep breath and then punched in the numbers. When she heard her mother's voice on the other end of the line, she felt an overwhelming urge to be a child again—to lay her head in her mother's lap and wait for her to make everything right. Then she stifled the weakness and put a lilt in her voice when, in truth, she wanted to cry.

"Mother! It's me."

Edna Dudley grinned. "Darling! You're back! How was Rome?"

"Wonderful, and so spiritually rejuvenating. Say, Mother, I would love to visit longer, but I'm late now. We're going to Children's Hospital this morning, and I don't want the van to leave without me, but I need a favor."

"Anything," Edna said.

"Do you remember where my old yearbook is from Montgomery Academy?"

"I'm not sure, but I think it's still on a shelf in your room. Do you want me to look?"

Sister Mary hesitated.

"It won't take a minute," Edna said. "I'm already upstairs."

"Then yes, would you please? It's important."

Edna laid down the phone.

Sister Mary could hear her mother's receding footsteps and then, a minute later, the loud, positive clip of shoes against the floor. She could just picture her mother's stride on the shining hardwood in the old upstairs hall.

"Yes, it's here," Edna said.

Sister Mary sighed with relief. "Okay, great! Now open it up and look for our class picture. There will be a smaller picture right below it."

"Just a minute," Edna muttered. "I need to lay down the phone."

Sister Mary glanced at the clock over the office door and then said a quick prayer.

"Yes! Here it is," Edna said. "Oh...I'd forgotten how tiny you girls were at six. You and that little Shapiro girl were inseparable. I seem to remember she's working for a newspaper now, is that right?"

Sister Mary took a deep breath, trying to make herself stay calm when all she wanted to do was scream at her mother to stop chatting. People were dying, and she didn't know why.

"Yes, she's a reporter for a paper in St. Louis," she said. "I got a Christmas card from her last year. Now, could you read off the names of the girls who were in that special class with me?"

"Is that the little picture right below the one of the entire class?" Edna asked.

"Yes. Please, Mother, I'm in a hurry."

"Okay, here goes. Do you have a pen?"

"Mother...please...just read."

"Let's see, there's Emily Patterson, Josephine Henley, Lynn Bernstein, Frances Bahn, Allison Turner, Virginia Shapiro and you. Seven in all."

Sister Mary had to swallow to keep from screaming. For some, names had changed due to marriages, but her memory hadn't failed her. Every one of the women who'd died had been a part of that class.

"Is there anything else you need, dear?" Edna asked.

"Yes. If you don't mind, would you please overnight the yearbook to me?"

"Overnight? Those charges are so high. Why don't I just—"

"Mother, please. I need it."

"All right. I'll go straight down to FedEx as soon as we hang up."

Sister Mary sighed. "Thank you, Mother. Thank you a thousand times."

Edna laughed. "You're welcome, dear. We miss you, you know."

Sister Mary's voice began to shake. "I miss you, too, Mother. Oh...Mother?"

"Yes, dear?"

"I love you, you know. I love you very much."

Edna smiled. "I know you do, sweetheart. God bless."

Sister Mary's eyes filled with tears. "Yes... God bless," she echoed, and quietly hung up the phone.

She stared first at the letters, then at the list of names her mother had given her. The truth was there, but it didn't make sense. Unless the laws of coincidence had been violated more harshly than she could believe possible, someone was behind those deaths, and she and Ginny Shapiro were the only two left alive. Within the past two months, five young and vital women with everything to live for had taken their own lives. She couldn't help thinking that she and Ginny would be next.

Then her rational mind shifted into action, and she began to think back over what she'd just learned. There were two common threads that she was aware of: the special class they'd been in, and the fact that each death had happened after a phone call.

But who could have called? Even more puzzling, what in God's sweet name could they have said to trigger something as horrendous as this? Something was wrong—horribly wrong—and she didn't think prayers were enough to stop what was happening. She needed to get help before she and Ginny also succumbed.

After a quick search through her address book, she dialed Ginny's number at home. When the answering machine came on, she slapped her head in disgust. What was the matter with her? Ginny would be at work. She made the second call, this time to the *St. Louis Daily,* where Ginny worked, only to find out that Ginny was out of the office for the day. She left a message for Ginny to call her and then hung up. Now she was really scared.

Immediately her thoughts shifted to Sullivan Dean, her brother's best friend. As a child, Sully had been her white knight. She'd given up her dreams of marrying him on the day she'd given her heart to the Lord. But Sullivan Dean was still a white knight. The only difference now was that his metaphorical sword came in the form of a badge, compliments of the Federal Bureau of Investigation. Yes, Sullivan Dean was a Fed. A hard-nosed, implacable cop for Uncle Sam. He would know what to make of all this, but to do so, he would need all the information she had.

She quickly made copies of everything she'd received, along with a brief note telling him of her fears, and then sent a duplicate set of the information to Ginny, as well. Ginny had to be warned immediately. She would drop the packages off at FedEx right now, on the way to the hospital to visit the children.

Later she went to the evening meal with a lighter heart. The burden of what she suspected had been shared, and if she knew Sullivan, he would be calling as soon as he got her package. When Mother Superior gave the blessing, Sister Mary Teresa added a small prayer of her own.

Please, God, help us in our hour of need.

"Sister Mary Teresa, would you please pass the bread?"

Sister Mary raised her head and grinned at the woman on her right. Sister Frances Xavier was very fond of bread, as her round little body attested.

"Certainly," she said, and passed the bowl of rolls just as the sound of a jackhammer abruptly broke the peace within the room. She jumped, almost dropping the bowl.

"It's only the workmen," Sister Frances said.

"What workmen?"

"The ones down in the basement. There's something wrong with the plumbing, I think. You know how old the pipes must be in this place." Then she leaned close and dropped her voice to a whisper as she lifted a roll from the bowl Sister Mary was holding. "Mother Superior was all in a fuss about it. Said they're disturbing the sanctity and peace of Sacred Heart." Then she giggled and added, "But Father Joseph said that one hundred and twenty-three nuns and no bathrooms or running water would be what constituted a real disturbance, not this little bit of noise."

Sister Mary Teresa giggled. "That must have been when I was at the children's hospital. Wish I'd seen those two squaring off. They're always at cross-purposes. You'd think, since we're all in the same calling, so to speak, that they'd get along a little better."

Sister Frances shrugged as she tore her roll apart. "Just because they both love the Lord does not necessarily mean they love each other," she said, and then quickly added, "symbolically speaking, of course." She pointed. "Would you please pass the salt?"

Thirty-six hours had come and gone without a word from Sullivan or Ginny, and Sister Mary Teresa was starting to get concerned. She'd tried again to call Ginny at the *St. Louis Daily*, only to be told that her friend was out on assignment. She could only guess at why Sully hadn't called, but knowing the line of work he was in, he could be anywhere in the U.S. at this moment, completely unaware of what was happening.

She thought twice about contacting the local authorities and then dismissed the idea. All the deaths had been witnessed and ruled accidents or suicides. She had no proof that anything was wrong except a gut instinct that she and Ginny would be next.

Two days ago, she'd asked to be relieved from her duties in the office for fear of having to answer the phones. When Mother Superior had asked her if she was ill, she'd lied and said yes. Now her conscience was bothering her. With a heavy heart, she exited the main building and headed toward the chapel on the far side of the grounds, thankful that the rains they'd been experiencing for the past week had finally subsided. Her eyes were on the path before her, her thoughts focused on a long-overdue confession. Although there were a number of vehicles parked in the visitors' lot, she bypassed them with little notice. Visitors were common to Sacred Heart. She walked with her head down, taking hasty steps, the hem of her habit swishing busily against her ankles; unaware of the person sitting on the bench beneath the trees to her left. From a distance, she could hear footsteps on the path behind her, but the sound was unremarkable and gave her no reason to turn.

As Sister Mary Teresa entered the chapel, her anxiety began to dissipate. She drew strength from this place, and from the peace that dwelled within.

Several people were scattered throughout the pews, some with their eyes upon the magnificent stained glass window directly over the altar, others sitting quietly with heads bent in supplication to the Lord. She paid them no mind as she genuflected, made the sign of the cross, then kissed the figure of the Blessed Jesus hanging from the end of her rosary before heading toward the confessionals in the back of the room.

Although Father Joseph heard confessions at this

time every day, he was nowhere to be seen. Sister Mary didn't care. He would eventually show up, he always did, and she was happy just to be in the House of the Lord. Taking a seat within one of the confessionals, she shut the door and then clasped her hands in her lap and bowed her head. When Father Joseph saw that the door was closed, he would know someone waited within. For now, she would exercise patience. It was something she'd learned during her time as a novice. Everything comes in its own time, including priests.

A minute passed, and then another. The panic within her heart was all but gone. God was around her and within her, and she had no sense of fear. When she heard the sound of approaching footsteps and then the door opening in the cubicle next to her, she knew Father Joseph had come. With tear-filled eyes, she took a deep breath.

"Forgive me, Father, for I have sinned. My last confession was three days ago."

Instead of the familiar rhythm of Father Joseph O'Grady's voice, she heard a faint but heavy rumble, like the sound of distant thunder. Then, between one breath and the next, a part of Sister Mary Teresa's past, belonging to the child that she had been, wrapped around her mind and pulled her under. There was no time to panic, because she was already gone. In a matter of moments, Sister Mary Teresa was lost to a master who'd claimed her long before the One she now served.

The thunder was gone now. Slowly she opened her eyes and opened the door. As she stepped outside the confessional, someone took her by the arm.

"Forgive me, Sister, I was unavoidably detained. Please take a seat and I will hear your confession," Father Joseph said.

But the little nun gave no sign that she'd heard a word he said.

"Sister Mary Teresa!"

She kept on walking, leaving the aging priest to make what he would of her behavior.

Father Joseph watched in disbelief. Just as she reached the exit, something—maybe the voice of God Himself—told him to follow her. By the time he reached the doorway she was nowhere in sight. More than a bit concerned, he went down the steps, taking them two at a time as he scanned the grounds. Pausing to look again, he turned, taking in the lay of land that ran in a gentle slope from behind the old cathedral to the river below.

Shrugging, he started to leave when a flash of black appeared and then disappeared within a copse of trees above the river. It was her, of that there was no doubt. But why would she be walking down there? Again an inner voice pushed at him to follow, although it made no sense. There was nothing down there but the river, and it was in flood.

Suddenly, within his mind came a word, so forceful and frightening that he knew in his heart it had come straight from God.

Go!

Without thought for his old joints, he started to run. The closer he got to the river, the faster he moved. By the time he exited the trees on the bank above the fast-running water, he was moving at an all-out lope. Breathing heavily, he stopped, bracing an arm against a tree as he searched the area with a worried gaze.

Then he saw her about a hundred yards downstream, standing on the edge of a precipice that jutted out over the river, poised like a small blackbird about to take flight. In the riverbed below, the water roiled, sweeping past huge boulders at a deadly pace.

Cupping his hands to his mouth, he shouted her name, but it disappeared within the roar of the rushing water. His heart sank. She would never be able to hear him. When she suddenly swayed, his concern turned to panic.

"No! Dear Lord, no!"

He began to run, oblivious to everything but the woman on the rocks. Moments later, she slowly lifted her arms to the heavens, turned her face to the sky and then leaned forward.

He froze in midstride, watching in disbelief as she

fell into space. Although it took only seconds for her body to hit the water, he would remember it later in a series of perfectly framed stills.

The smile on her face, her eyes closed as if in slumber.

Her arms horizontal to her shoulders and unmoving, like the image of a crucified Christ.

The flutter of her clothing, dark and molded to her body like a shroud.

The way the water parted to accept her presence.

A flash of white, a momentary shadow beneath the thick, muddy flow, and then...nothing.

The little nun was gone.

"No!" he screamed, as he fell to his knees. "Dear merciful God, no!"

Twenty-four hours later, Washington, D.C.

Sullivan Dean shoved his key into the lock, taking satisfaction in the distinct click of the tumblers. Shouldering the strap of his duffel bag, he pushed his way inside his apartment, slamming the door behind him as he went.

An old, musty scent pervaded as he moved from room to room. An ivy plant hanging in a nearby window was drooping like Santa's mustache as he set his bag on the floor and tossed the armful of mail that had collected while he was gone onto a nearby table.

Rolling his eyes at the condition of the plant, he realized he'd forgotten to take the darn thing to his neighbor's before he left. This was the fifth, or maybe sixth, one he'd killed since he'd moved to this place. He shrugged. Maybe he should quit replacing the damned things; then he wouldn't have this worry.

Lifting the ivy down from the hook on which it was hanging, he carried it into the kitchen and set it in the sink, giving it a liberal dousing of water, although he suspected it was going to be a case of too little too late.

Eyeing the limp leaves, he gave one a tug. It came away in his hand. "Sorry, buddy. I'm not cut out for roots of any kind...not even yours."

A short while later, he strode into the kitchen and opened the fridge, quickly wrinkling his nose in disgust. Whatever it was that he'd wrapped in that plastic had turned to a green, soupy liquid. He dropped it in the trash and slammed the door before turning to survey his surroundings.

Well, the best that could be said for the apartment was that the rooms were dusty and empty. He sighed. This was one of those times when the thought crossed his mind that it would have been nice to come home to something besides echoes, which reminded him of the last relationship he'd tried to have. At that point, he decided that dead plants and dusty furniture weren't so bad after all. And there was the fact that he didn't have to go in to the office until Monday. By then all would be back in order.

Satisfied that he'd solved all his problems, he reached for the phone. He would order in a pizza tonight, call a cleaning service tomorrow, and shop for groceries, then take his clothes to the cleaners on Monday. Maybe tonight he would call his brother. They hadn't talked in months. He also reminded himself that he needed to call the nursing home tomorrow and check on his mother's condition. She wouldn't miss him, but he missed the person she'd been. Alzheimer's had robbed him of his last living parent, and what he needed right now in his life was less chaos, not a lover to mess up his life.

A couple of hours later, after a shower and a meal, Sully settled down to go through his mail. The inevitable bills would need to be dealt with, and there was no time like the present. He sat on his sofa with the mail in his lap, sorting through the stack. Bills to his left, newspapers at his feet, personal mail to his right, catalogues in the trash.

About halfway through sorting, he came to a letter-size pack from FedEx. Curious, he glanced at the return address and started to smile. It was from Georgia. Almost immediately he amended the thought to Sister Mary Teresa, although in his heart, she would always be Tommy Dudley's little sister Georgia.

Setting aside the rest of the mail to be sorted out

later, he tore into the packet and pulled out a handful of papers with a brief, handwritten letter from Georgia on top. Scanning the papers, he quickly saw that they were Xeroxed copies of newspaper clippings. Curious, he picked up her letter and started to read.

Almost instantly, the smile he was wearing went south. He sat up with a jerk and reread her note before scanning the clippings, taking note of the areas she had highlighted.

"Well, hell," he muttered, and looked back at the letter. The last line on the page stopped his heart.

Sully, please help. Ginny or I might be next.

He bolted to his feet and raced to the bedroom. His address book was still on the dresser where he'd tossed it last week. Shuffling through the pages, he found her address, as well as the phone number to Sacred Heart Convent. A sick feeling was building deep in his belly as he punched in the numbers. Surely to God he was making too much of this. Georgia would answer and then laugh when he called, telling him she'd jumped to too many conclusions. That was it. As soon as he heard her voice, they would be laughing together. Yet when his call was answered, he found himself stumbling for words.

"Sacred Heart Convent. How may I help you?"

"I need to speak to Georgia...I mean, Sister Mary Teresa."

He heard a soft gasp and then, "One moment please."

In the background he thought he could hear hasty whispers, and his stomach knotted. When a different person suddenly came on the line, he knew something was wrong.

"Mother Superior speaking. Who's calling, please?"

The woman's voice was stern, and he had instant flashbacks of a ruler popping on his head and being sent to stand in a corner. It took all he had to get out of that juvenile frame of mind and back to the problem at hand.

"This is Sullivan Dean. I'm a family friend of Sister Mary Teresa. I need to speak with her."

"I'm sorry, it's..."

"Please," Sully said. "It's important."

The woman sighed, and Sully was surprised to hear tears in her voice.

"You don't understand," she said. "It's not that I won't allow it. It's just that—" She stopped suddenly, changing her focus. "If you're a family friend, you should already know."

Sully dropped to the edge of the bed, his legs too weak to hold him.

"I've been out of the country. What should I know?"

"I'm so sorry," she said, "but we lost Sister Mary."

Sully's ears were roaring as he pinched the bridge of his nose to stop a sudden need to cry.

"What do you mean, lost her?"

"She's dead, sir."

Sully's lungs deflated. A long moment of silence passed as he struggled to find breath with which to speak. Finally the word came out in a harsh, ugly groan.

"How?"

"It's not for us to judge. All we can do is pray for her soul."

Rage shifted the pain. "To hell with prayers. I want answers!" he shouted.

"Father Joseph witnessed her death," she said, still hedging.

"Mother Superior, I am an agent with the Federal Bureau of Investigation, and for the last time, I'm asking you how Georgia died."

There was another long moment of silence, followed by a word that rocked Sully's world.

"Suicide."

"No. Not only no, but hell no. The woman I knew would never kill herself. Not in a million years."

"She jumped into a flood-swollen river."

"She couldn't swim," Sully said.

"Yes, we know."

Sully's thoughts were spinning. He needed to concentrate. But on what? Georgia had asked him for help, and he'd been too late.

"Her things. What happened to her things?" he asked.

"Her family is coming next week to pick them up."

"I'll be there first thing in the morning. Don't move a thing until I get a chance to look at them."

"Oh, but I..."

"She was murdered," Sully said. "I don't know how, but if it's the last thing I do, I will find out. Are you going to help me or not?"

3

Ginny was late for work. The thunderstorm that had rolled through St. Louis last night had knocked out power in her area just long enough to mess up her digital alarm clock. It was still blinking madly as she rinsed the toothpaste out of her mouth and then ran a brush hastily through her hair. When it caught on a tangle, she winced, then cursed.

"Crap," she muttered, yanking the brush back through the spot without care for the pain.

It served her right for succumbing to the storm. For as long as she could remember, the sound of thunder had always given her a lethargic feeling, which often escalated into long, dreamless sleep.

Grabbing her raincoat and umbrella, she dashed from the bedroom. If the traffic went her way, she would make it to work on time, but barely. She was reaching for the knob when a knock sounded on the door. Startled, she jerked, then stood on tiptoe to look through the security peephole.

"Crap again," she muttered, recognizing the superintendent of her apartment building. He'd been hitting on her for months and didn't seem to recognize the fact that she wasn't interested. She opened the door abruptly, hoping her impatience showed.

"Yes?"

He stripped her naked with a healthy leer before returning his gaze to her face.

"Good morning, Virginia."

"Stanley...as you can see, I'm in a bit of a hurry."

"Yes, well, aren't we all?" Then he whipped a large express envelope out from behind his back. "About this delivery...I found it on the floor behind the wastebasket this morning. I don't know how it became so misplaced, but since it was marked Urgent, I felt it my duty to get it to you at once."

"Thanks," Ginny said, as she took the envelope, glancing at the return address as she closed the door in his face.

Almost immediately, her mood shifted. Sacred Heart Convent. It must be from Georgia! Then she amended that to Sister Mary. It still seemed impossible that Georgia Dudley, the girl who had stripped off her sweater at a New Year's Eve party and danced on her boss's table had become a nun. Then she grinned to herself. Maybe that was *exactly* why she'd done it. Knowing she would never work at the Dudson, Dudson and Gregory law firm again and having to explain to her next employer why she'd been fired, would have made job hunting quite difficult.

Then Ginny sighed. That just wasn't true. She knew

why Georgia had chosen her life's work. She'd seen it on her face the day she'd told everyone about her dream and the ensuing vision. The change in her had been internal, but it had radiated throughout. With a halfhearted glance at her watch, Ginny dropped her stuff on the sofa. She was already late. A few more minutes couldn't matter.

Sitting down, she tore into the packet with a smile on her face and pulled out the handful of papers, paying little attention to anything except the letter on top.

Dear Ginny,

I don't know how to start except to say that I think we're in danger.

Ginny frowned. Her gaze slid to the next sentence, then the next and the next, and by the time she'd come to the end of the letter, her stomach was in knots. Hastily, she glanced through the accompanying pages, counting off the names of the deceased. They seemed familiar, but who...?

Memory surfaced as she reread the note from Georgia. The gifted class! They were all in that gifted class together!

"No," she muttered. "It can't be."

But it was the same group, and five of them were dead! Emily. Josephine. Lynn. Francis...and Allison. Dear Allison. This made no sense.

She reread the letter, her focus lingering on two particular sentences.

Whatever you do, don't answer your phone unless

you know for certain who's calling. I sent a copy of all this stuff to Sullivan Dean, as well.

She didn't know who Sullivan Dean was, but she would find out when she talked to Georgia. Surely she had jumped to conclusions. Yet as Ginny dug through her desk for her address book, she kept thinking of the copied newspaper clippings. There was no denying the deaths of five of her childhood friends, and all within the space of a couple of months.

"Where the heck is that...oh, here it is," she muttered, as she yanked the address book from the back of the drawer.

With shaking fingers, she punched in the number to Sacred Heart, then closed her eyes and took several slow, calming breaths. Even though she was expecting to hear a woman's voice, when the call was answered, her heart skipped a beat.

"Sacred Heart Convent."

"Yes...um...hello. This is Virginia Shapiro, I'm a good friend of Georgia...I mean, Sister Mary Teresa. I don't know what your rules are, or where she is at the moment, but it's imperative that I speak with her."

There was a distinct gasp at the other end of the line, then silence.

"Hello? Hello? Are you there?"

"Yes, I'm sorry. Would you please hold?"

Ginny glanced at her watch and then rolled her eyes as a recording of "The Hallelujah Chorus" came on in her ear. This was going to be okay. As soon as Georgia arrived and Ginny could hear her voice, everything would be okay. She just knew it.

"Hello. Mother Superior speaking. Who's calling, please?"

Ginny glanced at the letter in her hand. "Virginia Shapiro. I need to speak to Sister Mary Teresa. It's urgent."

"Are you family?"

"No, but we are really old, really close friends. Please, I won't keep her long, but..."

"I'm sorry, dear," the nun said. "It's not that I won't let her take the call, it's that she can't."

The knot in Ginny's stomach tightened. "Why?"

"Because Sister Mary is no longer with us."

Ginny breathed a sigh of relief. "Oh...you mean she's moved? I didn't know. Was she transferred, or whatever you call it? If you could give me her address, I would really appreciate it."

"I'm sorry, dear. I didn't make myself clear. Sister Mary didn't transfer. She died."

Ginny slid to the floor, her knees beneath her chin as she struggled to breathe.

"I don't understand. She can't be dead. She just wrote me a letter."

"I'm sorry, but it's true."

Ginny's gaze fell on the Urgent notice on the outside of the envelope and bit her lip to keep from screaming. Would it have made a difference if she'd gotten this on time?

"Please...how? How did she die?"

"Technically...she drowned."

Shock sent Ginny scrambling to her feet. "That's not possible. Georgia couldn't swim. She was afraid of water. She wouldn't have gone anywhere near it."

This last was something Mother Superior had not known, and the knowledge troubled her. She thought back to her conversation with the FBI agent who'd called earlier, claiming Sister Mary had been murdered. Could it be?

"Still, it's so," she added.

"I don't believe it," Ginny said, her voice shaking with disbelief and growing anger. "Was there someone else with her? She must have been pushed."

"Oh, my dear! You don't know what you're saying. Father Joseph saw her with his own eyes. He shouted at her to stop, but she didn't seem to know he was anywhere in sight."

Bile rose in the back of Ginny's throat. "Saw her do what?"

"Why...she jumped. Straight off a cliff into a flood-swollen river. There wasn't a thing that could be done to save her. Now all we can do is pray for her soul not to be lost."

"I don't understand."

"She took her own life, my dear. Suicide is not

condoned by the Holy Church. I'm afraid her soul is lost to God.''

It was ten minutes after eleven when Ginny came to her senses, and then only because her phone began to ring. She got up from the sofa, her eyes swollen from the tears that she'd shed, and staggered toward the phone. Her hand was on the receiver when the line from Georgia's letter popped back into her head. *Don't answer the phone unless you know who it is.* In sudden panic, Ginny yanked the jack from the wall and then started to shake. This was crazy! What had Georgia meant? There were too many unanswered questions. She needed to talk to someone, but who?

Immediately she thought of Harry Redford. Harry was not only her boss, he was the coolest man under pressure that she'd ever known. Staggering to the bathroom, she splashed cold water on her face and managed to pull herself together. A few minutes later she was out the door with the packet of papers Georgia had sent clutched tightly to her chest. She would show this stuff to Harry. He would know what to do.

Harry Redford took one look at the expression on Ginny Shapiro's face and stifled the sarcastic remark he'd been about to make. He bolted from his desk, shoved her into a chair and shut the door to his office.

''What?''

Ginny looked up at him, taking refuge in the familiarity of his craggy face, and handed him the envelope full of papers.

"What the hell's this all about?" he growled, as he spread the stack across his desk.

"I don't know," Ginny said, and then started to cry again. "Harry, I'm scared."

Harry read the letter first, then quickly scanned the copies of the newspaper clippings. Knitted brows forming a solid bushy line above his eyes, he continued to read. Finally he looked up, the letter from Sister Mary Teresa still in his hand.

"Is this on the up-and-up?"

She nodded.

"What does your friend...this Sister Mary Teresa have to say about it?"

Ginny's tears started anew.

Harry groaned and then handed her a box of tissues from his desk.

"Here, damn it," he muttered. "Blow your nose and then talk to me."

Ginny blew.

"You *have* talked to her, haven't you?" Harry asked.

"She's dead."

Harry leaned forward, the palms of his hands flat against the surface of his desk.

"The hell you say! Since when?"

"I don't know the exact date, but it was sometime

after she sent this.'' Ginny took a shuddering breath. ''Harry...I'm scared.''

''Yeah, I can see why.'' He frowned, then raked a hand through his thick, graying hair. ''Talk to me. Tell me about these women. Exactly how were you connected?''

''We were all enrolled in a private school in upstate New York. That's where I grew up, remember?''

''Yeah, go on. So you were classmates.''

''Not only that, but there was the special class.''

''What special class?''

Ginny took another tissue and dabbed at her eyes. ''When we were six, they began a special class...they called it a gifted class. There were seven students, all girls.'' She pointed to the list of names in Georgia's letter. ''Except for me...they're all dead, and all within the last couple of months.'' She drew another shaky breath, waiting for Harry to make it all right.

Harry blanched. ''Son of a bitch,'' he muttered. He glanced back at the letter. ''Who's Sullivan Dean?''

''I don't know. I was going to ask Georgia...Sister Mary...but now I—''

She shook her head, unable to go on.

''I don't get the deal about not answering the phone, either,'' Harry said. ''But I do know something you *can* do.''

''What?'' Ginny asked.

''Get to your desk and make some calls. Follow up on these stories. Talk to their families. Find out what

you can about the phone calls. Sister Mary died before
she could fully explain what she knew, but she gave
you a place to start. Now go do what you've been
trained to do. Investigate!''

Ginny stood. Harry was right. She'd been in shock
before, that was all. There had to be an answer to this.
All she had to do was find it.

"Let me know what you find out," he said.

Ginny nodded.

"Oh, and, kid…''

Ginny paused.

"Just to be on the safe side…maybe you really
shouldn't take any calls, okay?''

Ginny swallowed nervously. "Right! I'll have everything switched to voice mail.''

''No, just let someone else take your calls. As far
as the world needs to know, you're on assignment and
can't be reached.''

It was almost five o'clock when Ginny hung up the
phone for the last time. It had taken her more than
two hours before she'd located anyone in Oklahoma
who could verify the story the *Oklahoma Dispatch*
had done on Allison Turner. She'd had to call back
four times before the reporter had returned, then he
had to look up some notes to refer her to Allison's
friend, who had witnessed it all. Ginny rubbed her
eyes and then rolled her neck to release some of the
kinks.

Her gaze fell on the notes she'd been making, as well as the stuff Georgia had sent her. This was so bizarre. From the first victim, whose husband had come home to find his son with the neighbor and a phone lying on the kitchen counter, to Allison, who'd driven straight into the side of a gasoline truck with her arms outstretched, she had to admit that Georgia's warnings about the phone calls held merit. The only one who had broken protocol was Georgia, herself. The priest at the convent, a Father Joseph, stated that she'd come out of the confessional, walked past him as if he'd been invisible, and headed straight for the river. There were no phones in confessionals. For that matter, there weren't any phones in the entire chapel, only in the convent office itself. But Ginny knew that, somehow, whatever had happened to the others had happened to Georgia, as well.

Resting her head against the palms of her hands, she took a slow, weary breath. Had it been only this morning when her world had turned upside down? Her eyes were burning and puffy; her head was pounding. She'd cried more today than she'd cried in years, and all she'd gotten for her efforts was a re-sounding headache. If she didn't answer any phones, maybe she would be okay, but she couldn't go through life like this. She had to figure out what was happening and who was causing it.

The phone rang on a nearby desk, and she jumped as if she'd been shot.

I can't live like this. I've got to get away, at least for a while. And I've got to tell Harry what I found out.

Gathering up her notes and her purse, she headed for her boss's office.

"It's not good," she said, as she plopped down in a chair in front of his desk.

Redford looked up, shoved aside the papers that he'd been working on, and kicked back in his chair.

"Talk to me," he said.

"This is what I know for sure. There were seven of us in the first gifted class that Montgomery Academy had. Actually, the only gifted class, since the school burned down before the school year was over. Of those seven, six have died within the past couple of months. I'm the only one still living. Also, Georgia's theory that they each had a phone call right before they died is true." Ginny took a deep breath and then leaned forward. "Harry, I'm scared, and I don't like being scared. I'm taking all of this information to the St. Louis Police Department, and then I'm leaving town. I don't know where I'll go just yet, but I'll check in with you from time to time. What I need to know is…will I still have a job when I get back?"

Harry snorted beneath his breath. "Hell, yes, you'll have a job…and, I hope, an exclusive story to go with it. I want you to promise me that you'll check in at least once a week so I'll know you're okay."

Ginny stood abruptly. "I promise," she said, blinking rapidly to clear her vision through a fresh set of tears. "And, Harry…"

"Yeah?" he said gruffly.

"Thanks."

He came around his desk and gave her a hug. "Hang in there, kid, and if it gets to be too much, you get yourself back here ASAP. You don't have to do this on your own, you know. We'll figure something out."

"I know, but for now, I think I'll feel safer if I can just disappear for a while."

Having said that, she gathered her things and walked out the door.

"Hey, kid!" Harry called.

Ginny stopped and turned.

"You *are* going to the cops, aren't you?"

"Yes. Whether they believe me or not is another story."

"They mess with you, I'll tie knots in their asses they won't ever get out."

Ginny grinned all the way to her car, but the moment she got inside, she locked the doors and then gave the parking lot a more than cursory glance before driving away.

Sullivan Dean was at Chicago's O'Hare airport, mentally cursing the snafu that had become his flight. Already on the second hour of an unscheduled delay, he headed for a pay phone, desperate to make contact with Virginia Shapiro. He'd already tried her apartment with no luck; then, when he'd tried the paper, he'd gotten nothing but voice mail. If he could only connect with her, he would feel a hell of a lot better.

He hung up in defeat and went back to his chair, trying to ignore the squalling baby and its harried mother across the aisle from where he was sitting. In a moment of frustration and grief, he leaned forward, resting his elbows on his knees and covered his face with his hands.

Ah, God. Georgia, Tom's little sister, was dead. He could only imagine the family's grief. And then there was his guilty conscience to deal with, as well. He'd been promising Georgia for years that he would come visit, yet had never made time—until now. Having to walk into her room and see the plain and simple life that she'd chosen for herself, all the while knowing the joy she'd derived from the decision, made it hard to draw breath. He'd gone through her personal belongings, almost expecting her to come bursting through the door at any time and berate him for digging through her things, then having to blank his mind to the knowledge that they were hers. As he'd searched, he had to admit that Georgia had been thorough in her amateur investigation. Although she'd made copies of everything she knew about the women who'd died, except for a school yearbook that had arrived after her death, he found nothing new.

Struggling with grief, he'd gone to the chapel,

prayed to the same God to whom Georgia had pledged her life, and made a promise to both. Whatever it took, he would find out who was behind these deaths and save Ginny Shapiro in the process. With the year-book tucked safely at the bottom of his duffel bag, his next stop was St. Louis, Missouri.

Detective Anthony Pagillia had a headache and the beginnings of another afternoon of heartburn when he saw a woman approaching his desk. Frowning, he tried to figure out why her face looked familiar. When she introduced herself, he remembered. She worked for the *Daily* and had covered the Bruhns kidnapping case last year.

"Miss Shapiro, what can I do for you?" Pagillia said.

She laid a large brown envelope before him. "Start by calling me Ginny," she said. "And then finish by telling me I'm not losing my mind."

He smiled. "I make a point of *never* telling women anything that could get me hurt." He dumped the contents of the envelope onto his desk. "What's this about?"

"I think someone wants me dead."

His smile froze, his eyes widening. "Are you serious?"

"Just read. When you've finished, I'll answer any questions I can."

A few minutes later, Pagillia rocked back in his

chair and looked up "You have my attention. Start talking."

"Having read those, you know almost as much as I do."

"Your friend, the nun, what does she have to say?" he asked.

Ginny's chin quivered once, but she held herself back. This was no time to give in to new grief.

"She's dead. As of a day ago, she supposedly committed suicide by walking off a cliff into a flood-swollen river." Ginny leaned forward, tapping her finger angrily against the surface of his desk. "Georgia Dudley—or Sister Mary Teresa, as the case may be—would never kill herself. Never."

Pagillia's chair came down with a thump. "They're all dead...these girls from that class?"

"Except for me, yes, and all within the last two months. I did some checking before I came here. Besides the class connection, there is another common denominator."

"Like what?"

"Every one of them received a phone call before she went off the deep end. We know because their family either found the phone off the hook or they were seen talking on the phone just prior to their deaths. Every one, that is, except for Georgia, and that's just because I can't prove it."

"I don't get it. How could a phone call make six separate women in different parts of the country go out and commit what amounts to suicide?"

"I don't know," Ginny said. "That's where you come in. Will you help me?"

"Of course," Pagillia said. "I wonder...are other police departments aware of this connection?"

"I don't think so," Ginny said. "The incidents were so scattered, and as you can tell from the newspaper clippings, they were all ruled as accidents or suicides. They have no reason to suspect any different."

"Then that's where I start," Pagillia said.

"Thank God," Ginny said, and then stood.

"Where can I reach you?" the detective asked.

"You can't," Ginny said. "I'm leaving town and, needless to say, I won't be taking any phone calls."

"But what if I need to talk to you?"

"I'll call you," Ginny said. "That's the best I can promise. Oh...and you can keep the letter and clippings. I made copies for myself, just in case."

Pagillia nodded. "Just stay in touch."

"Count on it," Ginny said, and walked away.

It was five minutes past 11:00 p.m. when Ginny pulled beneath the canopy covering the entrance to the Hideaway Motel. Half of the neon letters on the motel sign were burned out, leaving it to read HIDE MOTEL. Well, she thought, it seems I'm in the right place after all.

The desk clerk looked up as she came through the door.

"I need a room," Ginny said.

"One night?" the clerk asked.

Ginny hesitated, then nodded.

"Smoking or non-smoking?"

"Non, please."

"Single?"

Ginny stared. What the hell did it matter whether she was married or not? "I'm sorry? What did you say?"

"Do you want a single room, or is there someone with you?"

If she hadn't been so exhausted, she might have laughed.

"Oh…no…there's no one but me."

"How will you be paying?" he asked.

She laid a credit card on the counter and then turned to scan the lobby while the clerk continued his work. Her eyes were burning, her belly grumbling from hunger. It took her a few moments to realize she didn't even know where she was.

"Where am I?"

The clerk looked up. "Excuse me?"

Ginny sighed. "I know I'm at a motel. What I need to know is where the closest city is located."

"I wouldn't call Hoxie a city, miss, but that would be it. It's about fifteen miles back that way."

He pointed west. She nodded, absorbing the fact that she had already passed through it.

"What's the next city east?" she asked.

He squinted as he thought. "That would probably be Memphis."

Suddenly Ginny had a faint mental image of where she was and made a note to herself to get a map tomorrow. Driving headlong into nowhere would gain her nothing but more trouble.

"Thank you," she said, ignoring the wary look he kept giving her. She wasn't drunk, and she wasn't high, and to hell with what he thought. She just needed a place to lay her head.

He laid a credit card slip in front of her. "The room rate is forty-five dollars a night. Sign here."

Ginny signed.

A few minutes later she stuck the key in the lock and entered her room, locking and chaining the door behind her. The color scheme screamed at her. Ignoring the noise, she staggered to the bathroom.

Emerging a couple of minutes later, she fell facedown on the bed without removing her clothes. Within seconds she was fast asleep.

High above the city of St. Louis, a 747 was entering the flight path for landing. Sullivan Dean glanced out the window, then looked down. The night was clear. The lights of the city below lay like diamonds on a bed of black velvet, and yet all he could see was the distance between him and his goal.

I'm coming, Virginia. Please don't be dead.

4

Sully had retrieved his baggage and was exiting the airport when it began to rain. He paused beneath the canopy, trying to decide what to do first.

Problem number one: Virginia Shapiro wasn't answering her phone, which made him nervous. What if she couldn't? What if she was already dead?

Problem number two: Problem number one.

The way he figured it, her apartment had to be first stop on the list of things to do. He had her address. The rest was simple. At that point, he hailed a taxi, and after giving the driver the address, leaned back in the seat and closed his eyes, but his mind wouldn't let him relax. He kept seeing Georgia at five years old, chasing after him and Tommy when they were kids—the crush she'd had on him during his sixteenth summer, while her twelve-year-old body hovered on the brink of womanhood, still wrapped in freckles and braces. The look on her face when she'd told him that she was going to become a nun. The passion in her eyes had been as fervent as always, but it was the quieting of her spirit that had humbled him. For the first time he had seen her as a woman in her own right and not just as Tommy Dudley's little sister.

Now the authorities wanted him to believe a woman like her was capable of taking her own life? Not now. Not ever.

Then he sighed. He wouldn't deny the how of her death. After all, a priest with no reason to lie had seen it all. But what in God's sweet name would it take for her to walk off a cliff into a flood-swollen river? At the thought, he shuddered, then wiped a hand across his face. Nothing short of the Devil.

He clenched his jaw. *God help us all.*

One thing was certain: when he got to a hotel, he was going to call Tommy. The family deserved to know what was going on, and from the little he had gained from Georgia's letter, he didn't think she'd shared her suspicions with them.

His mind was still lost in the past when the cab took a sudden swerve to the right. He looked out the window and then up, peering at the three-story building. Although his view was somewhat marred by the rain, this was not where he'd supposed Virginia Shapiro would live. It was a Victorian home in an ordinary neighborhood, as opposed to a high-rise apartment befitting a hard-nosed, hardworking journalist.

"That'll be fifteen seventy-five," the cabby said.

Sully handed him a twenty. "Keep the change."

As he got out of the cab, a pizza delivery car pulled up behind them at the curb. Mentally thanking his luck, Sully followed the delivery boy up the steps. When the boy buzzed to be let in, he followed him inside, then took the stairs as the delivery boy rang the bell on the downstairs door. It soon became apparent that there were only three apartments plus the super's room in the whole of the house, and Virginia's was the one on the second floor.

He paused at her door and rang the bell, then stood in the shadows of the hallway, listening to the echo of the bell on the other side of the door. It was now five minutes after midnight. If she *was* in there, probably the last thing she would do was come to the door, but he'd come too far to stop now. He rang again and when there was still no response forthcoming, began to knock.

Now his imagination was starting to kick in, imagining her unable to answer—imagining her dead—and he damn sure wasn't leaving until he knew for sure. Dropping the duffel bag near his feet, he reached in his jacket pocket. Moments later, he inserted a small lock pick into the keyhole and gave it a couple of twists. The click of the tumblers seemed loud in the silence of the small hallway, and he glanced over his shoulder before stepping inside. No alarms went off. No bells and whistles sounded.

After one quick glance back at the stairwell, he closed and locked the door behind him. Motionless, he stood with his back against the door, listening for sounds of life, but heard nothing. Not even a dripping faucet. Hesitantly, he turned on the lights.

Within seconds, he knew she was gone.

There was a throw pillow on the floor, and a drawer in a nearby table was only half shut, as if someone had grabbed something out of it and, in their haste, had not pushed it shut.

Following the layout of the apartment, he began to move through the rooms. Her bed was made, but there was a large indentation in the middle of the spread that would accommodate the size of a suitcase. Her closet door was half-open, a dresser drawer still ajar. A pair of shoes lay in the corner of the room, as if they'd been tossed aside for something else. In the adjoining bath, her cosmetics were gone.

There were a dirty bowl and glass sitting in the kitchen sink and nothing else. Absently, he ran a little water in the bowl to soak loose the dried cereal and rinsed out the glass, then stood in the middle of the floor, mentally mapping her progress through the house.

Moving to the living room, he began a more thorough search.

As he was looking, a phone began to ring in an apartment downstairs. The faint sound jarred his memory about Georgia's warning to avoid taking calls, and he thought of Virginia's phone.

At first glance he didn't see it. On closer inspection, he found it on the floor by the sofa. He picked it up and set it back on the table, then lifted the receiver. The line was dead. Tracing the cord to its end, he soon saw that the jack had been pulled from the wall. A small smile crossed his lips as relief settled in his gut.

She knew! By God...she knew!

Now the urgency to find her was over. He didn't know how, but somewhere within the next couple of days he would locate her, only not tonight. And, since it seemed obvious that Virginia Shapiro was not coming back any time soon, he saw no reason to let a perfectly good bed go to waste. He thought of his promise to call Tommy and decided it was too late for that now. He would do it in the morning, before he left.

As he turned toward the bedroom, a picture on the wall caught his eye. He moved closer for a better look and caught himself staring at the trio—an older man and woman, and a young, dark-haired woman caught in the middle of their embraces.

Me, Mom and Dad: Yellowstone—1997

The woman in the middle had to be Virginia. He took a step closer, curiously examining her face. The picture was about four years old, but she couldn't have changed that much. The image was grainy, obviously an enlargement from a smaller snapshot, but the joy and vibrancy on her face were impossible to miss. He couldn't help but superimpose what she must be feeling now. Fear. Confusion. Helplessness.

He reached out and touched her smile, frowning at the obstruction of the glass between him and her image. She seemed so real.

As he stood, the air-conditioning unit suddenly kicked on, and he became aware of the wet clothing on his back. Sully gave her picture a last thoughtful glance before striding toward the bedroom. It was time to get out of these clothes and into a bed.

It was 2:15 a.m. and Sully had yet to fall asleep. The faint scent of her shampoo was on the pillows, while echoes of her perfume stirred through the air. Frustrated, he rolled onto his belly and shoved her pillow onto the floor. Never in his life had he fixated on something as juvenile as a pretty girl's picture, and he wasn't going to start now. The only thing wrong with him was that he'd been too long without a woman.

Just before three, he finally drifted off to sleep, but Virginia Shapiro was still in his dreams, mixed up in the nightmare that this trip had become—a beautiful smiling face, staring sightlessly up at the sky and covered in blood.

Bainbridge, Connecticut

"Emile, not that tie, dear. Wear this one. It's much more dignified."

Emile Karnoff traded ties with his wife and smiled.

"Lucy, darling, what would I do without you?"

Lucy Karnoff hung up the other tie and then turned to her husband, giving him a judicious stare.

"Maybe if you change the—"

Emile held up his hand. "Relax. The rest of my attire is fine. It's just another press conference, after all."

"It's no such thing," Lucy argued. "You're an important man. People deserve to hear what you have to say."

Emile smiled as he began to knot the new tie.

Lucy fussed about the room, picking up a sock from beneath the bed, then rearranging Emile's shoes inside their closet. He seemed easier with his new-found fame than he had in weeks. When the buzz began that he was up for the award, Emile had suffered many sleepless nights, often waking up in a cold, shaking sweat. She'd begged him to see a doctor, but he'd refused, calling it nothing but a case of nerves. As the weeks had progressed, so had his troubles. Only in the last few days had he seemed more at ease with himself and what he'd become. She could only imagine how difficult it would be—going from an obscure physician to having his picture on the front of all the news magazines.

She brushed a piece of lint from the back of his jacket as he smoothed down his thin, graying hair. Not only was it her job, but it was her joy, to have Emile presented to the world in perfect order. After years of financial struggle and behind-the-back ridicule from the women in their social circle, her husband, the man her family had disowned her for marrying, the man who'd so often been the butt of her friends' bad jokes, had won the Nobel Prize for Medicine. That the call had come more than a month ago and the story was beginning to be old news didn't matter. Lucy Karnoff had come into her own.

"Don't fuss," Emile said. "I'm fine."

"I only want to help," she said.

Emile turned and touched the side of his wife's face with his forefingers, tilting the saddened corners of her lips into a smile.

"Lucy, my love, you are always a help to me."

Emile smiled as she giggled. In his eyes, she became a girl again, rather than his sixty-eight-year-old wife. It was a blessing that Lucy was so easily pleased. He suspected it was the single reason their marriage had lasted. In the early years his passion for his studies had overflowed into his personal life to such a degree that his son, Phillip, was almost a stranger. But Lucy's faith had never wavered, and for that he was truly thankful.

He turned to the mirror for one last look at himself as Lucy hastened from the room, murmuring something about making sure the drawing room was in order and the flowers in place. Only in the past couple of years had they been able to afford a cleaning lady, and while Lucy liked the picture it presented to her friends, he suspected she resented another woman's presence in her house. However, the fact that they now had help was an important factor in keeping their lives in order, because the truth was, Phillip had become a burden to them both. Unable to maintain a job, his periodic bouts with depression seemed destined to keep him under their roof, and neither of them was getting any younger. Because of Phillip, Lucy had been tied to their home, unable to travel with Emile for any length of time for fear they would come home to a family disaster.

Emile yanked at his tie, pulling it straight, and then reached for his cuff links. It was too bad that the discovery that had netted him the Nobel Prize had no effect on mental instabilities, although in the early days he had pursued that train of thought. After realizing the dangers that hypnosis represented to those in an unstable state of mind, he had quickly foregone the theory.

The sound of footsteps in the hall outside his door sent his focus in another direction, as did the familiar hesitation in his son's voice.

"Father?"

Emile turned, wondering again, as he had for almost thirty years, how he could have sired a son such as this. He was tall, good-looking in an effeminate sort of way, yet he hadn't a clue as to what life was really about.

"Yes, Phillip, what is it?"

Phillip Karnoff shifted from one foot to the other and hated himself for being such a wimp where this man was concerned. He was forty years younger, half a head taller, and just once he would like to be the one to stand unflinchingly beneath that all-seeing gaze instead of always, always, being the first to look away.

"I was wondering...about the press conference, I mean. Do I need to be there this time? I don't really—"

"You are family! You will sit at my side!"

Come on, wimp. Tell him how you feel. If you're too big a coward, then stand back and give me a chance at him. Phillip's gut knotted, ignoring the constant presence of the voice inside his head.

"Why, Father? I am nothing. Compared to you I am a failure. I have no focus—no dreams. I still live at home, and I haven't held a full-time job in four years."

Yeah, but I can show you how to have fun.

"You are my son," Emile said. "You will find your way when it's time."

"And what if I don't?" Phillip asked.

Emile shook his head in denial, as if the thought did not bear consideration.

"This is not the time for such discussion," Emile said. "Some other time, when we aren't so rushed."

He strode past his son, giving him a halfhearted pat on the shoulder in passing.

Phillip sighed. Time never turned in his favor.

There was no reason to assume anything would change. Especially now. He would never be able to come close to what his father had done, let alone top it. His shoulders slumped as he followed his father downstairs. How did one compete with a man who had discovered how to unleash the healing power of the human mind when he couldn't even control his own thoughts?

Sully came awake suddenly and sat straight up in bed. He'd been dreaming, but about what? Already the dream was fading from his memory, but he remembered it hadn't been good. Glancing at the clock, he swung his legs out of bed and strode to the bathroom, turning on the shower as he passed. Outside the old Victorian house, a new day had begun. It was time he joined it.

He dressed quickly after showering, anxious to get back on the road. But he had a call to make first, and it wasn't going to be easy. He sat down on the side of Virginia Shapiro's bed and picked up the phone. It was time to talk to Tom Dudley. The phone rang twice, and then a woman answered.

"Susan, this is Sully. I need to talk to Tom. Is he still there?"

"Sully! How wonderful to hear your voice," Susan said. "He's here, and he'll be so glad to hear from you." Then she added in a lower tone, "You know about Georgia?"

"Yes, that's why I called."

"Just a minute, I'll go get him."

Sully waited. This was the kind of call he hated. There was nothing to say but "I'm sorry" when someone died, but when it was a member of your very best friend's family, the words came even harder.

"Sully, is this really you?" Tom Dudley asked.

Sully grinned despite the sad circumstances. "Yeah, it's me. How have you been?"

There was a pause, and then it was as if the life had gone out of Tom's voice. "We've certainly been better," he said.

"Look, that's why I called. There's something about Georgia's death that I think your whole family should know, but I'm leaving it up to you to spread the word."

"What do you mean?" Tom asked.

"I'm not officially working on the case, but—"

"What case? What the hell are you talking about? Georgia killed herself. Father Joseph witnessed the whole thing."

"Just listen," Sully said. "And trust me."

He repeated everything he knew about what Georgia had learned, right up to where he'd received her letter too late to help, then explained that he was trying to find the last classmate before it was too late.

"Oh God, Sully. You don't know what this is going to mean to our mother—hell, to the whole family. We've been struggling with a way to rationalize what she did, but it just didn't jibe with the woman we knew.''

"I can only imagine," Sully said. "Look, I want you to do me a favor. Sort of keep this to yourselves for the time being. I'm not certain whether the Bureau is officially involved or not yet, but I'm sure it's only a matter of time. You'll probably be contacted by an agent at some time during the investigation. Tell them any and everything you can remember, no matter how small and insignificant you think it might be.''

"Yes, of course," Tom said. "And, Sully…well, you know how I feel about you…how we all feel about you. You've been a good friend to me all these years and—"

"You don't have to say anything," Sully said. "I loved her, too.''

"Yeah. Right. Well, I'll let you go. I'm going to call Mom right now.''

"Give her my love," Sully said.

"You already have ours, and more.''

They disconnected, and for a few moments Sully just sat in the quiet room and thought about what lay ahead. Then his gaze fell on a ruffled pillow that he'd tossed on the floor and he stood. Picked up the pillow and put it back on the bed. He paused in the doorway, making sure that he was leaving things as he'd found them.

As he gathered up the rest of his things and moved through the apartment, he imagined Virginia's fear as she'd gone from room to room, wondering what to take, fearful of leaving the life she'd built for herself. He stopped again at the picture, tracing the shape of her face with the tip of his finger.

"Hang in there, honey. I'm on the way."

"Boss, some guy named Sullivan Dean wants to talk to you. I told him you were busy, but he insisted."

Harry Redford glanced up at his secretary and frowned. "I know that name. Why do I know that—" Suddenly he bolted to his feet. "Send him in!"

Harry's pulse rocketed as he watched the man make his way across the room. Damn, damn, damn, the man from Ginny's letter. Please God that didn't mean something had happened to her.

"Mr. Redford, I appreciate you taking the time to—"

"Is she okay?"

Sully frowned. "I'm sorry?"

"Ginny! Is she okay?"

Sully was beginning to feel like Alice must have felt when she fell down the rabbit hole.

"I think we need to start over," Sully said. "My name is Sullivan Dean. I'm with the FBI and—"

"So that's why the nun sent you the papers!"

Sully felt as if he'd been kicked in the gut.

"You know?"

"Some," Redford said. "Ginny showed me everything."

"You're speaking of Miss Shapiro? Virginia Shapiro?"

Redford nodded. "Yeah, but don't call her Virginia unless you're ready to get a piece of her mind."

"Where is she?" Sully asked.

Redford shrugged. "Hell if I know. She lit out of here yesterday afternoon. Said she was going to the police and then leaving town. Promised to stay in touch. Other than that, I couldn't say."

Damn it. "Do you know who she talked to at the precinct?"

Redford nodded. "Yeah, I checked. Detective by the name of Pagillia. Anthony Pagillia. He's good, but other than a bunch of dead women, they don't have much to go on."

Sully handed him his card. "If you hear from her, will you give me a call? It's important that I find her."

"Yeah, I'll call, and I'll tell her to stay put, but that's only if she calls. I can't make any promises."

"Fair enough," Sully said. "Got a phone book? I need to call a cab. I'm going to talk to this detective before I leave town."

"I've got a reporter who's going that way to pick up some court reports. Hang around a couple of minutes and you can hitch a ride."

"Thanks," Sully said. "I appreciate it."

"Anything for Ginny," Redford said.

Sully thought of the smiling woman from the photograph he'd seen last night. "I take it she's well-liked?"

"Oh yes, and a damn good reporter to boot. You go find her, and when you do, make sure you bring her back in one piece."

"That's certainly my plan," Sully said.

Minutes later he was on his way to the headquarters of the St. Louis Police. Upon his arrival, he soon realized that Redford must have made a few phone calls. Anthony Pagillia was waiting for him at the main entrance.

"Agent Dean, it's a pleasure to meet you," Pagillia said.

"Word does get around," Sully said. "I'm assuming Redford gave you a call."

"He's concerned for Miss Shapiro, as we all are. Out of curiosity, what's your tie to this mess?"

"I grew up with Georgia Dudley, uh...Sister Mary Teresa. Her brother was my best friend. She knew I would help. Unfortunately, I didn't get the information in time to help her."

"Yeah, tough break about that," Pagillia said. "It's a little hard to imagine a nun committing suicide."

Sully's lips thinned. "She was murdered."

"Do you know something I don't?" Pagillia asked.

"Yeah," Sully said. "I knew Georgia. She couldn't swim and was afraid of water. The last thing she would ever have done was kill herself, and even then, never by drowning.''

"We have information that a priest witnessed her death.''

"I'm not saying she didn't drown. All I'm saying is, someone made her do it.''

"That's going to be a hell of a thing to prove,'' Pagillia said.

"Not if I can find Virginia Shapiro,'' Sully said. "As far as we know, other than the person who's doing this, she's the last living link to this mess.''

"I've notified all the other police departments concerning the deaths, and there is a central task force here in St. Louis that will be coordinating the gathering of information. Since this has become an interstate crime, I'm assuming the Bureau will take control?''

Sully shrugged. "Maybe, but not through me. This is too personal for the Bureau to let me on the case. What I'm doing is strictly off the clock.''

"I understand, but just know that if you need it, you have our full cooperation.''

"Thanks,'' Sully said.

"What are your plans?'' Pagillia asked.

"I'm going to rent a car and keep a promise to a very old friend.''

The yellow lines on Mississippi Highway Number 48 were in need of repainting, and Ginny's car was in need of some gas. It was fifteen minutes after three in the afternoon, and both the gauge and her belly were hovering on Empty. As she rounded a curve, she realized she was approaching a town. Her shoulders slumped with relief as she slowed down to read the sign.

Collins, Mississippi, population 2,541.

It was small, but certainly large enough for what she needed. As she wheeled into a small service station and parked at the pumps, a man exited the building.

"Fill 'er up?" he asked.

"Yes, please," Ginny said. "And check the oil, too."

"Yes, ma'am, I'll sure do that. Right hot for July, isn't it?"

She nodded. "Is there an ATM nearby?"

He pointed up the street. "See that bank there on the corner? If you go around to the side, you'll see it."

"I'll be right back," Ginny said, and walked up the street while the man began filling her tank.

He was washing her last window when she came back at a jog, only slightly winded.

"How much do I owe you?" she asked.

"Twenty-three fifty."

Ginny counted out the money, giving him exact change. "Oh...I almost forgot. I need a map, too."

He went back in the station and came out with a neatly folded map of the state of Mississippi.

"Heading anywhere in particular?" he asked, as she paid him for the map.

"Not really," she said, and got in the car and drove away. A couple of blocks down the street she pulled into a drive-in and ordered a hamburger and a milkshake to go. The scents of charbroiling meat mingling with the heat of the day made her think of family cookouts and picnics. She leaned back against the headrest and closed her eyes, resisting the urge to cry. If only her parents were still alive. If only...

She sat up with a jerk. Self-pity would get her nowhere. Compared to her old friends, she didn't have anything to complain about. At least she was still alive.

A teenage girl came out of the drive-in, carrying a tray. Ginny reached for her purse. After situating herself so that she could eat and drive, she backed out of the parking slot and drove away, quickly leaving the town of Collins behind.

The urgency to get somewhere fast and then hide from the world was overwhelming. Before, she'd just been running, trying to get as far away from St. Louis as possible, but she couldn't keep driving forever. Inevitably, she would have to stop. What she needed was a place off the so-called beaten path—a place she would normally never go. But where might that be?

She took a big bite of her hamburger, then began

to chew. By the time she was through, she felt much better. In fact, she was confident that when it mattered, something would turn up.

Storm clouds had been building on the horizon for a couple of hours now, and Ginny was starting to get nervous. At best guess, she was driving directly into its path and that was not wise. She had to get out of her car and into shelter before it hit. Just thinking about the impending thunder and lightning gave her a feeling of sick lassitude. She pulled over to the side of the road and opened her map, trying to ascertain where she was, and then where the nearest shelter might be. She knew she was in the DeSoto National Forest and had been for some time. And that she was on Highway 29, a good distance north of Biloxi.

As she studied the map, the first drops of rain began to fall. Nervous, she looked up to see that the storm was almost upon her. Tossing the map aside, she pulled back on the old two-lane highway and accelerated swiftly. Surely there would be some place to stop.

Twenty minutes later she saw a sign through the downpour and slowed so she could read it.

Tallahatchie River Fishing Dock—One Mile. Cabins For Rent.

"Thank you, God," Ginny muttered.

Sure enough, she saw another sign, this time, a

large wooden arrow that had once been painted yellow, pointing down a road to her left.

Tallahatchie River Landing, it said.

The car dragged on the high center ridge between the ruts as she left the pavement for an old graveled road. Water splashed up around the tires as she split large standing puddles, while the windshield wipers swiped squeakily against the glass.

"Please, please, please," she muttered, unaware that she'd spoken aloud, or that her desperate request was so vague. Her head felt light, her focus slipping, as if she was about to faint. She had to get out of this car.

And then she saw it: a small cluster of old rustic cabins nestled against a backdrop of trees. There was one standing apart from the others, which she took to be the office, and she turned in that direction.

Bolting from the car, she dashed through the rain. Within minutes she had a key in her pocket and was pulling up to cabin number ten, which was at the end of the row. She grabbed her suitcase and got out on the run. The irony of her new home away from home was not lost on her. For some time now she'd been running out of hope and time, and now she was, quite literally, at the end of the line.

5

It was a few minutes after midnight when Ginny awoke. Disoriented, she staggered from the bed, staring around in confusion. A flash of lightning momentarily lit the room, and when she saw the rough-hewn walls and the drab, hardwood floors, she remembered. She was on the run.

With the memories came grief. Georgia was dead.

With her belly in a knot, she stumbled to the bathroom, stripping off her clothes as she went. Ignoring the moldy grout between the aging tiles, she soaped her skin as if she would never get clean. The fear and the filth of this horror were like stains upon her soul. How could she fight an enemy she couldn't see?

Finally the water began to run cold and she realized she'd probably emptied the hot water tank. Reaching through the plastic shower curtain, she felt along the rack until she came to the towel, then grabbed it and began drying off.

Naked now, her skin pink and chafed from the rough terry-cloth fabric, she dug through her suitcase for something clean to wear. Although she could no longer hear the sound of rain upon the roof, she knew the storm had yet to pass. The wind still blew, and the limbs from the trees sheltering her cabin still scratched against the shingles like a wandering ghost, begging to be let in.

Pulling on a pair of sweats and a soft T-shirt, she moved to the window and pulled aside the curtains, looking for the switch to the window-unit air conditioner. Ignoring a thin layer of dust, she turned it on in hopes it would both cool off the cabin and drown out the sounds. Wrinkling her nose at the musty smell emanating from the unit, she went back to bed, pulling the covers up beneath her chin. Even as she felt herself drifting back to sleep, the need to stay hidden was uppermost in her mind.

It was a little past noon when Sully pulled off Interstate 55 into Grenada, Mississippi. He needed some fuel, and it was long past time to check in with the director. It wouldn't be long before his presence would be missed, and since the Bureau had more than likely taken on the case, he didn't want this to look as if he was stepping on someone else's toes. Explaining why he'd started this without notifying the boss might get touchy, but the way he figured it, his time was his own.

After topping off his tank and getting a bottle of pop and a package of peanut butter crackers, he pulled over to the shoulder of the road and took out his phone. As he waited for his call to go through, he popped a cracker in his mouth and then unscrewed the lid to his pop while he chewed. In the middle of a drink, he heard the familiar voice of the director's secretary, Myrna Page.

"Myrna, it's me, Sully. I need to speak to the boss."

"Good afternoon, Agent Dean, one moment please."

Smiling to himself, he shook his head as he waited. He'd known the woman for almost six years, and she had yet to call him by his first name.

"Dean. I expected you to call in yesterday."

Sully set his pop in the cup holder and then shoved a hand through his hair. Although his boss couldn't see him, the need to stand at attention before this man was ingrained.

"Yes, sir, I know, but something came up."

"Is the something female?"

Sully sighed. "Yes, but not in the way you're thinking."

"Then enlighten me."

Sully took a deep breath. "I'm in Mississippi."

There was a brief silence on the other end of the line and then a slight snort of disgust.

"And the reason is?"

"It began as a personal trip, sir, but I suspect it's evolving into business...our business."

"I'm listening."

"I'm certain that by now you've been made aware of the Montgomery Academy deaths, the last of which was a Sister Mary Teresa at Sacred Heart Convent in upstate New York."

"How the hell do you know about those?"

Sully hesitated. Here was where it got sticky.

"It began with a letter from a friend, and it was only after I visited Sacred Heart that—"

"You've been to the convent? Do you know what you're messing with?"

"Yes, sir, and that's why I'm calling."

He began to explain, and by the time he was through, he detected a less abrasive edge to the director's voice.

"So, you see, sir, I feel it's not only my duty to find Miss Shapiro and keep her safe until this mess can be solved, but it's the last thing I can do for my friend Georgia." He waited a moment, then added, "I need to do this, sir. For my own peace of mind. I couldn't save Georgia, but Virginia Shapiro still has a chance."

"Do you know anything I don't?" the director asked.

"No, sir. Detective Pagillia with the St. Louis Police knows as much as I do—and, I might add, as much as Miss Shapiro. She's on the run, sir, and bound to be scared half out of her mind. Let me find her. If it's safe, I'll bring her in. Otherwise, let me stay with her until this is over."

"Yes, I see your point, although I can't say I'm

completely sold on your thinking. Next time it would behoove you to pick up the phone before you act on something as explosive as this.''

"Absolutely, sir, and thanks.''

"I expect you to stay in touch.''

"Yes, of course.''

"Is there anything you need?'' the director asked.

"Well, yesterday I ran a trace on her name, checking for a paper trail or traffic tickets. I got one hit off her ATM card. She used it in a place called Collins, Mississippi, which is where I'm headed now.''

"I'll have Myrna do a little checking. Have you notified the highway patrol?''

"Not yet. I wanted to check in with you first.''

"Then wait and see what Myrna finds out first,'' he said. "As of now, you have my authorization to pursue whatever you must to find and keep her safe. However, if any new information comes to you, call it in. Agent Howard has the case.''

Dan Howard was a good man. Just knowing who was on the case made Sully feel better.

"Yes, sir, I will.''

"Okay, that's all for now,'' the director said. "Just keep your nose clean on this. After the last White House scandal, the press has been hounding every department like flies on shit. I don't want any bad press.''

"You can count on me, sir, and thank you.''

"Yes, well…just go find her.''

The line went dead in Sully's ear. Tossing the cell

phone aside, he popped another cracker in his mouth and put the car in gear.

Within the hour, his phone rang. He pulled over to the side of the road before answering, in case he needed to make notes.

"Sullivan Dean."

"Agent Dean, this is Myrna. I have some information for you."

He reached for a notepad. "Okay, I'm ready."

"Miss Shapiro's credit card was used two more times. Once last night at a place called Tallahatchie River Landing. A cabin was rented under the name Leigh Foster, which happens to be Miss Shapiro's mother's maiden name. Then again, only a hour or so ago, at a grocery store in a place called Wingate. One would assume she's gone to ground."

Sully grinned. Despite never having worked in the field, Myrna had the lingo down pat.

"Got a location for this Tallahatchie River Landing?" he asked.

"Of course." She gave him the coordinates.

As she finished, he added, "You're good, Myrna. If you ever get tired of answering the boss's phones, maybe you'd like to be my partner."

"No."

He chuckled. "I'm not that bad."

"Of course you're not, sir. Will there be anything else?"

"Not for now. I'll let you know if something else comes up, okay?"

"Yes," Myrna said, and then hung up in his ear.

Sully's worries eased yet another notch as he pulled back onto the highway. He knew where she was! Now all he had to do was get there.

Ginny locked herself back in the cabin as she carried the last bag of groceries inside. The one saving grace of this place was the tiny kitchenette just off the bedroom. Being able to both eat and sleep in the same place made the landing the perfect hideaway. The absence of phones in the room was also a plus. If she needed one, she would use her cell phone, which she'd left in the car. Or, in case of an emergency, there was the pay phone at the office. At least this way she wouldn't turn over in the night and answer a ringing phone before she was awake enough to remember that it might get her killed.

The cabinets were small, but large enough to hold the food she'd just purchased. Milk went in the refrigerator, along with some eggs, juice, a small sack of vegetables and a couple of packages of lunch meat. Besides the ice cube trays in the tiny freezer, there was just enough room for a quart of chocolate ice cream. She emptied the last sack, putting her meager assortment of canned goods to the right of the sink. As she was about to shut the door, she noticed a piece of paper stuck to the bottom of one can. Curious, she peeled it off, only to realize it was her credit card receipt, which she needed to save.

She turned toward the table and reached for her purse, intent on putting this receipt with the others she'd gathered during her trip, when she suddenly stopped. Her eyes widened and her heart started to thump as she stared down at the receipt. With shaking hands, she dug through her purse and pulled out the others, quickly spreading them on the table. The evidence of her mistake was right before her eyes.

"Oh God, oh God…what have I done?"

Unwittingly, she'd laid a paper trail that was as good as any road map, beginning with the receipt from the gas station nearest her house, then south to a Git and Go in Arkansas, to Collins, Mississippi, to her final destination—the Tallahatchie River Landing—and a grocery story in Wingate. She might just as well have pinned a target to her back.

In a panic, she ran toward the window and peered out through the curtains. There was no one in sight. Except for the manager, a man named Marshall Auger, who lived on the premises, she was still the only customer. But how long would that last? Should she go? If she did, where? This place had been ideal until she'd messed it all up.

She glanced back at the bed, wondering how long it would take to get packed and how much of her groceries she would have to leave behind. As she stood, a familiar sound penetrated her panic. She spun around, looking frantically up at the sky and the gathering clouds. Another impending thunderstorm. Was this streak of inclement weather never going to end?

Not trusting the single door lock to keep out the world, she shoved a chair beneath the knob and then plopped down on the bed. Leaving now was out of the question. That horrible lassitude she endured during storms made driving almost impossible. She was in enough danger as it was. Adding to the problem by having a wreck was out of the question.

She wanted to cry. Instead, she lay back on the bed and rolled up in a ball. Her eyes were wide and fixed on the door, her body trembling. For the time being, she was here, whether she liked it or not.

Sometime later, it began to rain. Not the wild blowing rain from the night before, but a slow, steady downpour that raised the level of the Tallahatchie to new and frightening depths.

Sully pulled up to the office of the Tallahatchie River Landing and killed the engine. He never realized how tightly he'd been gripping the steering wheel until he tried to turn loose of it. His fingers were cramped, as were his legs, but he was here. Even though it was dark, he could see the outline of a car at the far end of the row of cabins. Ducking his head, he got out on the run and then found himself standing on the stoop and pounding on the manager's door to get in. He waited a minute, then pounded again. When a light came on inside and then a grizzled bear of a man opened the door to let him in, he bolted through the doorway without waiting for an invitation.

"Name's Marshall Auger," the old man said. "You're out kinda late, ain't ya?"

"Got caught in the rain," Sully answered. "I need a place to stay."

"You alone?" Marshall asked, peering over Sully's shoulder into the dark.

"Yes."

"Extra charge if you got someone with ya," Marshall persisted.

Sully looked up, his hand on his wallet. "I said I was alone. If you want to check, feel free. The car's not locked."

Marshall eyed the downpour and then the water running out of Sully's hair onto his face and shrugged.

"It'll be twenty-five dollars a night, plus tax."

Sully slid a hundred-dollar bill onto the counter.

"How long you stayin'?"

"I'll let you know," Sully answered.

Marshall pocketed the money and then handed Sully a key.

"I'd like the last cabin, please," Sully said.

"Done taken. How about the one next to it?"

"Yeah, all right," Sully said. "As long as there's not some family with a bunch of kids," he added.

"Nope. Just one woman. Real quiet."

Ha. Got my answer without even asking. "Okay, then," Sully said, and picked up the key.

"Ain't no phones or TVs in the rooms," Marshall added. "This here's a fishin' camp, so if you was expectin' somethin' else, you're outta luck."

"Just a place to sleep," Sully said.

"Sweet dreams," Marshall said, baring yellowed teeth as he grinned a goodbye.

Within moments Sully was back in his car and driving down the row of cabins, only he didn't stop at the one he'd been given. Instead, he drove down to the last and parked directly behind the car. A quick check of the license tag told him it was hers, and for a moment all he could do was sit and stare at the cabin. Praise the Lord, he'd found her.

He started to get out, then hesitated. The windows were dark. She was bound to be asleep. Should he wake her now and risk scaring her even more, or should he wait until morning? Instinct told him to do it now. Too many people had died for him to worry about etiquette.

As he walked toward her door, he kept picturing her as she'd been in the photo with her parents. Happy and laughing. Then he shrugged the thought aside. At least she was still alive. Doubling up his fist, he began to pound loudly.

Ginny came awake with a start, clutching the covers up to her chin. Someone was pounding at the door! She lay without moving, her heart hammering against her chest. Maybe it was a mistake. Maybe they would just go away.

The noise stopped and she felt a moment of hope, but moments later, the pounding was renewed, and this time she thought she heard someone calling her name. That wasn't right! She'd signed in at the office under her mother's maiden name, Leigh Foster. But she'd distinctly heard him say Virginia Shapiro.

In a panic, she rolled out of bed in one leap and began searching the room for something to use as a weapon. Just as her fingers curled around a fireplace poker, she heard him again.

"Miss Shapiro! Miss Shapiro! Please let me in!"

Creeping toward the window, she peeked through the curtains. All she could see was the dark outline of a man standing on the stoop.

"Go away!" she yelled. "There's no one here by that name."

The pounding stopped. She crept to the door and laid her ear against the wood, praying for the sound of receding footsteps.

Sully exhaled slowly, trying to ignore the water running off the roof and down his neck.

"Miss Shapiro, I'm Sullivan Dean. Georgia was my friend. She sent me the same information she sent you. I've been looking for you for the better part of two days. Please let me in. We need to talk."

Ginny moaned. Oh God, could this really be the man to whom Georgia had referred in her letter? If only she dared believe.

"How can I trust you?" she asked.

Sully sighed. "I don't know what to tell you," he said. "Maybe if you'll turn on the porch light, you can see my badge."

"Badge?"

"Yes, ma'am," Sully said. "I'm an agent with the Federal Bureau of Investigation. Please, ma'am, if you would just—"

The light nearly blinded him. Sully covered his face with one hand, allowing his vision to adjust as he reached for his badge. To his right, the curtain slowly parted, and he had a vague impression of dark eyes in a pale face. Then the curtain fell shut. He caught himself holding his breath.

"Oh Lord, please let this be all right," Ginny muttered, and slowly opened the door.

Sully saw her then, standing in the shadows of the cabin with a poker in her hand. In spite of the deadliness of her makeshift weapon and her height, he was more than a little startled at how frail she looked.

"Miss Shapiro?"

"Yes."

"May I come in?"

Ginny hesitated, then stepped aside, still clutching the poker.

Sully turned on the light as he entered, then shut

the door behind him. Water puddled instantly at his feet and began to run toward the corner of the room.

"If you have a mop or something, I'd be glad to—"

Ginny shook her head, then motioned toward a nearby chair.

"Please…sit down."

"I'll get *it* wet, too," he said.

"I imagine it will dry."

He sat.

Ginny ran a nervous hand through her hair, suddenly remembering that she'd been asleep. Lord only knew what she looked like. Tapping the end of the poker against the floor, she glanced nervously at him and then looked away.

Sully stared, studying her sleep-softened face and wondering what it would be like to wake up beside someone who looked like that every day for the rest of his life.

"Would you—"

"Do you mind if—"

They spoke in unison, both starting and then stopping at once.

Sully swiped a hand across his face. "You first."

Ginny hesitated. "I'll get you a towel."

Sully watched her walking from the room, and when his thoughts began to center on the length of her legs, he looked away, reminding himself that he'd come to help her, not sleep with her.

Ginny handed him the towel and then stepped back, still wondering if she'd let in a murderer instead of a savior.

Sully toweled his hair first and was drying his face when she spoke.

"If Georgia was your friend and she's already dead, then why did you come looking for me?"

He paused, considering the fear in her voice. He supposed he understood it, although in a way it hurt his feelings to think of how frantically he'd been searching for her, and here she was questioning his motives.

"She asked me for help, and I was too late to save her. She obviously cared about you, and I cared for her." His voice broke and he looked away, unwilling for her to see his emotions so close to the skin.

But it was too late. Ginny had seen the quick flash of tears in his eyes and heard the tremble in his voice. It was enough. She took a step forward, briefly touching Sully's shoulder before moving away.

"I'm sorry," she said. "But you see…I've been so scared."

Something in her eyes brought him to his feet.

"I know," he said softly. "I came as fast as I could."

Suddenly Ginny was crying and Sully was holding her.

"I'm going to get you all wet," he said gruffly, and tried to step back.

Ginny hiccuped on a sob, her gaze fixed on his face. The condition of his clothing was the last thing on her mind.

"You won't let me die?"

He cursed beneath his breath and pulled her back in his arms, this time, wrapping her completely within his embrace.

"I swear on my life, I won't let you die."

Ginny stiffened as the weight of his words settled in her mind.

"That might be more difficult than you think."

"What do you mean?"

She gestured toward the table where the receipts were lying.

"The credit card receipts. I didn't think."

"Yeah, I know about them," he said. "It'll be okay."

"You know?"

He almost smiled. "How do you think I found you?"

She cast a nervous glance at the door.

"It's not that easy," he added, wanting to assure her. "I have more access to that sort of information than the ordinary person."

"And what makes you think the person responsible for what's happening is ordinary?"

Sully sighed. "I didn't mean that as facetiously as it sounded. I'm sorry."

"Apology accepted," she said, and then added, "I think I owe you one, too."

Sully's brows knitted. "For what?"

"I have yet to thank you."

This time he did smile, but only a little. "I haven't done anything yet."

"Oh, but you have," Ginny said. "You're here."

He stared at her then, seeing her almost anew. Her dark shoulder-length hair and rather startling blue eyes set in a heart-shaped face were unforgettable, of that there was no doubt. But it was the thrust of her chin that was the most telling. The lady was no quitter.

"Yeah, so I am," he said, then lightened the moment by looking down at his feet. "This puddle I'm standing in is growing deeper by the minute. I think I'd better go change my clothes before I float us both down the river."

Ginny looked startled. He'd just gotten here, and now he was talking about leaving.

"Where are you going?" she asked, hating the tremble she heard in her voice.

"Next door. I rented the cabin next to you. You're going to be okay now, Miss Shapiro, but if you get scared, all you have to do is yell. I'm only seconds away."

Loath for him to leave, she blurted, "I could fix you some soup."

Sully hesitated. He wanted out of his wet clothes

and into a bed in the worst way, but he could tell she wasn't ready to let him go.

"Tell you what," he said. "How about if I get settled in and into some dry clothes? Give me fifteen minutes and I'll be back."

Embarrassed now that she'd all but begged him to stay, she felt obligated to add, "Okay, but only if you really want something to eat. If not, I'll be fine."

She was trying so damned hard to be brave, he couldn't help but admire her.

"Yeah, I know," he said. "But I think I could really go for that soup."

Her eyes widened in relief, and there was a smile on her face as she turned toward the kitchen.

"I won't be long," he added, but she was already dragging out a pot and digging through the meager contents of a utensil drawer in search of a can opener.

He didn't bother running back to his car. There was no way he could get any wetter. Instead, he strode through the rain, got his bag and then walked over to the next cabin without bothering to move his vehicle. If someone drove up looking for Ginny, seeing two cars instead of one would definitely give them pause. It might be the difference between life and death for both of them.

The hinges squeaked as the door swung inward. He flipped on the light and grimaced as he shut the door behind him. The place didn't look a damn bit better than hers did, but he hadn't come for the accommodations. Tossing his bag on the bed, he quickly located the bathroom and began stripping off his wet clothes as he went. Less than ten minutes later he had showered and dressed and was headed back out the door.

The rain was letting up, but he still ran toward Ginny's cabin, his boots splitting the puddles as he went. He knocked quickly, then turned the knob. To his relief, she'd left it unlocked. He came in on the run.

Startled by the noise, Ginny turned, then relaxed when she saw it was him.

Dean. Sullivan Dean. She was still trying to get used to the thought of his name.

"The soup is done. Do I call you Mr. Dean, or Agent Dean or—"

"Sully. Call me Sully."

"If you'll call me Ginny."

He grinned. "Yeah, Harry Redford said you wouldn't answer to anything else."

Ginny's eyes widened. "You know Harry?"

"We met," Sully said briefly. "He's concerned about you."

Ginny began dishing the soup into bowls.

"He's a good man to work for. I like him."

Sully nodded. "Smells good."

Ginny set the bowls down on the table. "It's just vegetable beef out of a can. All I did was add water and heat it. Want some crackers?"

"Sure," Sully said. "Can I help?"

She shook her head. "I've got it. Do you take anything in your coffee?"

"Just black," Sully said, as she set the cup near his bowl.

They sat across the table, eating in silence, with only the occasional clink of a spoon against a bowl for punctuation.

Ginny had seen the long thin scar near his left ear and traced the path of it across his neck with one brief, telling glance, trying not to imagine how he'd acquired it. All in all, he was a big man. Broad shoulders, big-boned. His legs were long and heavily muscled. She could tell he worked out, although in his line of business, she supposed he had to stay in good shape. His hair was short, straight and thick, a dark chocolate brown just a couple of shades lighter than his eyes, which appeared almost black. Suddenly, she realized that he'd caught her staring.

"Sorry," she said. "I didn't mean to stare, but has anyone told you that you look a lot like Harrison Ford?"

He grimaced wryly. "Maybe."

She shrugged. "Just an observation." She stood and picked up her bowl and cup and carried them to the sink. "More coffee?"

"If I do, I won't sleep," he said.

Ginny glanced at her watch. "Speaking of which, you must be exhausted. It's after 1:00 a.m."

Sully took that as his cue to leave. "Thank you for the food."

Ginny took the dishes out of his hands. "I'll do that," she said. "And you're welcome."

Now that it was time to go, Sully found himself vaguely regretful that he was going to leave.

"I'll just be next door."

She nodded.

"If you need anything, anything at all, let me know. I'm a light sleeper."

"I will."

"Well then...if you're sure you're going to be okay?"

Ginny folded her hands in front of her like a child about to recite.

"I'll be fine...now that you're here."

The trust on her face was frightening. Sully's heart gave a hitch as he headed for the door. *Please, God, don't let me screw this one up.* He opened the door and then stopped and turned. Ginny was staring at him from across the room. He started to speak and then realized he had nothing left to say. Instead, he nodded, then closed the door. Seconds later, he heard the tumblers turning in the lock.

Wind lifted the hair from his forehead as he stood in the darkness, waiting for her light to go out. Mist blew against his face, but the rain was gone. In the distance, he could hear the roar of a flood-swollen river. Seconds later, her cabin went dark.

He turned, staring about the area until he was satisfied there was no one around. Then he walked to his
cabin, sat down on the edge of the bed and took his
cell phone out of his pocket. It was time to make the
call.

"Sir, it's Agent Dean."

The director rolled over to the side of the bed and
lowered his voice so as not to disturb his sleeping
wife.

"Do you know what the hell time it is?" he muttered.

"Yes, sir, I'm sorry, sir, but I thought you'd want
to know. I found her."

"Good job. I'll notify Agent Howard tomorrow."

"Yes, sir."

"What's your read on this?"

Sully sighed, thinking of the woman who'd cried
in his arms. "She's scared, but pretty tough, all things
considered."

"Is the location secure?"

Sully eyed his surroundings and resisted the urge
to snort.

"That's debatable, but I'll let you know if we move
on. I don't suppose you have any breaks in the case?"

"No. Get some rest."

"Yes, sir, I plan to do just that."

"Oh...Sully?"

Sully's face mirrored his surprise. The boss wasn't

in the habit of calling any of his agents by their first name.

"Yes, sir?"

"Good job."

"I'd say thank you, but truthfully, the credit should go to Sister Mary Teresa. She put this all together. I'm just sorry as hell I didn't get there in time to save her, too."

"Yes, well, sometimes these things just happen. Get some sleep and keep in touch."

Sully laid the phone down on the bedside table and then walked to the window, giving the rain-washed parking lot one last look. The single security light near the manager's cabin left tiny refractions of light in the lingering puddles, while the hum of Ginny's air conditioner broke the silence of the night.

Satisfied that all was well, he turned away from the window and started to turn on his air-conditioning unit, as well, when he realized that, if he did, he might not be able to hear her call.

Shedding his clothes as he went, he opened the window beside his bed instead, laid his handgun and holster on the table beside his phone and crawled between the sheets. Exhaustion claimed him as he closed his eyes, and yet, as weary as he was, it was a long time before he slept.

6

Rain was everywhere, seeping through the walls, coming up through the floors. The roof was melting, the colors of the furniture bleeding one into the other in a tie-dyed nightmare. The ground beneath her feet began to give, and Ginny felt herself sinking. At first it was only a frustration, getting mud on her shoes, but it soon changed to terror as she struggled futilely to hang on to solid ground. Thunder suddenly sounded, rolling throughout the heavens above her head and sapping her strength until she was too weak to move. Out of nowhere, water rose to her knees, then soaked the front of her shirt. Clawing at a steadily dissolving shoreline, she began to cry. When the water lapped at her chin, then at the edge of her mouth, she threw her head back and screamed.

"Help me, please help me. Don't let me drown. Don't let me die."

Ginny woke on a gasp and sat straight up in bed. The bedclothes were tangled about her legs, and in spite of the air-conditioning, her hair was sweat-streaked and stuck to the back of her neck. Still shaking, she sat up on the side of the bed, then leaned her elbows on her knees and covered her face with her hands.

A dream. It was just a stupid dream.

When she'd gained some equilibrium, she stumbled to the bathroom, splashing her face and neck with tepid water before scrubbing herself dry. Unwilling to go back to bed with that memory so fresh in her mind, she turned the light on in the kitchen and made coffee instead. As she did, the two unwashed bowls from last night's late supper reminded her that she was no longer alone. The knowledge sat lightly on her heart as the dark, fragrant brew began to drip from the maker into the glass beaker below. After pouring herself a cup, she slipped on her sneakers and then unlocked her front door. Curious as to what kind of a day it would be, she stepped outside and inhaled. The sky was clearing, although a scattering of gray, wispy clouds still littered the morning sky. Behind them, the first gray fingers of dawn were tearing at the blanket of night, making way for the sunshine to follow.

Ginny took a careful sip of the coffee, relishing the warmth and the kick of caffeine as it slid down her throat. After careful inspection of the rickety stoop, she settled down on the top step to finish her coffee. Only then did she realize that Sullivan Dean had parked his car behind hers. She glanced over at his cabin but saw no evidence of his presence. Probably still asleep.

A slight wind ruffled through her hair, drying the lingering dampness. She lifted her face, studying the sky. It seemed to be clearing. That was good. No more storms. No more rain.

Storms gave her such an unsettled feeling, and things were already unsettled enough. As she sat, she became aware of the faint sounds of a radio and decided that the manager's alarm had probably gone off. When the sounds suddenly disappeared, she grinned and took another sip of coffee. Sounded like her theory was right. He hadn't wanted to awaken any more abruptly than she had.

A bird called from a nearby tree, and another answered from somewhere behind her cabin. Curious, she set down her cup and then strolled around the corner and walked a short distance behind the cabin to peer up through the limbs. As she did, she became aware of another sound. One that was more ominous. More threatening. The sound of rushing water.

The river! Of course. After all the rain they'd been having, it must be rolling at the banks. With the thought came the memory of another flood-swollen river and the image of Georgia falling through space, her habit billowing behind her like outspread wings.

She turned away, her joy in the morning over, and as she did, heard the sound of an approaching vehicle. Although she felt reasonably safe, she couldn't help remembering that Sullivan Dean had found her, and if he could, then so could anyone else. And, with no face to put to the danger she was in, Ginny bolted toward her cabin.

She emerged from between the cabins just as a one-ton dually pulled up at the manager's office. The truck bed was full of fishing equipment, which fell with a clatter as the driver hit the brakes. As Ginny watched, three men spilled out of the cab, laughing and talking loudly. One of them tossed an empty beer can on the ground and then reached over the side of the truck bed and pulled out another beer from a partially buried ice chest.

As he popped the top and turned to take the first drink, he saw Ginny. The grin that spread across his face made her nervous. In that moment, she knew she never should have stopped to watch. Trying to look nonchalant, she made herself walk toward the cabin when she wanted to run.

"Hey, baby! Wait for me!" the man yelled. "I've got something that'll put a sway in your step."

Ginny thought she heard the other two men telling him to shut up, but whatever they said, he seemed bent on ignoring.

She was gauging the distance to her front door as no more than forty feet when she heard footsteps approaching on the gravel. She spun. He was coming toward her on the run.

She didn't think, she just reacted. Sully had told her if she needed him, just yell, so she did.

Twice.

At the top of her voice.

It was hard to say who was more startled, Ginny or the stranger, but the half-naked man who came flying out of the cabin between them was armed and running. Sully's hair was awry, his feet and chest bare, but the look on his face and the gun in his hand said it all. He spared her one quick glance, assuring himself that she was still in one piece, and then barked out an order.

"Get in the cabin."

Ginny spun around and didn't stop until she'd slammed the door behind her. Quickly she ran to the window and peered through the curtain. Sully had the stranger on the ground and was going through his pockets, while holding the other two men at bay with his gun, although she couldn't hear what was being said. A few minutes later he yanked the man to his feet and then stood and watched until they all drove away. Once the pickup had disappeared, he turned and looked straight at her.

Ginny found herself wanting to run to him in thanksgiving. When she saw him coming toward her cabin, she settled for something less dramatic and just met him at the door.

"I suppose I overreacted."

He needed to tell her that she'd nearly stopped his heart. That the fear in her voice had yanked him out of a deep sleep with no mercy. That he'd stumbled into his jeans without thought for anything but her and getting to his gun, and that he'd been so damned scared he wouldn't get to her in time. Instead, he just shrugged and shook his head.

"You did what I told you to do."

Ginny nodded, then shivered suddenly and wrapped her arms around herself.

"Was he drunk?"

"And high."

"Lord," she muttered. "Do you think they'll come back?"

"Probably. The manager is their father."

Ginny winced. "Nothing like making points with management."

"I told them you belonged to me and to leave you the hell alone." He wasn't surprised by the startled expression on her face, but he didn't bother to explain. She could figure it out for herself.

Strangely enough, Ginny chose not to comment, which did surprise him. Then, when she pointed toward the porch behind him, the last thing he expected her to say was, "Would you please get my cup?"

He turned, saw the empty coffee cup and picked it up.

"Want some?" she asked, as he walked inside and handed it to her.

Her words curled around his belly and pulled his nerves in a knot. Some what? What he wanted right now had nothing to do with caffeine.

"Yeah, sure," he said. "If you've got extra."

Ginny nodded. "I owe you again."

Sully touched her then, on the shoulder, and only briefly. It was all he could afford.

"We're not keeping score on this one, okay?"

She smiled, then ducked her head and went to get his coffee.

Sully sighed as he watched her walk away. Her T-shirt had a hole near the hem and was faded to a dull, ugly gray. Her sweatpants weren't much better. Tall and lithe to the point of being almost skinny, she was still so damned beautiful she made him ache.

Laying his gun on the table, he combed his fingers through his hair. As he sat, he chose a chair that would give him the optimum view of her as she worked. It didn't take five seconds for him to know this was getting too personal.

He sighed.

Son of a bitch.

He shouldn't have slept in her bed.

When she turned around, he masked his emotions with a yawn and nodded his thanks when she handed him the coffee.

"Since you're up..."

He grinned.

"I'm going to fix some eggs. Are you interested?"

Weighing the possibility of a couple more hours of sleep against sitting across the table from her again, the food won.

"Sounds good. Need any help?"

Ginny's attention focused. "Can you cook?"

"I'm not bad."

"That's more than I can say," she muttered. "Bring your coffee. You can do the bacon."

"What are you going to do?" he asked.

"Watch?"

Sully arched an eyebrow as she led the way into the kitchen. Damn, but he was in over his head.

While they were cooking breakfast, the trio Sully had run off from the landing were cooking up something of their own. Carney, Dale and Freddie Auger didn't cotton to being run off of their own daddy's place of business. All they'd been looking for was a place to sleep off their three-day fishing party. It wasn't the first time they'd spent more time drinking than fishing, and it wouldn't be the last. But they all knew better than to go home in this condition. Their old ladies would never let them hear the end of it. Carney, the one who'd taken a shine to Ginny, was the most pissed and had spent the better part of the last hour talking about it.

"Goddamn it! I'm tellin' you both...ain't no son of a bitch puttin' me on the ground and livin' to tell the tale."

Freddie was driving and didn't bother to comment, leaving the commiserating up to their youngest brother, Dale. Dale was a yes-man from way back; no matter what they did, he always went along with the stunts, even when he knew he was making a mistake. Freddie didn't have much respect for Dale, although he didn't mind him hanging around.

"I don't blame you," Dale said. "He didn't have no call to pull a gun on you like that. You wasn't doin' nothin' but havin' yourself a little fun."

"Damn straight!" Carney said, and took another swig of his beer.

A few more miles passed, during which time Carney kept getting drunker and drunker. Suddenly he slapped the dashboard of Freddie's truck.

"Turn this som'bitch around," he mumbled. "I wanna see Daddy. We went to see Daddy, I wanna see him."

"Dang it, Carney, you'll put a dent in my truck. Calm yourself down. We'll see Daddy tomorrow after you've sobered up some, all right?"

"No, I wanna see my ol' daddy right now. He's gettin' on in years. What if he goes and dies on us tonight and I don't get to tell him goodbye?" The tears in his voice changed to fury as his drunken thoughts continued to scatter. "It'd be that bitch's fault. Her screamin' like that and all. What the hell did she think I was gonna do?"

Freddy glared. "You know how you get when you've done too much dope. Probably thought you was gonna rape her, you dumb ass, and I can't blame her. I wasn't so sure about you myself."

"Yeah, Carney, you as much as told her what you was comin' to give her," Dale said.

Carney slapped the side of Dale's shoulder. "Shut the fuck up," he muttered, and tossed his empty beer can out the window. "We're goin' to get us a motel room and sleep it off. We'll see Daddy tomorrow, and that's that."

Both brothers hushed for the moment, but Carney's anger continued to simmer. He would make that woman and her old man sorry or know the reason why.

Sully had almost finished dressing when his cell phone rang. He rounded the bed and grabbed it on the third ring.

"Sullivan Dean."

"Hey, Sully, Dan Howard here. How's it going?"

Sully sat on the side of the bed. "All right. I suppose the boss called you?"

"Yes. Thought I'd check in and let you know what's going on. I've got people in all six cities, gathering information on each of the victims. You know, this thing gives me the creeps. While their deaths seem self-inflicted, they're damned bizarre."

"Yeah, I know what you mean," Sully said. "And if you ask me, the most bizarre was Sister Mary's."

"I heard she was a friend. I'm really sorry."

"Thanks. Actually, she's the reason I even got involved."

"What about the Shapiro woman? Do you think she knows anything?"

"No. She's scared to death, hiding from the world and anything connected to telephones, but I'll have to give it to her, she's tough."

"That's all right. Being tough might be what it takes to keep her breathing."

"I hear that," Sully said.

"Anything else I need to know about?" Dan asked.

"Had a run-in this morning with three locals. I don't think it's anything serious, but I'm going to run a check on them just to make sure."

"Do you think they're connected to this?"

"No. Their dad manages the place where we're staying. I think it's just a case of bad luck and bad timing all the way around."

"Okay, but if you learn anything, let me know."

"Same to you," Sully said, and hung up.

He sat for a moment, contemplating the best way to run a check on the three brothers, then decided to call Myrna. If he went through the local authorities, then that would be more people who knew Sully was a Fed, and that would spark curiosity they didn't need. He punched in the number for the director's office and waited for her voice.

"Federal Bureau of Investigations."

"Myrna, it's Sully."

"Good morning, Agent Dean. I'm sorry, but the Director is on the Hill in meetings all day."

"I didn't call to talk to him. I called to talk to you."

"What do you want?"

Sully grinned. The woman was a shark.

"I know this isn't really in your job description, but I've got three brothers I need to run a check on. Do you think you could run the plate for me and see if these jokers have rap sheets?"

"Yes, I could."

When she put her emphasis on the word *could* rather than *yes,* Sully grinned.

"Then *will* you?" he asked.

"Will this piss off my boss?"

Sully's smile widened. Darned if Miz Myrna didn't have more vinegar in her than he'd imagined.

"No, ma'am. I wouldn't do anything to get you in trouble with the Director. Besides, Agent Howard knows about this, and he's in charge of the case."

"Then I need the number and the names."

"Yes, ma'am," Sully said, and reeled them off.

"Will that be all?" Myrna asked.

"You sure you won't reconsider working with me?"

Sully thought he heard a small snort just before the dial tone buzzed in his ear.

He grinned as he stuck the phone in his pants pocket and then headed out the door toward Ginny's cabin. There were decisions to be made regarding her safety. He was leaning toward taking her to a safe house. At least there, the perimeter would be easier to monitor.

"It's me," he said, knocking once on her door before entering.

Ginny was seated in the middle of the bed with a notepad in her lap and the pages that Georgia had sent her scattered about her. She didn't even look up when Sully entered.

"What are you doing?" he asked.

"Making lists."

"What kinds of lists?"

"Similarities. Differences."

He glanced at the notepad, impressed by the meticulous notes she was making.

"How did you know that?" he asked, pointing to one item about Jo-Jo Henley that she'd listed on the Differences side.

"I asked the owner of the place where she was working."

"She had ovarian cancer?"

"That's what he said. He also said that no one else knew."

Sully pulled up a chair and sat down, his interest growing.

"That could change a lot of people's perceptions about her death. You know...maybe she flipped out and decided to take her own life."

"Yes, I know. But if she was so bent on just killing herself to keep from suffering later, then why not take some sleeping pills or something? If she was averse to suffering, I don't think she would have chosen to hug a truck as a means of leaving this earth.'' She looked up at him then. ''None of this makes any sense.''

''Okay, granted there are a lot of variables. None of them actually put a gun to her own head and pulled the trigger, but each and every one of them did put herself in a situation that caused her own death. I mean...where else can you go but down if you're jumping from a bridge...or, in Georgia's case, into a river?''

Ginny tossed her notepad aside and bolted from the bed, too antsy to sit.

''I don't know, damn it! If I had answers, I wouldn't be hiding, afraid of my own shadow.''

Sully let her vent. Getting mad was a hell of a lot healthier than being scared half to death.

''What else do you know that I don't?''

Ginny threw up her hands. ''I don't know! I made calls to the families of the deceased. Did you?''

Sully rocked back in the chair, his eyes widening.

''When did you do all this?''

''Before I left St. Louis. After I found out that Georgia was dead.''

''Did you make notes?''

''I'm a reporter, Agent Dean. What do you think?''

''I think I've underestimated you, and the name is Sully.''

Ginny's anger slid out of her in one breath. "I'm sorry," she said, and slumped down on the side of the bed, only inches away from his knee.

Sully could see a vein throbbing in her neck, and there were beads of sweat along the upper edge of her lip. They would be salty.

He jerked as if he'd been slapped, although Ginny Shapiro had no idea where his thoughts had gone.

"No apologies needed. We just need to get on the same page."

"I'll get my notes," Ginny said, and leaned backward on the bed, reaching for the notepad she'd tossed aside.

As she did, his phone suddenly rang. She gasped and then froze, her eyes wide with shock as she watched him reaching into his pocket.

"Ginny...don't! My phone can't hurt you."

She went limp, embarrassed that she'd reacted in such a terrified manner. Of course his phone couldn't hurt her. What was she thinking?

"I knew that," she muttered, and strode outside, leaving him alone in her cabin.

Sully cursed beneath his breath and then answered. It was Myrna.

"The '94 model Ford extended cab, Mississippi license number 4XJ99, belongs to Freddie Joe Auger, of Hemphill, Mississippi. He's been arrested a couple of times for Drunk and Disorderly, but nothing major. Dale Wayne Auger, also of Hemphill, has nine speeding tickets. Nothing more. Carney Gene Auger has a rap sheet longer than Lady Godiva's hair. Should I read them all off?''

Sully's gut clenched. He should have known this wouldn't be as simple as he'd first believed.

"No, just give me the highlights."

"Lots of possession charges, drug-related arrests, theft, assault with a deadly weapon. He's a real Boy Scout."

"I don't suppose there are any outstanding warrants?"

"No."

Sully sighed. "Of course not. That would have been too easy."

"Their father, Marshall Auger, is the brother of a local judge. He owns and manages a fishing area on the Tallahatchie River, about a hundred miles north of Biloxi."

That much he'd already known. "Okay, Myrna, I owe you big, this time. When I get back to D.C., I'm buying you the biggest steak in the city."

"I'm a vegetarian."

Sully laughed. "The hell you are. I personally saw you downing a good half-dozen shrimp at last year's Christmas party."

"I backslid. I'm over it."

"Myrna, can I ask you a personal question?"

"No."

The line went dead in his ear. Sully disconnected,

making a mental note to himself to send her flowers when this was all over, and went to look for Ginny.

She was sitting on the stoop, staring down at the ground.

"I want to move you to a safe house."

Startled, she jumped up. "Why? What was that phone call about? Do they know who's causing—"

Sully took her by the arm. "No, no, calm down a minute and just let me talk."

She went silent, but she didn't relax. He could feel the tension in her muscles.

"That wasn't about the deaths, it was about the guy who accosted you this morning."

Ginny frowned. "What's he got to do with all this? I thought he was just some local who—"

"He is a local. The manager here is his father, which means he might come back and take another run at us. I pissed him off pretty good this morning."

Ginny sighed and then combed her fingers through her hair in frustration.

"No! Damn it to hell, no!"

"What do you mean, no?"

"I'm already running from someone I can't identify. I'm not going to start running again. Better the enemy I know than the one I don't. I'm not going to a city. There are too many people and places to be careful of. I don't want to go to some safe house where people watch me from dawn to dark, taking note of everything from the fact that I cry in my sleep to how many times I go pee.''

Sully couldn't think. She'd taken him off guard with her honesty.

"You cry in your sleep?"

She shrugged. "Sometimes."

He wanted to touch her, but something told him to keep his distance.

"Why?"

"I don't know. Dreams, I guess. I never remember them, but the tears are there when I wake up."

"Jesus," he muttered, thinking of the other six women and wondering if they'd cried in their sleep, too.

"Don't make me leave," Ginny said, hating herself for begging, but something inside her said to stay where she was, and she'd been a reporter too long to ignore her gut instincts.

Sully sighed. "We'll see," he said. "If things escalate with those men, you won't have a choice."

She shrugged. "Fair enough."

"Now, about your notes. Want to share them with me?"

He'd asked, not demanded, and Ginny's estimation of the man went up yet another notch. He was darned good-looking, and if this morning was any indication, he looked even better out of his clothes. He'd come to her rescue, not out of duty, but from love and honor for their mutual friend, Georgia. And he was still coming to her rescue. She was going to have to be careful not to let herself get emotionally involved with a virtual stranger.

Ginny waved her hand toward the cabin. "After you...Sully."

She'd called him by his name. He looked at her and then grinned. Slowly.

Ginny's breath caught in the back of her throat. Oh man, why couldn't he have looked like Walter Matthau instead of Harrison Ford?

7

Phillip Karnoff's fingers were flying over the keyboard of his computer, his eyes fixed on the screen. Unable to sleep, he'd been up for hours, "talking" in a chat room. Now, only he and one other net junkie, a user named CyberRat, were still up. Phillip found himself unloading fears on an stranger that he could never say aloud.

Babydoc: "The pressure is getting to me. I don't know how much longer I can hang on."

CyberRat: "You'll do what you have to do, man. It's your life. Don't let them call all the shots."

Babydoc: "Yeah, but you don't understand. I can't hold a job. Every time I get one, something inside me starts pushing and pushing and I screw it all up."

CyberRat: "That sounds serious, Dude. Maybe you need to see a doctor? Ever try therapy? I've been in therapy for years."

Tears rolled from Phillip's eyes. See a doctor? That was rich. He lived with one, and it had yet to do him any good.

Babydoc: "Different strokes for different folks. I'm not into that."

CyberRat: "Come on, man. You need to spill your guts or bad karma will eat you alive."

Phillip hesitated. Saying more could be dangerous, but the urge to unburden his soul was overwhelming. And what could it hurt? He didn't know this person—would never know this person. Anonymity would protect him, and maybe CyberRat was right. Maybe he did need to unload. At this point, what the hell could it hurt?

Babydoc: "I think I'm going insane."

CyberRat: "Why?"

Babydoc: "I hear voices."

CyberRat: "This is serious, man. Ever been checked out? Ever take any meds for that?"

Babydoc: "No."

CyberRat: "Does anyone else know you're tuned in to something else?"

Babydoc: "No."

CyberRat: "Look, dude. I don't know you personally, but if you were my friend, I'd be saying, get yourself to a shrink. You don't want to freak out on yourself or your family, do you?"

Phillip was shaking so hard he couldn't think. His eyes were focused on the keyboard. He could see his fingers above the keys, but he couldn't make himself move. God. Oh God. What was happening?

Disconnect, Phillip. Do it now, you sniveling little bastard.

CyberRat: *"Dude? You still there?"*

Phillip shook his head, as if trying to shake out the sound of the other man's voice. And then he sobbed. Other man? What other man? There was no one here but himself.

CyberRat: *"Dude! Dude! Talk to me, man."*

Phillip shuddered, then slumped forward. When he lifted his head, the smirk on his face said it all.

Babydoc: *"Babydoc can't talk to you anymore. He's gone and you're pissing me off. Get lost. I'm the one in control."*

Phillip shut down the computer and stood abruptly, yanking off his clothes as he went.

Phillip is a wimp. I'm sick and tired of putting up with his crap and wearing these damned preppy-looking clothes.

He strode to his closet, shoving his clothes first one way and then another. Finally he saw what he wanted in the back of the closet. He pulled a pair of black slacks from a hanger and put them on. They cupped his buttocks and emphasized the size of his cock, just the way he liked it. He pulled up the zipper and then smoothed a hand down the front of his fly before diving back into his closet. Shuffling through the stack of clean and folded shirts and sweaters, he found a black knit T-shirt that emphasized his flat belly and pulled it over his head. Striding to the full-length mir-

ror on the back of the bathroom door, he combed his
fingers through his hair, rearranging his staid, busi-
nesslike haircut into a bad-boy, windblown appearance. Then he smiled.

"Tony, boy, you're one good-looking ."

"Phillip! Are you awake?"

The knock at his door, accompanied by Lucy's
whining question, sent him spinning around. In a few
short strides he was at the door.

"I'm up," he said, shortly, staring at Phillip's
mother. In his opinion, it was her fault that Phillip
was so damned inept.

Lucy Karnoff frowned when she saw her son's
clothes.

"Phillip, those clothes just won't do. You have to
take your father to the airport this morning. He has
an important consultation in Ireland tomorrow and little time to waste."

"He can take a cab. I've got things to do."

Lucy grabbed her son's arm, determined he would
not leave until she'd had her say.

"Whatever it is, surely it can wait," she said. "After all, it's not like you're clocking in somewhere, is
it?"

His fingers curled into fists, and it was all he could
do not to hit her.

"You don't know anything about *my* business, so
back off, old lady."

Lucy gasped as Phillip shoved her aside. Over the past few months he'd exhibited periodic bouts of this type of behavior, but this was the first time he'd ever laid a hand on her.

"Phillip! How dare you?" she cried. "After all we've done for you, the least you could do is—"

"Phillip is gone, bitch. And you will be, too, if you don't get the hell out of my life."

The hate on her son's face was frightening, but not nearly as much as the look in his eyes. It was like looking at a stranger. And what did he mean, Phillip was gone? By the time she got her wits together, he'd already driven away. The urge to run crying to Emile was overwhelming, but she couldn't. Not when he was about to leave on this very important trip.

Smoothing her hair away from her face, she made her way downstairs. By the time she reached the kitchen, she had convinced herself that the incident had never really happened.

It was only hours later, after Emile was gone and there was no one left but her and the hired help, that Lucy let herself think of the morning's events. Something was wrong with Phillip, she could tell. It was almost as if he were two separate people.

With the thought came a newer and more frightening fear. What if Phillip was ill, really ill? What if he was so mentally unstable that he might do something untoward that would bring the media down around their ears?

Lucy wrung her hands as she began to pace. This couldn't happen. Not now! Not when their every move seemed to be documented by the press. She had to do something, but what?

If only Emile's work could apply to other illnesses besides physical ones. In the early days, when they'd worked side by side, she as his assistant and secretary, he'd had several theories leaning in that direction. She paused, frowning, and trying to remember where Emile might have kept his notes on those experiments. Maybe if she...

Within seconds her rational self was back in control. She resumed her pacing, mentally chiding herself for even considering such an act. This was their son, not some lab rat on which to experiment.

Down the hall, the grandfather clock struck two. Lucy glanced out the window, praying she would see Phillip's car coming down the drive. There was nothing in sight but the neighbor's gardener pruning a hedge. If only Emile were here. She should have said something this morning before he left. Nothing could be more important than their own family—than their own son. She dropped into a nearby chair and began to cry. Everything was so messed up. It shouldn't be this way. She'd worked so hard to make sure they had the perfect family, and now this. What on earth was she to do?

Carney Auger woke up on the floor and for a moment couldn't remember where he was. A snort, coupled with a foul-smelling fart from the bed above, was enough to tell him that, wherever he was, he wasn't alone. Rising to his hands and knees, he peered over the bed, straight into his brother Dale's face.

"Well, hell," he muttered. That just ruled out the hope that it might have been a woman.

~~Pissed~~ off about the smell and the lack of a place to put his ~~hands-on~~, he slapped Dale in the face and then dragged himself to his feet.

Dale Auger woke up in a panic, his fists doubled, his eyes red-rimmed and bleary.

"Somebody hit me!" he yelled, which roused their other brother, Freddie, who was sleeping on the couch on the other side of the room.

"Shut up," Freddie mumbled, and pulled a pillow over his head.

"Somebody went and hit me," Dale muttered, staring angrily at Carney, who was on his way to the bathroom.

As soon as the door shut on Carney's departure, silence resumed. Dale glared one last time at the bathroom door, then rolled over on his side and settled back into his comfort spot. Within a minute, he was fast asleep again.

Carney, however, was in no mood to sleep. His nerves were jumpy, and his head was pounding. He needed a drink, and he needed to score. He was coming down and in no mood to start puking his guts.

Naked as the day he was born, he stepped into the shower and began scrubbing himself, noticing, as he did, the dirt and bits of grass and leaves gathering in the bottom of the tub. It must have been one hell of a tear they'd been on, but he couldn't remember where they'd been.

The hot water felt good as he scrubbed at his skin, using almost all the motel minisoap. It wasn't until he bent over to wash his feet that he had a flashback of falling forward. Slowly, he straightened, then stood without moving, trying to focus on the fuzzy images floating through his brain. Water pelted his belly. The washcloth hung limply from his hand. As the steam rose around him, he closed his eyes and saw a face. A woman's face. His forehead furrowed. But where? Where had he seen her? He took a deep breath and made himself relax, using the needle-like spray of water as a point of concentration. For a few seconds he saw nothing but the back of his eyelids, and then suddenly another face flashed before his eyes. This time of a man—a big man. There was a gun, and someone yelling.

Carney's eyes flew open. He saw himself being thrown facedown on the ground and could almost taste the coppery tang of his own blood as he had bitten his tongue. But where in hell had...

The Landing. They'd been at the Landing all night, drinking and watching flotsam from the flood-swollen river, making bets on how many beers Dale could drink before he puked. Someone, maybe him, maybe Freddie, had suggested they go clean up in one of Daddy's cabins before they took themselves home to their respective wives.

He stared at the wall, oblivious to the mildewed grout between the tiles or the squeak of rusty pipes as the water pelted down. A car horn honked outside the bathroom window. Startled, he turned toward the sound, and as he did, he remembered.

That bitch! She'd screamed like bloody murder and brought the bastard from hell out of hiding. He'd tried to tell them he was just fooling around, but no one would listen. That half-naked SOB had put his face in the dirt and then threatened to shoot off his balls if he so much as moved.

Carney dropped the washcloth into the tub and reached down and turned off the water. Grabbing a towel from the rack, he began yanking it across his body in angry swipes. With water droplets still clinging to his skin, he strode from the bathroom, letting the door hit the wall with a thump.

When Dale jumped out of bed with his fists doubled, Carney sneered.

"You stink, little brother. Get yourself cleaned up. I got someplace to go."

Freddie rolled over and gave Carney a disgusted look.

"In case you don't remember it, you're flat broke,

and I'm not giving you a dime to put up your nose or down your gullet."

"I don't want no damned dope," Carney said. "I want payback."

This time Freddie sat up. He'd seen that look on Carney's face before.

"The last time you wanted revenge, you wound up in jail. You willin' to give it another go?"

Carney didn't hesitate. "No man puts my face in the dirt and lives to tell about it."

Dale blanched. "I ain't havin' nothin' to do with no killin'."

Carney sneered. "I don't remember askin' you, little brother. Now get your clothes on. You, too, Freddie. I've got a notion to go pay Daddy a visit."

"You can leave me out of it, too," Freddie said.

Carney turned to his brother and grinned. "No way. You're going to take me out there. I can't drive, remember? Not since I got that last DUI."

"No, I'm not," Freddie said. "You're doped up crazy. Just let it go."

Carney's grin widened. "I wonder what Wanda would think if she knew her sweet little Freddie was fuckin' the checker at the Supermart?"

Freddie's face turned a bright, angry red as he stood.

"The day you was born, Daddy should'a put you in a burlap sack like he once did my pups and tossed you in the Tallahatchie."

Carney's eyes narrowed angrily. "Maybe so, but he didn't. Now, you gonna do what I said, or you wanna go down to the motel office and pay yourself up for the month? 'Cause if I have to start talkin', Wanda ain't ever gonna let you back in the house."

Freddie stalked into the bathroom, slamming the door behind him.

Carney looked at Dale.

Dale paled and started grabbing at his clothes.

"You're the one that oughta been drowned," Carney said. "I'm goin' across the street to get myself some coffee. Give me some money."

Dale dropped his wallet on the bed between them, wincing as Carney tore out the bills and then tossed it aside.

"You took my gas money, Carney. I need gas money to get to work next week."

"You ain't never been short on gas. Just fart into the tank," Carney said, and strode out of the room, slamming the door behind him.

"Shut your mouth," Dale muttered, although he purposely waited until Carney was too far away to hear what he said.

"Wait," Ginny said, and stopped beneath a tree. "Something's sticking my ankle."

"Let me look," Sully said, and squatted beside her. "Put your foot on my knee."

"My shoes are muddy. It will get your pants dirty."

He looked up. "They'll wash."

Ginny did as he asked, bracing herself by holding on to his shoulder as he settled her shoe on his knee. They'd been walking for the better part of an hour, talking about what she remembered of the six other girls in that ill-fated class, but without much luck. They'd been so young, and it was so long ago.

A puff of breeze slipped beneath her hair, lifting the weight of it from her neck. She chewed the edge of her lower lip and tried not to focus on the width of Sullivan Dean's shoulders as he slipped a finger between her sock and her skin.

"Here it is," Sully said, as he stood. "A sharp piece of grass had gone through your sock. Does it feel better?"

Ginny found herself staring—subconsciously waiting for something more from him than just words. Finally she realized he had asked a question.

"I'm sorry, what did you say?"

"Your leg...does it feel better?"

"Yes, thank you," Ginny said, and looked away. "The river must be close."

Sully tried not to frown, but his frustration level with this woman was growing. One moment she would be friendly and at ease with him, and the next she seemed nervous and distant. He was tired of walking on eggshells around her.

"Virginia?"

That got her attention.

"I'd rather you didn't—"

"I know all about what *you* don't like," he said shortly. "What I don't know is what *I'm* doing wrong. If I've offended you, or said something that hurt your feelings, I apologize."

Ginny looked startled. "Of course you haven't. Why would you say something like that?"

"Because of the way you've been acting. If it's not that, then what? We've got to get through this time together whether you like it or not, and it would be a hell of a lot easier on both of us if you would just tell me when to back off instead of clamming up and changing the damned subject."

Ginny sighed. He made her nervous, but she didn't know why, so how was she going to explain it to him?

"It's not you," she said. "I swear." She slipped her hand in the crook of his elbow and gave it a tug. "Walk with me," she said. "I think better when I'm moving."

"Yeah, so do I," he said.

"See, already we have something in common," she said.

"We already had something in common," Sully countered.

Ginny stopped. "What?"

"Georgia. You forget. She's the reason I'm here."

Ginny's eyes filled with tears. "I don't forget anything,'' she said briefly, and started walking without looking to see if he would follow.

He did.

''Talk to me, Ginny. Tell me what's on your mind. Why do you keep turning hot and cold on me? This isn't good, you know. I can't protect you if you don't trust me.''

Ginny hesitated, then turned, facing him with a determined tilt to her chin.

''I do trust you.''

''Then what?''

''I'm not used to depending on anyone but myself. I've been alone most of my adult life. My parents are dead. I have few living relatives, none of which I see.''

''Isn't there someone special? Maybe a man in your life? Is that what this is all about?''

The minute Sully asked, he found himself holding his breath, almost dreading the answer.

Ginny snorted in an unladylike manner. ''The last man in my life slept with the woman who lived in the apartment across the hall from me. That was four years ago, and I haven't bothered getting to know another one since.''

Sully felt guilty at the spurt of pleasure he had in knowing she was unattached.

''That must have been tough.''

She shrugged. ''I learned a hard lesson that day,

and I have no intention of ever repeating the mistake.''

The moment she said it, she knew what was wrong. She was keeping her distance from Sullivan Dean because she was attracted to him and she didn't want to be. She didn't want to be hurt like that ever again.

Sully took her hand and gave it a tug as they resumed their walk. Startled by the feel of his fingers curling around her palm, she almost stumbled. But he caught her beneath her elbow, steadied her without comment, and then once again resumed the lead, still holding her hand.

A couple of minutes later, Sully suddenly stopped and turned. Ginny pulled out of his grasp and earned herself another hard glance, which she promptly ignored.

"I'm curious," he said. "I never heard Georgia speak of you, yet you must have been quite close at one time in your lives."

"I never heard Georgia speak of you, either, but it's obvious you cared a lot for her."

"Her brother, Tommy, was and is my best friend. I met them when they moved to Connecticut. She was almost seven, I think."

Ginny's eyes widened. "That was right after the fire at Montgomery Academy. Before that, we lived next door to each other. After they moved, I still visited her in the summers, and we were roommates in college for one semester until I changed my major."

"It's strange we never met. I visited Georgia at college more than once."

Ginny frowned. "She used to have a crush on this one guy, I remember. Only he was older than her, and she said he couldn't see her for the trees."

He looked away. "That would have been me. I saw her, all right, but not as a sweetheart. I'd watched her grow up, for God's sake. To me, she was just Tommy's little sister."

Ginny's eyes widened. "How ironic. I had a crush on Tommy once. I think I was nine or ten. It lasted until the day he dropped a cricket in the pocket of my shirt. After that, I thought boys were stupid." The corner of her mouth tilted in a wry grin. "Some days, I still think that."

Sully laughed aloud, and Ginny's heart stopped. It was the first time she'd seem him really laugh, and the expression completely changed his appearance.

"You should do that more often," she said.

"What's that?"

"Laugh. It looks good on you."

Disgusted with herself for having said too much, Ginny started to look away when Sully's hand suddenly cupped her cheek.

"You're doing it again," he said. "And don't pretend you don't know what I'm talking about. You say something nice and then you get all prickly. What are you thinking?"

Her eyes narrowed angrily. "I thought you were my bodyguard, not my shrink."

"Ginny."

She sighed. "It has nothing to do with you," she muttered. "It's me."

"I disagree. I'm the one who's on the receiving end of your attitudes, honey."

The sarcasm in his voice pushed her last button. She spun on him then, her fists doubled, her voice shaking.

"You want to know what's wrong? I'll tell you what's wrong! I'm attracted to you, and I don't want to be attracted to you. Someone is trying to kill me, and I'm getting all moony-faced about some Fed who's going to disappear from my life the minute this is over! That's what's wrong with me! I'm certain it's that...that...that China Syndrome thing, but it doesn't make it any better."

"Stockholm," he muttered, too shocked to say more.

"What the hell are you talking about?" she snapped.

"*The China Syndrome* was a movie. I think you meant Stockholm Syndrome, where a victim forms a romantic attachment to her captor."

Ginny threw up her hands in mock defeat. "Oh! Well! Thank you for correcting me as I make an ass of myself, which only heightens my stupidity!"

Having said all she could say without bursting into

tears, Ginny pivoted angrily and stalked back toward the cabin, her head held high.

Sully stood and watched her go. It was either that or shoot himself now and put himself out of his misery, but he wasn't ready to check out. Not yet. Not when the prettiest woman he'd met in years had just said she was attracted to him.

A slow grin began to spread across his face. Damn. She liked him. She really liked him. Of course, he was going to have to find a way to get past her grudges, and she had a few to get past. But he liked a challenge. Always had. And finding a way to get past Virginia Shapiro's hangups might just prove to be the biggest challenge of his life.

When he realized she was almost out of sight, he started after her. As he moved back onto the path, a twig snapped in the trees to his right. He paused, staring curiously into the underbrush. When a rabbit suddenly bolted out of the thicket, he relaxed. It didn't occur to him then that the rabbit was too small to make that kind of sound. His thoughts were on Ginny.

Carney breathed a sigh of relief when the big man moved away. He'd come close to blowing it, and if it hadn't been for that rabbit, he would have. He'd been too far away to hear most of what was being said, but he'd seen enough to know that they'd been arguing. He'd also seen enough to change his mind about the angle of his retribution. He would hurt the man—he would hurt him bad. But not before he took away his woman. A man was most vulnerable when he was in love.

"You're gonna be sorry," he muttered, watching until Sully was out of sight. "Come nightfall, you're gonna wish you'd never been born."

8

Although hours had passed since their flare-up in the woods, Ginny was still withdrawn, and Sully was smart enough not to push the issue. Instead, he'd sat her down as if she were a suspect in a crime and grilled her unmercifully over the minutiae of her childhood. While the interrogation had been grueling, in an odd way, it had settled Ginny's nerves, as if reminding her why they were even together and what needed to be done to make this all go away.

However, she had yet to come up with anything new. The one thing Sully thought strange was Ginny's lack of memories regarding the special class at Montgomery Academy. Other than that it met once a week and lasted only for an hour, she couldn't remember anything of what they'd studied or even why she'd been picked. An ordinary child, she had claimed no special talents or skills and was certainly no genius. In truth, she had often been sickly, suffering from periodic asthma attacks, which thankfully, had lessened in severity, ending completely by the time she'd reached her teens.

Finally he'd relented, and Ginny had gone into the kitchen to make them some sandwiches. He'd offered to help but had been turned down flat. Instead of being offended, he'd grinned. So he made her nervous. Good. Better that than be ignored.

"Do you want coffee?" Ginny asked, as she assembled their sandwiches.

"I'd rather have a beer, but I'd settle for a Coke."

"What you'll settle for is what I've got."

Her sarcasm raised his ire just enough to make his behavior careless.

"That sounds like a bargain to me," he drawled. "From where I'm standing, you've got what it takes. I'll just have some of that."

Ginny froze, her back to the man, a slice of bread in one hand, a knife in the other. She caught herself grinning and then stifled it before he could see. He was giving back as good as he got. She'd always admired that in a man. She turned, her expression bland.

"Don't flatter yourself, Agent Dean. I might be attracted to you, but I'm not in heat. Go pour yourself a glass of whatever and set your butt down in that chair. Your meal awaits."

Sully's grin widened as he strolled past her to get to the cabinets and took out a couple of glasses. Opening the refrigerator, he peered inside.

"Milk, orange juice…hey! You've been holding out on me," he said, as he reached to the back of the shelf and pulled out a couple of wine coolers.

Ginny put the sandwiches on the table and then nudged him aside to get to the plates. Sully purposefully moved slowly, taking juvenile pleasure in the round softness of her backside brushing against his thigh.

"Want one?" he asked, holding up a bottle.

"No, thank you, I'm having milk."

"Lord," he muttered, as he set one of the drinks back and took out the jug of milk. "You really like this stuff?"

"I am not in the habit of putting things in my mouth that I do not like. I think I passed that stage at about two or three."

Sully stared at her lips, picturing himself putting his mouth on hers and wondering what kind of a reaction that would bring—wondering if her kisses would be as fiery as her words.

Ginny offered him her glass, but he seemed to have lost his focus on liquid refreshments, so she took the jug from him and poured her own milk.

"Cheers," she said, and toasted thin air before taking a sip. "Ummm, good and cold. Come on, hotshot, let's eat."

She sat herself down at the table and put half a sandwich on her plate, then added a handful of potato chips out of a newly opened bag beside it. When she opened her mouth to take the first bite, Sully's concentration snapped. He unscrewed the lid to his wine cooler and took the other chair, piling two sandwich halves onto his plate and then turning the open bag toward his plate for easy access. Thrusting his hand inside, he pulled out several chips and thrust them all into his mouth in one bite.

"Tastes good," he said, as he chewed.

Ginny arched an eyebrow. "That's because I didn't make them."

Sully grinned and took a bite of the sandwich. Something crunched as he chewed, which surprised him. He hadn't seen her put anything in there but mayonnaise, meat and cheese.

"Uh...something crunched," he said.

"That would be the radishes."

He swallowed without choking and then laid his sandwich down on his plate, curious as to how he could dissect his food without insulting her. She saved him the trouble.

"If you don't like them, then just take them out."

Sully nodded as he lifted the top slice of bread and began removing the white, red-rimmed orbs that were stuck to the mayonnaise.

"Uh, Ginny, don't take this wrong, but can I ask you something?"

She nodded as she chewed.

"I'm not saying I don't like them. I've just never had them on bologna and cheese sandwiches before."

"Really?"

He nodded. "So, uh...why do you make sandwiches this way?"

She opened her sandwich and pointed. "It's all about the basic food groups. Bread and meat, of course. The cheese would be dairy, as well as another form of protein, the mayonnaise is a fat, and the radishes are the vegetables. I have apples for dessert, which is a fruit. So...bread, meat, dairy, vegetable, fruit and fat. A balanced meal, right?"

At a loss for words, he watched as she put the top back on her sandwich and took another bite. Even from where he was sitting, he could hear the faint crunch of radishes as she chewed. He looked down at the one on his plate and shrugged, then started replacing the radishes he'd taken from his own.

"Change your mind?" she asked.

"When in Rome," he muttered, then took another bite and began to chew.

Her heart gave a leap. Not once in her adult life had a man ever finished a meal that she'd made, not even her father, who had loved her most of all. Sullivan Dean didn't know it, but his shining armor was taking on quite a glow.

In the midst of their dessert, they were disrupted by a series of rapid knocks. Sully was on his feet and striding to the door before Ginny could move. He peered through the curtain and then looked back at her, motioning that it was all right. It was the manager, Marshall Auger.

"Just checking to make sure everything is okay before I make a run into Wingate."

"Yes, we're fine," Sully said.

The old man tried to peer over Sully's shoulder but had little luck. Sully had put himself directly between Ginny and the outside world. The image of him standing tall within the doorway, feet slightly apart, hands braced against the door frame as if holding it up, made her heart skip a beat. In a fit of being hateful, she'd called him her bodyguard and not her shrink, and now it shamed her to realize that was exactly what he'd set himself up to be.

"Well, then, I'll just be running along. Won't be gone more than two or three hours. If you have an emergency, there's a pay phone just outside the office."

"Yes, thank you," Sully said. "We'll be fine."

"All right...see you later."

Sully started to close the door when the old man suddenly grabbed it, holding it ajar.

"I almost forgot," he said. "I was wondering, how long you planning to stay?"

Sully frowned. "I'll let you know," he said, and shut the door in the old man's face, then watched at the window until he drove away.

He turned back to Ginny and realized she was carrying dishes into the kitchen.

"Hey," he said. "You cooked. I'll do dishes."

"I dirtied a knife, two glasses and two plates. That's not cooking, that's making a mess."

Sully slid a finger underneath her chin, tipping her face until she was forced to meet his gaze.

"You fed me."

"And you're taking care of me."

Her soft words countered everything he'd been trying to balance.

"And it's the best damned job I've ever had." Then he cupped her face and brushed his lips across her forehead.

Ginny froze. The feel of his mouth against her skin was intoxicating. When he raised his head, there was an unmistakable look of wanting more in his eyes. To his credit and her dismay, he didn't say what he was thinking, and the moment passed, leaving an awkward silence between them.

"Go take a break. Read a book. Take a nap. I'm going to do these dishes, and then I've got a few calls to make, okay?"

Ginny wanted to put her arms around his waist and lay her head on his chest. Instead, she nodded.

Needing to put some distance between them, he turned away and began running water into the sink. Ginny stood there for a moment, watching the way his fingers curled around the glasses then walked out of the little room.

By the time he was through, she was on her bed, pretending great interest in a book. Sully paused.

"I'll be right back," he said.

She nodded without looking up.

Once again, she'd slipped back in her shell, but not as far as before. Hoping to learn something new from Dan Howard, he stepped out on the little stoop to make some calls. As he did, he thought he saw movement in some trees on the far side of the parking area, but when he looked closer, he decided it was nothing but the flight of some birds from one tree to another. Still cautious, he watched for a while until he was confident there was nothing out of the ordinary to be seen. What he did notice was that a couple more cabins had been rented. There was a sport utility vehicle pulling a boat at one cabin and a Jeep beside another. Both were loaded with fishing gear, and even though the level of the river was going down, he couldn't imagine the fishing being any good with it running so fast and so high. After a few minutes, five men emerged from the two cabins and began moving gear into the SUV. When they saw Sully, they waved in a friendly but distant sort of manner and then drove away, following a narrow dirt road that led behind the cabins toward the river beyond.

Satisfied that all was well, Sully made his calls. Dan Howard had nothing new to pass on, nor did Detective Pagillia in St. Louis, although Sully did learn that they had bugged Ginny's phones, both at home and where she worked, but had yet to come up with any useful hits. His frustration was mounting as he finally disconnected and went back inside the cabin.

Ginny's name was on his lips as he opened the door, but he forgot what he'd been going to say. She'd fallen asleep. The book was on the floor, and she had curled up in a ball with her feet tucked under a pillow and her hands curled beneath her chin, as if she were cold. Sully quietly closed the door and then moved to where she lay. The loneliness of his life hit him as he stood watching her sleep. What would it be like to be able to have the freedom to crawl into bed beside her and curl his body around hers like a shield—to warm her body and his soul without thoughts of conse-quences or anger? Instead of giving in to the urge, he pulled a blanket up over her shoulders and then walked out of the cabin while he still had the good sense to move.

Carney was hot and tired and sick as a skunked dog, which only served to make him angrier. Freddie and Dale had dumped him out about a quarter of a mile from the cabins and left him to stew in his own revenge, vowing to have nothing to do with any of it. To add insult to injury, his old man had refused him a cabin, saying he needed them free to rent. Carney had stomped out of the office and into the woods, muttering a "to hell with all of them." He would give that big SOB at the farthest cabin something to cry about and then tell them all to kiss his ass, because he was leaving Mississippi for good. There wasn't anything here for him but more grief. If a man couldn't count on his family, then he couldn't count on anyone. As for his wife, he wouldn't care if he never saw her again. All she did was bitch at him to get a better job. Hellsfire, it wasn't his fault that roofers didn't work regular hours like everyone else. Their work depended on good weather, and when it rained or was too cold, it wasn't happening.

As he sat nursing his grudges and a sickening headache, he saw his old man come out of his house and then walk down to the far end of the row. A few minutes later he walked back, got in his car and drove away.

Carney stood abruptly, then started grinning. After making sure that he wasn't observed, he circled his father's house and slipped in the back door. The house smelled of burned bacon grease and damp, musty wood, but Carney wasn't picky. He knew where his Daddy kept his liquor, and he needed a drink. After two quick shots of Tennessee Red, he began rummaging through the refrigerator for something to eat. Settling down in the living room in Daddy's easy chair, he picked up the remote and turned on the TV. Might as well enjoy himself until it got a little darker. He knew the old man's routine, and chances were that he wouldn't be back for at least two or three hours. With the cool air circulating in the small dusty room and his belly full of liquor and food, Carney leaned back in the chair and closed his eyes.

* * *

When he awoke, it was almost dusk. He stretched
in the recliner and scratched his head, trying to figure
out what had awakened him so abruptly. At the same
moment, he heard a car door slam and sat up with a
thump. Daddy was home! Scrambling for the remote
that had fallen into his lap, he turned off the TV and
slipped out the back door as his father came in the
front. Moving quickly, he headed for the trees behind
the cabins and disappeared. As soon as he was certain
he hadn't been seen, he circled back through the
woods until he was directly behind Ginny's cabin and
then settled down to wait. Eventually the lights would
go off. After that, it was but a matter of time until he
paid that woman a little visit. A feral smile crossed
his face as he thought of her slim body and long legs.
This time he would give her something to scream
about.

Sully's phone rang as he was chopping vegetables
for the omelet he was making. Without thinking, he
yelled over his shoulder.

"Hey, Ginny, get that, would you?" The minute
the words came out of his mouth, he was running with
the knife still in his hand. "I'm sorry. I'm sorry," he
said, as he snatched the phone off the table. "I just
wasn't thinking."

"Don't worry. I was," she muttered, eyeing the cell
phone as if it were a snake. She took the knife out of
his hands and started into the kitchen.

"Just chop!" Sully yelled. "I'll finish the rest."

She grinned to herself as she kept on walking. He'd gotten the message real early about her cooking skills. She picked up the bell pepper he'd been slicing and resumed the task. So she couldn't cook all that well. So what? Maybe when all this was over she would take a cooking class. It wasn't as if she couldn't follow a recipe; it was more like she neglected to read them in the first place. Usually she remembered what went in a dish. It was the quantity and the timing that kept throwing her off.

Finishing the chopping, she laid the knife on the counter and rinsed off her hands. As she turned to dry, she noticed the expression on Sullivan's face and moved closer, trying to overhear what was being said, but then he hung up. As he did, he looked up and saw her standing there.

"What?" Ginny asked.

Sully inhaled slowly, judging the look on her face against what he was going to tell her. Would she panic, or was it just going to be another fact to add to the confusion of what was already known?

"I have a right to know," Ginny said.

"I have no intention of keeping you in the dark," he said, and tossed the phone on the bed.

"Then what? Was that Agent Howard?"

"No, it was Pagillia, with the St. Louis police." He eyed her curiously. "Did you know they'd put taps on your phone at home and the one at your desk?"

She shook her head.

"Well, they did. Pagillia said they went into your apartment, plugged the phone back into the jack and turned the answering machine on. There have been fourteen calls in the past couple of days, and all of them were hang-ups."

Ginny shivered and impulsively wrapped her arms around herself.

"Could they trace them?"

"No."

"I can't believe in this day and age there's not a way to at least figure out where the calls are coming from."

"Pagillia said something about a block on the other end of the line. However, they could confirm that it was an out-of-state call."

Ginny dropped to the corner of the bed. Sully put his hand on the top of her head.

"You all right?" he asked softly.

She sighed, then looked up and nodded.

"Is there anything I can do for you?" Sully asked, wishing he could make the despair in her eyes disappear.

She made herself smile. "Feed me?"

"Only if you keep me company."

He held out his hand, waiting. She slipped her hand into his, absorbing his strength as his fingers curled around her wrist and gave her a tug off the bed.

A few minutes later he turned a perfect omelette

out onto her plate and then began making one for himself.

"Don't wait for me," he said. "It'll get cold."

She picked up her fork and dug in, sighing with appreciation as the flavor of egg and melting cheese lingered on her tongue. The sauteed vegetables inside were done to perfection, as were the toast points he'd made to go with it.

"You know, if you ever decide to quit Uncle Sam, you could open your own restaurant. You're really good."

Sully turned, the spatula still in his hand. "I'm good at a lot of things, Virginia."

She gaped, her mind whirling with all the possibilities that remark had resurrected. Sully winked as he turned back to his task, calmly flipped the omelette over the filling and slid it out onto his plate.

He slid into the seat and picked up his fork, then gave her an innocent smile.

"What? You already full?"

She glared and then pointed at him with her fork.

"Don't play fast and loose with me, mister. I've heard it all."

Sully grinned and then took a big bite, rolling his eyes in mock appreciation as he chewed.

Ginny's impulse was to dump her food in his lap, but she was too hungry to give it up, so she settled for a second glare and then began to eat.

They finished the meal in relative silence. It wasn't

until they were cleaning the dishes that Sully dropped another bomb.

"Tell me about Yellowstone," he said. "What was your favorite part?"

Ginny stilled, her hands still in the dishwater, then, slowly, she turned and looked at him.

"How did you know I'd been to Yellowstone?"

"Saw the picture in your apartment."

"You've been in my apartment?"

The indignation in her voice was noticeable.

"I was looking for you, remember?"

"But why—"

Sully's hand encircled her wrist and gave it a gentle tug.

"Virginia, you don't understand. When you didn't answer the doorbell, I was afraid." He looked away, remembering, then shook his head, as if ridding himself of the fear that he'd felt. "I couldn't go to a hotel without knowing if you were all right, okay?"

"Oh. Right."

"So, about Yellowstone?"

Ginny sighed. "It seems like a lifetime ago. Mom and Dad were killed later that same year, just before Christmas."

"I'm sorry. How did it happen?"

Old anger welled inside her. "It was so preventable. Carbon monoxide leak from the heating unit in their house. They died in their sleep."

There wasn't anything to say, so Sully just let her talk.

"We'd had so much fun that summer. It was the first time in years that we'd done anything together...like a family, I mean. We spent two weeks at the lodge in Yellowstone and made plans to go back the next year." She shrugged and then looked at him, for the first time meeting his gaze straight on. "But you know what they say about the best laid plans. Anyway, I have that picture to remember it by, and that's my favorite thing."

"I'm sorry," Sully said, and opened his arms. "Feel like a hug?"

Her chin quivered once, and then she nodded.

The only way Ginny could have described being in Sullivan's arms was to say he enfolded her. The strength of his body and the powerful beat of his heart beneath her cheek were the bulwark between herself and defeat. They stood without speaking, each settling into the feeling of being so close and wondering what it would be like to take the hug a step further.

As they stood, Sully suddenly jerked. Gripping Ginny's arms, he pushed her back. "Son of a—! I can't believe I forgot."

"Forgot what?" Ginny asked.

"The yearbook!" Sully said. "Some Fed I am. I completely forgot about Georgia's yearbook being in the car."

"What yearbook?"

"A yearbook from Montgomery Academy."

Ginny's eyes widened in surprise. "Oh my God! I don't think I ever knew there was one."

"It was in Georgia's things at the convent. Apparently she'd asked her mother to send it to her. She died before it arrived."

"Are we in it?" she asked. "I mean...are you sure it's not one from before? You know, the school burned down before that year was over."

"Yes, I'm sure. I saw you." He tweaked a lock of her hair. "Pretty darn cute, if you like the no-teeth grin."

"Go ahead," she muttered. "Make fun. I'll bet your first-grade pictures aren't any better."

"They're worse," he said. "I had a black eye and a Band-Aid across the bridge of my nose, compliments of a new skateboard and an unopened gate."

Ginny smiled. "Ouch."

"Yeah, ouch is right. But the black eye was pretty cool. Turned a whole bunch of different colors before it healed."

Ginny was trying to picture this huge man as a little child, when Sully headed for the door.

"I wonder how the yearbooks survived the fire," she asked.

He stopped. "Yeah, I thought the same thing and checked. They were still at the printers when it happened."

"I wonder why I didn't have one?"

"Maybe your parents didn't order one. Maybe the school didn't have a forwarding address for where you moved. You told me that everyone went in different directions after the fire. Some to public schools. Some even moved out of state. I imagine it would have been difficult to track everyone down."

Ginny nodded. "Yes, I suppose." Then she clasped her hands together in anticipation. "I can't wait to see. Where is it at?"

"The trunk of my car. I'll go get it. Won't take but a minute."

"Hurry," Ginny said. "Maybe there's something in there that will help us sort out this hell."

"You want to lock the door behind me?" Sully said, as he opened the door.

"No need. You'll be right back."

He closed the door and then stepped off the stoop. Out of habit, he scoped out the area before heading to his car. The sky was clear and littered with stars. The air was muggy and still and filled with the sounds of everything from crickets to tree frogs. The Jeep and the SUV were still there, which told him that the five fishermen had yet to go home. He could just make out the faint sounds of laughter from one of the cabins and suspected they were up telling tales and drinking beer. From a male point of view, it was the best part of a fishing trip.

He was trying to remember where he'd packed the yearbook when he heard footsteps on the gravel behind him. The hair rose on the back of his neck as he turned, but his reaction was too late. Pain exploded on the side of his head and the world went black.

Ginny was in the bathroom when she heard the hinges squeak on the cabin door.

"I'll be right out!" she yelled, as she finished drying her hands. She frowned as the volume of the radio in the other room was suddenly turned up loud. Before she could comment, the bathroom door opened. Her surprise turned to shock and then fear.

"Don't bother," Carney Auger said. "I'm comin' in."

9

Ginny screamed, but the scream was cut short as Carney slapped her across the mouth and then grabbed her by the arms, slamming her against the wall. Her neck popped as her head collided with the mirror. She kept thinking that this couldn't be happening, but the sound of shattering glass brought everything into reality. She had a brief glimpse of his face before her attention shifted. Then he began grabbing at her breasts, tearing at her shirt and the waistband of her shorts.

"No!" she shouted, hitting at him with her fists, "Get out! Leave me alone!"

"I ain't goin' anywhere, bitch, and neither are you!" Carney growled, and shoved himself hard against her body.

Fury rose above fear as she lashed back, scratching both hands across his face and then jamming her thumbs into his eyes.

He screamed in pain and began to curse as he frantically grabbed at her hands, trying to regain control, but he'd underestimated his opponent.

She kicked and bit and clawed and screamed, intent on causing pain to every tender place on his body. At the same time, the toe-tapping music coming from the radio in the other room was an obscenity, becoming an accomplice to what was happening to her.

"Stop it! Stop it!" Carney yelled, still struggling to bring the woman under control.

Finally he succeeded in grabbing one of her hands. As he did, he grabbed the electric cord attached to her hair dryer with the full intention of using it to tie her up. He had it wrapped around her left wrist and was reaching for the other when Ginny doubled up her fist and hit him square in the nose. Blood spurted as Carney roared in pain and rage.

It was reflex that made him cover his nose with both hands, and as he did, Ginny gave him a shove. He staggered backwards into the shower stall, scrambling to stay afoot. Ginny bolted out of the bathroom, screaming Sully's name with Carney only seconds behind her.

The doorknob was beneath her palm when he caught her again, this time by the hair. Yanking her backward, he slammed her onto the floor. Within seconds, he was on top of her and Ginny's chances for escape were almost gone. No match for his superior weight and strength, her mind raced for a way out of this horror. He hit her again with the flat of his hand and as he did, Ginny went limp, pretending unconsciousness.

It took Carney several seconds to realize she was no longer fighting, and even then, he couldn't resist a last punch in her belly before he straddled her legs and rocked back on his heels.

Blood was dripping from his chin, and his eyes were already starting to swell. The bitch had broken his nose. Now he was really pissed. This went past payback for putting his face in the dirt. When he was through with her, there wouldn't be enough left for that bastard in the parking lot to bury.

As the country music station changed to a she-done-me-wrong ballad, he stuffed his hand down the front of Ginny's shirt and ripped it from neck to hem, revealing an expanse of smooth, creamy skin and a pink, lacy bra, which he quickly dispatched. It wasn't until he thrust his hand into the waistband of her shorts and started to pull that Ginny came undone. Windmilling both arms, she hit him first in the balls and then again in the nose. Momentarily blinded by the incredible pain, Carney gagged and slumped sideways, both hands on his crotch. At that point, Ginny managed to get one leg free.

It was nothing but bad luck when Carney caught her by the ankle. He staggered to his feet, almost doubled over from the pain, but he had a death grip on Ginny's leg.

"Help! Somebody...help me!" she screamed, kicking frantically at him with her other foot.

Carney reached over and turned the radio up to full

volume. Tears were streaming down his face, mixing with the constant flow of blood.

"You bitch, you bitch, you sorry bitch," he sobbed, then he reached behind his back and came back holding a knife.

Ginny watched in horror as the switchblade snapped out of its sheath. At that point she threw back her head and screamed as she'd never screamed before. The sound ripped up her throat and swelled above the music, shattering Carney's eardrums and making his head ache even more. He had never liked women all that much except when he was in need of a ▪▪▪. He didn't trust their lying ways, and he'd come to the conclusion that he probably hated this one most of all.

"There ain't no one left to help you, bitch, so you might as well shut up."

The gunshot was startling, as was the plastic that went flying when the bullet took apart the radio, instantly silencing the song.

Both Carney and Ginny froze, staring first at each other and then in the direction the shot had come from.

"You son of a bitch," Sully said.

Ginny had only a fleeting glimpse of the blood running down Sully's face before she saw the gun in his hand. A millisecond later he fired again, this time sending a bullet ripping through Carney's shoulder.

The knife he was holding fell to the floor, and he followed it with a lifeless thump.

For a second there was nothing but the labored sounds of Sully's breathing and the thunder of Ginny's heartbeat pounding against her eardrums. Then Sully staggered forward, pulled Carney's unconscious body off Ginny and lifted her into his arms. At that moment men began spilling into the doorway. It was the fishermen from the neighboring cabins, all talking and shouting at once.

Sully made it to the bed before his knees gave out. He sat, still holding Ginny so close she could hardly breathe.

"Someone call 911 and do it fast, because if that son of a bitch comes to before the ambulance gets here, I'm going to kill him."

Two men bolted toward the pay phone, while the others came inside to help. There was no mistaking what had happened, or what Carney Auger had tried to do. The state of Ginny's face and clothes was frightening, as was the look in Sully's eyes.

"What can we do, man?" someone asked.

Sully felt himself starting to black out and shook his head hard, knowing that pain would be the jolt he needed to stay focused. Clenching his teeth to keep from groaning, he pointed at a blanket that had been tossed on one of the chairs.

"Hand me that blanket," he muttered. "The bastard nearly stripped her naked." Gently, he covered her nudity and faced the fact that he'd come too late to keep her from harm.

Ginny's head was throbbing, her body a mass of pain. Added to that, shock was beginning to set in. When she started to shake, Sully pulled the blanket a little closer around her and began to rock her in place.

"It's all right, baby," he said softly. "It's all right. I've got you now. He can't hurt you again."

Ginny needed to talk, to find out why one side of Sully's face was covered in blood, but her teeth were chattering too hard for her to speak.

Someone laid a cold washcloth on the side of her face where it was starting to bruise. Ginny moaned.

"Easy, damn it," Sully said.

"Sorry," the man said. "Here, maybe you should do it."

With one arm still holding her close, Sully turned loose of her long enough to wipe the blood from her mouth. Just looking at the split in her lower lip and the blood oozing from her nose came close to sending him over the edge. He was contemplating the idea of putting another bullet into Carney Auger's body when the old man came running into the cabin.

"What the hell's been happening here?" Marshall cried.

Sully pointed. "Your son tried to kill us, and before you say a damned thing in his favor, you better know it took every bit of restraint I had not to put that bullet into his brain."

Marshall stared, momentarily too shocked to speak, and then his voice filled with tears as he shook his head in disbelief.

"Sometimes a parent knows things about his children that he don't want to face." He looked first at Sully, then at the woman in his arms. "Is she...? Did he...?"

"She's hurt, but he didn't get the chance to rape her, if that's what you're asking."

The old man's shoulders slumped, and it seemed as if he aged ten years before their eyes.

"I'm as sorry as a man can be." He looked down at the limp body of his eldest son. "You would have done us all a favor if your first shot had been his last." Then he lifted his head and took a deep breath. "I'm going to drive out to the main road and make sure the ambulance and the police don't miss this turn. It's hard to see in the dark."

The trio of fishermen were soon joined by the other two, and they stood guard at the door and around Sullivan and Ginny. Not because it was necessary anymore, but because it was the only thing they could do.

The paramedics took them by ambulance to Hattiesburg, running hot all the way into the city. The shrill bleat of the repeating siren was like a knife being thrust into Sully's brain, and yet the pain was nothing compared to the fear in his heart. The paramedics had tended his head on the scene. It would need stitches, and he knew from past experience that he had some degree of concussion. That would heal. It was what he'd let happen to Ginny that was a festering sore.

He should have known from Auger's rap sheet that he wasn't the kind of man to let someone put him in the dirt without payback. He should have moved them from the cabins the same day the incident happened, despite what Ginny had wanted. And he should have been more observant when he'd gone to the car to get that yearbook. He kept looking at her there on the stretcher as the ambulance flew down the highway. She had paid dearly for his mistakes.

By the time they reached the hospital, he knew he was fading fast. His thoughts kept going in and out of focus, and he didn't trust the local authorities to keep Ginny safe. As they unloaded the stretcher Ginny was on, he began to follow.

"Hold on there a minute, buddy," one of the orderlies said, and seated him in a wheelchair.

Sully tolerated it long enough to get him inside, but as they passed the front desk, he dragged his feet and got out, swaying where he stood as he reached for a phone.

"I'm sorry," a nurse said. "That's not for public use."

"Come on, buddy. You need to get that head

looked at,'' the orderly urged, and tried to get Sully back in the chair.

Ignoring both of them, Sully pulled out his badge. ''It's an emergency. How do you get an outside line?''

The nurse's eyes widened. ''Punch nine.''

He pointed at the disappearing stretcher with Ginny on board.

''Nurse, you stay with that woman and don't take your eyes off her until I say so. Don't let anyone near her but the attending physician.''

She hesitated but a moment, then called for another nurse, who was just coming down the hall.

''Watch the desk until I get back,'' she said, and took off after the paramedics who'd taken Ginny into the examining room.

Sully closed his eyes, trying to remember the numbers he needed to call, but they were all jumbled up in his head. If only he had his cell phone, he could have used speed dial and saved himself the trouble. Finally he took a deep breath, making himself relax, and as he did, the numbers fell into place.

The call was answered on the second ring.

''Howard.''

Sully stifled a groan as a sharp pain shot behind his eyeballs. ''Dan, it's me, Sully. We've had a situation here totally unrelated to the case, but I'm going to need help.''

Agent Howard frowned. Sullivan Dean wasn't the

kind of man to ask for help unless something was really wrong.

"What happened?"

"Long story," Sully muttered. "But we're in a hospital. I've got a concussion, and they're working on our witness right now."

"Damn it, Sully, what do you mean, working on her? Were you in an accident?"

"It was an assault by a local…completely unrelated to the other."

"Are you sure?"

"Positive. But I don't dare trust the local authorities on this one. There are too many variables that could mean the end of her life."

"Where are you?"

"Hattiesburg, Mississippi, but I'm not sure which hospital."

"Don't worry about that," Dan said. "I'll get it from my caller ID. You just sit tight, buddy. I'll have someone there within an hour."

"Thanks," Sully said. "I owe you."

"Uh…Sully…?"

"Yeah?"

"The woman…is she going to be all right?"

Sully sighed. "Physically, yes."

Dan Howard grunted. It was what Sully hadn't said that worried him.

"What happened to her?"

"She was beaten within an inch of her life in a rape attempt."

"Oh Jesus."

"Just get me some help," Sully said. "I can't talk anymore."

Howard was still talking as Sully slid to the floor.

Emile Karnoff frowned as he hung up the phone. Damn this age of answering machines. If he couldn't complete this call, he would never be able to rest. In less than fifteen minutes his driver was going to pick him up and take him back to the hospital. One last session today and he would be finished here in Dublin, although he had unfinished business at home. The young cancer patient was already showing signs of improvement. Her white count was up, and the fever was down. A couple of doctors in the Dublin Hospital were claiming it was nothing more than the results of chemotherapy finally kicking in, but most of the others were in awe of the results of his treatments. Although Emile never worked with anyone in the room besides him and the patient, he had allowed video cameras to film him in action.

It seemed so simple to the naked eye. Putting someone into a hypnotic trance, then basically telling them to get well. Only it wasn't that simple. It was a complex treatment—as complex as the mind itself.

He had discovered, during the experimental phases, that different parts of the brain responded to different musical tones. After that, he began to manipulate the mind with sound, using a series of chimes, not unlike running the scales on a children's xylophone. By programming the patient to listen for the tones, he obtained entrance into the subconscious and beyond. Past buried memories into the part of the brain that controlled the nervous system, then past that into the depths that sent out warning signals when the body was in danger of dying. And with each progressively higher tone, he obtained access to the places where pain was registered and recorded—and even into the convoluted whorls within the human mind that poisoned the body with stress and tension.

It was all about trust. He taught the patient to trust him. After that, they always let him in. Once inside the human mind, he set a series of commands in place in which the mind told the body how and where to heal itself.

It sounded preposterous—like something out of an old sci-fi movie. But there had been a time in history when people had thought it preposterous that there were things called germs that could make people sick—could even kill. How could something invisible be that deadly? But time had proven the far-seeing men who espoused the germ theory to be right. And it wasn't as if he had fought a completely uphill battle. Hypnosis had been used for years in the treatment of smoking and eating addictions, as well as a treatment for sexual traumas and the like. Many studies had been done on certain Asian religious orders and on the monks who could supposedly control pain and blood loss by the simple use of their minds.

All he'd done was take those theories a leap further. Using the human mind to heal the body seemed so simple—so logical. No transplants to be made. No anti-rejection drugs to take. And the only cutting to be done was by men like Emile, who cut through the trash littering up the human brain with softly spoken words and gentle commands. It was another step toward a perfect world, and Emile Karnoff was riding an accolade high.

Granted, he'd made some mistakes in the early years, but that was to be expected. All research had dead ends, some more dead than others. At least he hadn't spent a lifetime pursuing the wrong paths. That had become apparent early on. It wasn't until he'd done his first experiments on actual subjects with real illnesses that he'd begun to see the possibilities. He thought back to those times, remembering the faces of the children who'd so trustingly let him into their minds. Children were the easiest to treat and the most susceptible to his methods.

A knock on his door signaled his driver had arrived. Later, as he rode to the hospital, he thought of his son as a child and then frowned. It was a shame that the innocence of children disappeared with their maturity. Phillip had no focus—no dreams. He simply existed—a shadow of the love Emile and Lucy shared.

And as he thought of Lucy, he looked again out the window of the car in which he was riding, yearning for the countryside beyond the city.

Emile sighed. He had fallen in love with Ireland. The simple lifestyle and the beauty of the country, coupled with the genuine friendliness of the people, had spoken to his soul. All during his trips back and forth to the hospital, he kept thinking of ways to approach Lucy about buying a second home. It wouldn't have to be anything fancy, because life was simple here. He would have peace and quiet for his studies, and it would be as easy to travel from here as it was from Bainbridge, Connecticut, where they lived now.

It wasn't as if he had an office and a roster of regular patients. He'd been in research most of his life, and it was only after receiving the Nobel Prize that he'd started getting requests for consultations. If he wanted, he could easily become wealthy in a short space of time. It would be years before his methods could be taught to other qualified doctors, and by then, he would be too old to care about making even more money. Besides, he reminded himself, he'd done this for the good of mankind.

"Sir, we're almost to the hospital, we are," the driver said. "Will ye be wantin' me to wait?"

Emile glanced at his watch and then shook his head.

"No, thank you, McGarrity, you go on home. I'll catch a cab back to the hotel."

"I'll not be mindin' the waitin'," the driver insisted.

"No. I insist. I have no idea how long I'll be. Go home and spend an early evening with your family. I wish I could do the same."

"Yes, sir, thank you, sir," the driver said.

Moments later, Emile entered the hospital, his mind already shifting to the young woman and the work yet to be done. She was only thirty-two years old, with a family yet to raise. It did his heart good to know that her brain was already accessing a different route to healing her body. The proof was in her blood work as well as her appearance. The yellow, jaundiced look to her skin was almost gone. He predicted that before six months were up, she would be as good as new. Quite a miracle for a woman they'd given up as lost.

By the time he reached the fourth floor, his walk was almost a swagger, and why not? He walked with God. Only one other man on this earth had healed in that manner, and He'd been crucified. Emile was in no danger of that.

"Ummm, baby, are you awake?"

When a hand encircled his ▬▬, Phillip gasped, then fell out of bed.

"Who the hell are you?" he mumbled, staring down in disbelief at the skinny blonde who was lying spread-eagled in the bed he'd just exited.

"Come on, baby, I'm ~~horny~~," she whined, and began stroking herself as he watched.

"My God, my God," he moaned, and looked around for his clothes. They were nowhere in sight. And that wasn't the worst of his awakening. He had no idea where he was or how he'd gotten there.

"My clothes," he said. "Where are my clothes?"

The woman just made a face at him and then stuck out her tongue.

"Come play with Teena, then I'll tell you where they are."

Phillip's shock turned to panic. Play with her? Good lord, he couldn't even bring himself to touch her. There were needle-marks on her arms, and a multitude of small scabs on her legs that he didn't want to think about. Instead, he began tearing through the room, opening drawers and looking through her closet.

"Come on, baby, I'm getting hot, real hot," the woman said, closing her eyes as her fingers began to move faster.

Phillip wouldn't look at her for fear of gagging. He tore into the adjoining bathroom and then wished he hadn't. Filth was everywhere.

"No, no, no," he moaned, and dashed into the front room.

At first he didn't recognize them, but when he realized the black pants and shirt on the floor near the door were men's clothing, he grabbed them and began putting them on. To his horror, they fit perfectly. More pieces to a puzzle he couldn't explain. When he pulled out the ring of keys from the jacket hanging on the back of a chair, he recognized them. They were his.

In the other room, he could hear the woman's voice rising higher and higher in pitch as her orgasm started. He cast one last frantic look behind, him, praying that he was leaving nothing of his own behind and grabbed the doorknob.

She moaned and then started to scream.

He yanked the door open, slammed it firmly behind him and never looked back.

Lucy Karnoff slammed the phone down and then burst into tears. Everything had been so perfect, and now it was falling down around her ears. She'd spent two days trying to find Phillip, but to no avail. She'd called every place she'd ever known him to frequent and spent precious hours in taxi cabs, searching in places of such degradation that she'd burned the clothes she'd worn during the search.

It wasn't fair. It just wasn't fair. She'd spent her whole life making things perfect and pleasant for Emile so he could concentrate on his work, and now that he'd finally garnered the recognition he so richly deserved, everything was coming apart. It was her duty to make things right. She always made things right. But for the past two years she'd seen the changes in Phillip increasing in intensity. And each time the shift happened, she made sure her husband didn't know. She'd spent a good portion of their savings bailing Phillip out of jail and paying for everything from traffic tickets to fixing the damage to other people's cars so that it would not be reported to their insurance. Once it had cost her a thousand dollars to pay for the damage Phillip had incurred during a fight at a nightclub in a neighboring town. But he'd never disappeared before. Not for this length of time.

She slumped into the chair behind Emile's desk and covered her face. She couldn't find their son and was torn between the shame of what he might have done and the fact that she might never see him again. To her dismay, she caught herself leaning toward the last possibility as the best. Then she started to cry. He was her baby. Her precious only child. God forgive her for even thinking such horrible thoughts. She wanted him back, no matter what he had done.

Then she lifted her head and wiped the tears from her face. This was their child, not just hers. It was time that Emile shouldered some of the fear and responsibility. She opened the drawer to his desk, digging through the papers for the phone number and address of the hotel in Dublin where he was staying. A few moments later she found what she needed and then sat back in the chair, shaking with relief. Emile would know what to do.

She picked up the receiver and started to punch in

the first set of numbers when she heard the front door slam. She stood abruptly, her heart pounding.

"Phillip? Is that you?"

Footsteps sounded on the hardwood flooring, coming nearer and nearer to the study. Unable to stand the suspense, she started moving toward the door.

And then he was there, standing in the doorway with tears running down his face. His hair was a mess, his eyes wild and bloodshot. His lower lip quivered, and then he held out his hands.

"Mother?"

She caught him to her breast, holding him close and patting his back as she'd done so often in comfort when he was a child.

"Yes, darling, Mother's here. Whatever has happened, it will be all right."

10

Sullivan woke with a jerk, wincing as the light from the window to his right hit his pupils.

"So...you're awake. How are you feeling, Mr. Dean?"

"Feeling? Where am—" *Oh my God...Ginny!* "How long have I been here?"

The nurse checked his chart. "The better part of two days."

"Christ almighty!" Sully groaned. "I've got to get up."

He began throwing back covers and fidgeting with the IV they had inserted in the back of his hand.

"No! No! You can't do that," the nurse cried, and began pushing at his hand.

Sully's fingers encircled her wrist, but it was the calmness in his voice that told her he meant business.

"Lady, I'm getting up, whether you help me or not. Which is it going to be?"

Knowing she couldn't manhandle a man his size on her own, she reached for the call button, but it was too late. Sully was already pulling the tape off his IV.

"Wait! Wait!" the nurse said. "You'll have blood everywhere."

"It'll wash," Sully said. "I need to see Ginny."

"Who?"

"Virginia Shapiro. We came to the hospital in the same ambulance."

"Oh. Her."

Sully's heart sank. "What do you mean, her?"

"She's the one with the guard at the door."

He sighed. "Thank God. How is she? Her condition, I mean."

"If you'll give us a few minutes, you can see for yourself."

"That doesn't tell me anything," Sully muttered.

"That's because her condition is between her and her doctor."

"You don't understand," Sully said. "She was in my care when this happened. If I had—"

Suddenly, the nurse understood, and her frustration with the man disappeared.

"I didn't realize," she said softly. "Look, just let me find your doctor and get his okay. If he has no objections, you can visit her and see for yourself. But please don't get up until I get back. You have a concussion. It won't do anyone any good if you fall on your face and wind up back in bed."

Sully frowned. "I feel fine."

"You do not," she argued. "You're pale and

sweating, and I'll bet the only five dollars I have in my purse that you'll be dizzy when you stand up."

He glared.

She stood her ground.

"Are you going to stay in bed, or do I have to ring for the orderlies?"

The idea of being manhandled did not appeal to him. "I'm here, aren't I?" And then he added as she walked to the door, "But I'm not going to wait forever."

"You'll do what you're told," she said, and closed the door behind her.

Defiant to the end, Sully swung his legs over the side of the bed and stood up. True to *her* word, the room tilted beneath his feet. He sat back down.

"Son of a bitch."

It would seem she'd been right after all. Added to that, within ten minutes, a doctor strode into his room. Proof that the nurse was a woman of her word.

"So, Mr. Dean, I hear you're wanting to go AWOL on us."

"Are you going to take the IV out of my arm or is she?" Sully asked, eyeing the nurse, who had followed the doctor into the room.

The fact that he'd countered a question with a question was not lost on the doctor, nor was the look on Sullivan's face.

"You had a pretty good knock on the head," the doctor said.

"I've been hit before."

Well aware of Sully's occupation, the doctor smiled. "Yes, I suppose you have." He circled the bed and leaned over, checking Sully's pupils and then reading his chart. "Have you been up?" he asked.

"Yes," Sully said, ignoring the snort of disapproval from the nearby nurse.

"And how did you feel?"

"Slightly dizzy. Slightly weak."

The doctor grinned outright. "Thank you for being forthright, Mr. Dean. If you'd said anything else, I would have known you were lying."

"Oh, I'll tell the truth every time. It's entirely up to you whether you like what I say. And I *am* going to get up and go to Virginia Shapiro's room, with or without your permission."

The doctor frowned. "The question isn't really whether you're able to go. It's whether she will have anything to do with you."

Sully glared at the nurse. "I was given to understand she was healing. What the hell do you mean?"

"She's healing fine. But she hasn't said a word to anyone since the day she arrived."

"Oh hell," Sully muttered, then swung his legs over the side of the bed again and started pulling at the tape on his IV. "Either you get me out of this getup or I'll check myself out right now."

"Nurse, would you assist Mr. Dean before he makes a mess of himself?" the doctor said.

"Certainly, Doctor."

"Where are my clothes?" Sully asked.

"In the closet," the nurse said. "If you'll wait a moment, I'll get them for you."

"Understand, Mr. Dean...I'm not recommending this," the doctor said.

"Yeah, I know, and if I fall and bust my nose, I won't be suing anyone, okay? Just hand me my pants."

The doctor frowned at Sully's impatience. "You won't be doing her or yourself any good if you have a relapse, you know."

Sully stopped, giving the doctor a cool, studied stare.

"Then I'll have to be sure and stay on my feet, won't I?"

The doctor sighed. "Nurse, while he's dressing himself, ring for a wheelchair. The least we can do is give him a ride to her room."

The nurse nodded, laid Sully's clothes on the bed and left to do as she'd been told.

Ignoring the doctor, Sully slowly stood, hanging on to the bed to make sure he was going to be mobile. This time he experienced nothing more than a brief moment of lightheadedness, which passed.

"How do you feel?" the doctor asked as Sully started putting on his pants.

"Like hell," Sully said.

"Miss Shapiro...she means a lot to you?"

Sully stopped, then took a deep breath and nodded.

"Well, if you mean as much to her as she does to you, then I wish you both the best," the doctor said, patted Sully on the arm and walked out.

The imprint of the man's hand was still on his arm, but he couldn't move. Unknowingly, the doctor had hit the proverbial nail on the head, pinpointing the depth of Sully's concern. He grunted as if he'd been punched in the gut and sank back on the edge of the bed. His gaze fell on the linoleum floor, but he wasn't seeing it. He was locked into the last time he'd seen Ginny's bloody face. He closed his eyes, and as he did, he flashed on the picture of her and her family that had been taken in Yellowstone National Park.

God in heaven, what if she never smiled like that again? With fumbling fingers, he buttoned his jeans. He reached for his shirt, then saw the blood on the front and tossed it aside, opting to use the hospital gown as a shirt instead. He was at the door when an orderly arrived with the wheelchair.

"Hop in, man," he said. "I hear you're ready for a ride."

"Take me to Virginia Shapiro's room," he said.

"Yeah, they told me. The one with the guard."

A mop handle hit the floor in the hall outside Ginny's door. She jerked at the startling noise, the motion sending her whole body into spasm. A quick film of tears shattered her vision as she stifled a moan.

She was healing. Nothing had been broken, only terribly bruised, and nothing had required stitches. She considered herself fortunate, considering the size of the knife Carney Auger had pulled. If Sullivan hadn't come in when he had, the man would have cut her to pieces. At the thought, she closed her eyes, squeezing them hard against the horror of what she'd endured. But the images wouldn't go away. Not when she slept. Not when she was awake. They'd been with her every moment since they'd brought her to the hospital.

Added to that was the guilt of knowing she was the reason Sully had been injured. She turned her face to the pillow. She'd heard them talking when they thought she was asleep. Sully was unconscious. Had been since he'd passed out in the hall. What if he died? She couldn't live with that guilt on her conscience.

And then there was the other thing. Carney Auger was in this very same hospital. Under guard, they said, but he was here, under the same roof with her. Just the thought made her want to throw up. What if he slipped past his guards? What if he came after her or Sully to finish the job?

Doctors and nurses had been here and a man she thought might have been like Sully—with the FBI. He'd come twice the first day. She hadn't seen him since, but the others wouldn't leave her alone. They wanted her to talk about what had happened—to tell them all the gory details of how the man stripped her and beat her and put his hands on every inch of her body. They wanted her to say how he jerked and then screamed when Sully's bullet ripped a hole through his body. They wanted to know how his blood got on her face and hands. They wanted to hear it said in the name of medicine and the law. Why couldn't they understand that the words were poison on her lips? Didn't they know that saying them aloud would only give them life? That revealing what had happened to her would make it real, and that the only way she was still staying sane was by pretending this was a nightmare from which she would eventually wake?

Suddenly she tensed. She could hear voices outside her door, talking about things better left unsaid, as if people who were sick had also suddenly gone deaf. Usually they went away, only this time they didn't. The door was beginning to open.

She pulled the sheet up to her chin and held her breath, knowing she had no endurance left for anything, not even herself.

And then she saw him, getting out of a wheelchair and coming toward her bed.

Oh God. Oh God. Sully.

Her heart started to pound. The familiar swagger in his walk was missing, and the concern on his face shamed her. She was ugly. Ugly. She would never be pretty again.

She ventured another glance at his face, this time focusing on his eyes. He was crying. She'd never seen a grown man cry—not like this. Dear God, he was crying for her. She closed her eyes, unable to bear his pity.

"Ginny...Ginny, baby, look at me."

When his hand brushed her shoulder, she flinched.

"I'm sorry...I'm sorry," he said softly. "I didn't think about..."

She heard him sigh, and it was the defeat in the sound that made her ashamed. This man wasn't like Carney Auger. This man had promised he wouldn't let her die. He'd kept his promise. Now all he wanted was for her to look at him. It was the least she could do.

When she opened her eyes, Sully's whole body went limp. The stress of being up, coupled with his fear for her, had undone him. He swayed where he stood, and as he did, an orderly darted into the room. The moment Ginny saw the stranger, her eyes widened with unmistakable fear.

Sully turned, his voice tight with anger. "Get out. Get out and leave us alone. I'm fine."

"But, sir, you're too weak to be left—"

"Now!" Sully barked.

The door swung shut behind him.

Sully turned. Ginny was looking at him now, her attention completely on his face. He could see her searching out the injuries—the bandage on his forehead and the stitches that were beneath. Her lip started to quiver.

He groaned. "Baby...please... I swear to God I won't hurt you, but I need to touch you. Just to know." His voice broke. "It's my fault. I let him get to you and—"

Tears boiled to the surface, suddenly blurring Ginny's vision.

"You saved my life," she whispered, and reached for his hand.

Sully froze. Riddled with guilt, it was the last thing he'd expected her to say.

Ginny pulled his hand to her cheek, then turned her face into his palm.

Her tears were wet against his skin, her lips trembling as she struggled to speak.

"I thought he'd killed you. I didn't know where you were, and I thought he'd killed you."

"Jesus," Sully moaned, and sat down on the side of her bed before he fell.

Her pupils dilated with fear as her voice lowered to a mere whisper.

"He's here, you know. Right here in this hospital."

Sully stiffened. "Are you talking about Carney?"

Her fingers were clutching at his arm, fingering the fabric of his gown in nervous jerks.

"Don't go to sleep," she whispered. "It isn't safe."

"Christ almighty," Sully muttered, and then stood abruptly. "I'll be right back."

He strode to the door.

The guard on duty jumped and reached for his gun as Sully grabbed his arm, thinking something was about to go down.

"You go tell whoever is in charge of Carney Auger's detainment in this hospital that they'd better get that son of a bitch out from under this roof or I'll do it for them."

"I'm not supposed to leave my post," he said.

"You've got a radio on you, don't you?"

He nodded.

"Then use it. I want Auger moved. If someone has a problem with that, send them to me."

The young man had been an agent with the Bureau for less than a year, but he was well aware of Sullivan Dean and the reputation that went with him. The fact that the director himself was directly involved in this case told him not to argue. If Dean spoke, the young man knew enough to listen.

"Yes, sir. Right away, sir."

"One last thing," Sully said.

"Sir?"

"Thank you for taking care of her."

The young agent nodded. "Sir. It was my pleasure." Then he added, "I'm real sorry what happened to her."

"Yeah," Sully said. "So am I."

He stepped back inside the room and closed the door. Ginny was just as he'd left her. He started back across the room, feeling weaker with each step he took. But he couldn't give in to the urge to lie down. Not yet. Not until that horrible fear was gone from her eyes.

"He'll be gone before dark. I promise."

She nodded, then clutched at his hand again, curling her fingers around his wrist and tugging gently.

"Stay with me," she begged.

Sully's heart twisted. "Baby...I'm not going anywhere." Then he grinned wryly. "I'm so damned weak, I couldn't if I tried."

"Then lie with me."

Sully felt as if he'd just been punched in the gut. Lie with her? *Lord in heaven, give me the strength to do this thing right.*

"You sure?"

She nodded.

He took a deep breath and then exhaled slowly. "I don't know about this. What if I hurt you?"

"Please, Sully. I've been afraid to close my eyes."

It was the "please" that sold her case. He sat beside her first, then scooted his arm beneath her neck. When she flinched, he paused.

"It's not you," she said. "Just for a minute I could feel his hands on my—" She swallowed harshly. "Just hold me."

Sully scooted the rest of the way onto the bed, then pulled her close against him. The guardrail was up against her back. At least she wouldn't fall out.

"Am I too close?" he asked, fearing the simple

weight of his body against her would be enough to send her into a flashback of the assault.

She sighed. "No."

"I'm going to have to pull the guardrail up behind me or I'll fall," he warned.

"Okay."

He reached behind him, felt for the metal railing, then gave it a yank. It came up abruptly, then locked into place. Now they were cocooned within the narrow bed, connected in body as well as in spirit.

"Are you in pain?" Sully whispered.

"Not anymore."

He heard her sigh, then felt her body relax. Minutes passed in which he watched her eyelids begin to droop, finally fluttering to a close. Her breathing slowed, then evened out. Only now and then did a muscle tense and begin to jerk, and when it did, Sully held her that little bit tighter and whispered quietly into her ear, "I've got you, baby. I won't let you die."

And they slept.

Curious as to why the patient in room 411 had never come back to his bed, the nurse who'd been caring for him went looking.

She found them asleep, locked in each other's arms. She knew their history. She also knew the woman hadn't spoken a word to anyone since she'd been admitted, and she knew why. Rape, even if only attempted, was an ugly thing. And the woman had been beaten badly to boot. If she needed that man to hold her, then so be it. It was against every hospital rule and everything she'd been taught, but she turned and walked away as if she'd seen nothing.

Dan Howard stood just inside the hospital entry, waiting for his passengers to arrive. He could have sent someone else to pick Sullivan up, but he wanted to talk to Virginia Shapiro personally, and this seemed the best way to do it.

While he waited, the elevator doors inside the lobby suddenly opened. Sullivan emerged first, looked around the area and spotted Howard at the entryway.

"He's here," Sully said.

Moments later, Ginny emerged, seated in a wheelchair. After a week of being hospitalized, she felt as if she were being let out of jail.

"Let me walk," she said.

"As soon as I get you outside," the orderly said. "Hospital rules."

Heads turned as they passed, mostly out of curiosity that someone was being released, but there were some who gave the woman a second glance, wondering about the fading bruises on her face, and the healing cuts on her lip and eyebrow.

Ginny hated it all. The curiosity. The double takes. She felt as if they could, just by looking at her, know what had happened. It was like being stripped naked all over again and at the mercy of that man.

"Miss Shapiro, it's good to see you again."

She jerked. Again? Had she seen him before?

Dan Howard could tell she didn't remember him, and while he hated to remind her, it had to be done. He had more than one thing to ask her while they were en route to the safe house.

"I came to see you when you were first admitted," he said. "Maybe you don't remember. Those were pretty tough days for you."

"Oh. Yes. I remember."

"Let's get you inside the car, where it's nice and cool," he said. "Sully can sit up front with me, and that way you can stretch out in the back seat. It's going to be a short drive to the helipad, and then a couple of hours in the air until we get to the house."

Ginny gave Sully a nervous look.

"It's all right, Ginny."

Satisfied, she got inside the car and buckled up, but she didn't relax until they were underway. After that, she settled back and pretended to nod off, knowing she would learn far more about what was happening with the case that way than if she asked specific questions herself.

As they drove away, the irony of her situation struck her. She'd been a victim and survived, but the danger in her life was far from over. It seemed impossible to believe that anything else could possibly happen. She'd had her quota of traumatic injuries from the assault, and yet that might be nothing to what lay ahead. She was still in danger of losing her life, and her enemy still had no face. If not for the man sitting beside Dan Howard, she would certainly be in danger of losing her mind.

"Where are we going?" Sully asked.

"Closest unoccupied safe house is outside of Phoenix. I know it's hot as hell there this time of year, but the house has a pool and a great view."

"It doesn't matter where we go," Sully said. "Ginny just needs time to find herself again."

"I need to talk to her."

"Not now," Sully said.

"Damn it, Sully, it's her life we're trying to save here. I suggest we let her make the decisions."

Sully lowered his voice, not wanting Ginny to overhear. "You don't understand. Mentally, she's barely capable of getting through a day, and that's if no one rocks her world. You push her too hard and she could go over the edge."

"I'm not going to push. I'm just going to talk," Howard said. "When we get to Phoenix, we'll see. Okay?"

Sully frowned, but he knew Dan was right. They needed information to solve the case, and until it was over, Ginny had no life.

"Okay," Sully said. "There's the helicopter coming in for a landing now."

"Good. Right on time," Howard said.

"Hey, Dan, I meant to ask. Our things that were at the cabin...where are they?"

"In the trunk of my car."

"All of it? Even the stuff that was in my car?"

"Yes. We turned your rental in and put Miss Shapiro's car in storage in Biloxi. The receipt and keys are in your luggage."

"Thanks."

"You know the routine. You've done it yourself. Oh, and another thing. The old man back at the landing...he gave back the money you'd paid down and tore up Ginny's bill. He said it was the least he could do."

Sully nodded, then looked over his shoulder into the back seat, making sure Ginny wasn't listening before he asked.

"About Auger..."

"He copped a plea to attempted rape and assault, rather than face the attempted murder charge the D.A. was shooting for."

Sully's fingers curled into fists. "I should have finished the job when I had the chance," he muttered. "Just the thought of that man ever being able to walk the streets again makes me sick."

"Yeah, I know what you mean. The judicial system sucks, and we both know it, although he'll be out of commission for a few years."

The car stopped. Ginny roused.

"Sully?"

Instantly his hand was on her arm.

"Right here, Ginny. We're going to unload the luggage. Wait until I come get you, all right?"

"All right."

She watched the two men exit the car and then sat up. To her dismay, she really had dozed off, missing everything that had been said during the ride.

A short while later, Sully opened the back door.

"Come on, Cinderella. Your chariot awaits."

"Where are we going?" she asked, as he helped her out of the car.

He tilted her chin and then tweaked the end of her nose.

"To the ball."

Ginny smiled and then caught her breath on a sob. Two days ago, she would have sworn she would never laugh again. Maybe there was hope for her yet.

"But I don't have any glass slippers."

"Doesn't matter. That chopper's gonna turn into a pumpkin if we don't get a move on."

Ginny let him lead her, but she couldn't help glancing over her shoulder as they walked away. A couple of men had stopped working to watch, and there was a delivery truck coming down the road they'd just driven. She shuddered as they helped her up into the belly of the chopper and then buckled her in. When would this nightmare finally come to an end? Would she spend the rest of her life always looking over her shoulder?

Sully slipped into the seat beside her as Dan took

the co-pilot's seat. Ginny closed her eyes as the chopper lifted straight into the air. But her panic subsided as Sully gave her fingers a squeeze.

"You okay?"

Ginny swallowed the lump in her throat. "As long as this thing stays in the air and Agent Howard and the pilot don't turn into mice, I'm going to be fine."

Sully was still laughing as the chopper banked sharply and headed west.

11

"**M**r. Karnoff, do you have any more bags to be taken to the lobby?"

"No, just those two," Emile said. "I have a couple more phone calls to make, and then I'll be down. Oh…and I'll be needing a cab to the airport."

"Yes, sir."

Emile waited until the bellman closed the door and then pulled several items from his jacket, including an address book, before reaching for the phone.

"Operator, I need an outside line, please. I want to make a call to the United States."

"Yes, sir, one moment, sir," the operator said.

Emile waited for the tone and then dialed the number. A few moments later the phone began to ring.

When the call for Virginia Shapiro came in to the *St. Louis Daily,* the caller had no idea that the call was forwarded to the desk of Officer Bonnie Smith, of the St. Louis Police. The moment that phone began to ring, a number of events began to occur. As Officer

Smith answered, a tape began recording the call and another officer began a trace.

"*St. Louis Daily,* Shapiro speaking."

There was a brief moment of silence, and then something clicked. In the background, she thought she could hear rumbling, like the sound of distant thunder. And then another sound, similar to the chimes of a doorbell, only louder than the thunder. She frowned, waiting for someone to start speaking, but the chiming sound continued to repeat—once, then twice. When it began for the third time, she spoke.

"Hello? Hello? Is anyone there?"

She heard a startled gasp and then a click. The connection was gone.

"Did you get any of that?" she said.

"They didn't stay on long enough to get a trace."

"Blast it," she said. "Maybe they'll call back. In the meantime, make a copy of that tape and give Detective Pagillia a call. Tell him it's on the way."

Lucy Karnoff stood in the hallway just outside her son's room. She'd spent all morning tending to the details of keeping her home and family presentable, and now this! She absolved herself of guilt regarding the eavesdropping under the auspices of being a good mother. How else could she help if she didn't know what was wrong? But what Phillip was doing made no sense. She knew he was alone, and yet he was distinctly speaking as though someone was there. She pressed her ear closer to the door just as another outburst occurred.

"Listen, you crazy bastard, I'm getting sick and tired of having to clean up your messes! Haven't you heard of AIDS? And your taste in women... My God! Do you want your ▓▓▓ to rot and fall off?"

I'm not the one who's crazy, Phil. You're the one who can't keep his head on straight. I know who I am. I'm the one in charge. I'm the one who knows how to tell people to go to hell, which is more than you can do. If you had any backbone, you'd tell your old man to go ▓▓▓ himself.

"You're disgusting," Phillip said. "I don't have to listen to any more of this."

Oh, but that's where you're wrong. I'm Tony. I'm the player, and I'm not going anywhere, you idiot, because I'm inside your head.

The agonizing truth was more than Phillip could bear. He sank to his knees, his hands cupping his ears, as if he could block out the sound of the voice inside his head, but it didn't happen. Tony kept picking and digging at the scab between him and insanity and wouldn't let go. What frightened Phillip most was that Tony was getting stronger, he could feel it, while he was losing ground on a daily basis. There were days when he didn't think he could continue.

Oh, no you don't. You're not offing yourself. I won't let you. Besides, you're Mama's baby boy, remember? What would she do without her little boy?

"Shut up! Shut up!" Phillip mumbled.

Fine. I'm tired now, anyway. Why don't you go play with yourself, little boy, and when I come back, I'll show you what a real man is all about.

Phillip crawled on all fours to the edge of his bed, then pulled himself up and fell prostrate across the spread.

"Father in heaven, forgive me, for I have sinned," Phillip muttered, and closed his eyes.

Lucy pressed her fingers against her mouth and then slipped away. This was worse, much worse, than she had imagined, and more than she could handle on her own. She raced to a phone and called the number of the Dublin hotel where Emile was staying, but he'd already checked out. She had no way of knowing how to get in touch with him until he called. For all she knew, he could be on his way to another consultation, and this thing with Phillip couldn't wait. There had to be something in Emile's office that would help. After all, in the beginning, she'd been his assistant. She knew where he kept his ledgers and tapes. She'd even helped catalogue the ones from the early days. Without hesitation, she hurried to her husband's office, ignoring the fact that he would be very upset if he knew what she was about to do.

The tapes were well-marked as to dates and subject matter. What she needed was something on self-motivation. Yes. That should do it. All Phillip needed was a boost in the right direction. She began running her finger down the list, mentally reading them off as she went.

Exploring the Human Psyche.

Behavior Traits: Genetic or Learned?

Enhancing Personalities.

The list went on and on. Her fingers flew through the drawer, picking up one tape, then discarding it for another. It wasn't until she came to *Subliminal Messaging* that she stopped.

That was what she needed! Phillip would never agree to this on his own. She needed something that would work on him as he slept.

She popped it into the tape player and listened briefly, making sure the tape was not mislabeled. The familiar sound of her husband's sonorous voice brought tears to her eyes.

Oh Emile, Emile... I need you so.

Yes, this would work, of that she was certain. She took both the tape and the recorder. Tonight, when Phillip was asleep, she would slip this beneath his bed. Even though Emile was not there physically to help his son, she would use the wonders of his medicine to work its magic.

Detective Anthony Pagillia hung up the phone, his elation evident. He'd just talked to Officer Smith. The fact that they hadn't been able to trace the call was almost incidental to the fact that they had it on tape. He'd told Smith to make two separate copies of the

tape, one for him and one to be sent to FBI Headquarters in care of Agent Dan Howard. He clapped
his hands together in satisfaction and bolted up from
his chair. This was their first break in the case. He
needed to contact Howard now and warn him the tape
was on its way.

Dan Howard was helping Sullivan unload their baggage from the helicopter when his cell phone began
to ring.

"Go ahead and take the call," Sully said. "I'll get
the last one."

Sully started toward the safe house as Howard
paused to answer the phone.

"Howard."

"Agent Howard, this is Detective Pagillia, with the
St. Louis police."

"Yes, Anthony, what's up?"

"We got a hit on the phone at Miss Shapiro's
work."

Dan looked up. Sully was already in the house.

"The hell you say! Did you get a trace?"

"No, the caller hung up too fast, but we got it on
tape. Maybe your people at Quantico can make sense
of it. I'm told it's mostly sounds. If someone was
talking, my officer couldn't hear what was being
said."

Dan started walking rapidly toward the house.

"This is great news," he said. "Send the tape to my office in D.C. I'll be there by tonight."

"Yes, sir."

"Good work, Detective," Dan said.

"Thank you, sir. The sooner we catch this nut, the better we'll all sleep at night."

"You've got that right," Dan said.

"Oh... Agent Howard...if it's not out of line to ask, how is Miss Shapiro? I got your message about what happened to her."

Dan paused on the walk, unwilling to talk about this inside the house, where Ginny could overhear.

"She's hanging in there, and that's about all I can say. It was rough on her."

"And Agent Dean? I understood he was injured, too?"

Dan chuckled. "Oh hell, yes. The perp almost brained him, but he still managed to control the situation before it was too late. He's worse than a mother hen with his charge, if you get my drift."

"Yes, I can see that happening. The day I met him, he was pretty focused on finding Miss Shapiro. Well, thanks again for the information."

"And thank you for yours," Dan countered, then disconnected.

"Hey, Sully!" he shouted. "Good news."

Ginny had gone through every room of the safe house twice, familiarizing herself with the location of bathrooms and bedrooms, and seeing the inevitable guards that would be their companions for as long as they were here.

The house itself was nice. In fact, it was better than nice. In another situation, she would have enjoyed being here. The low-slung, adobe ranch-style house faced west toward the Maricopa Mountains, and she'd heard the men make mention of an Indian reservation to the east. Other than that, she had no earthly idea of where they were. What she did know was that whatever green there was around this house had to be the result of a watering system. The rest of the land was arid and desertlike, although she'd seen many fertile fields from the air as they'd flown over.

A veritable forest of giant saguaros surrounded the house in all directions, along with many other varieties of cacti she couldn't identify. But the tall, stately cactus, with its long, spiney arms pointing heavenward, was familiar, although she couldn't say why. Something she'd probably researched for a story and forgotten about until now.

Following the voices, she retraced her steps back into the main room of the house, once again noting the thick adobe walls, the tall, narrow windows and the high, domed ceilings. Energy savers.

She entered the living room just as Sully broke into a grin and clapped Dan Howard on the back.

"Did I miss the joke?"

Sully turned toward her, a quick smile on his lips.

"We've had a break in the case. They got a tape of a suspicious phone call made to your office at the *Daily*."

Ginny froze. "Tape? What kind of tape? What was on it? What did the caller say?"

"We haven't heard it yet," Dan said. "All I know is what Detective Pagillia told me. He said it was mostly background noise, but we may be able to make something out at our lab."

"What kind of noise?" Ginny asked.

"Well, let me think. The officer said she could tell that it was coming up a storm when the call was being made, because she could hear the distant sound of thunder. And then she kept hearing something like a doorbell ringing over and over. You know...when a caller won't go away. She thinks maybe the caller was disturbed by the arrival of an unexpected guest and disconnected."

A frisson of something long-ago buried shifted itself deep within Ginny's mind. She closed her eyes, trying to hold on to the thought, but it wouldn't come.

Sully saw the expression on her face.

"Ginny, what is it?"

She frowned, then shook her head. "I don't know. Nothing, I suppose. Are we going to get to hear it?"

"Yes, sure...as soon as I—"

Sully interrupted. "No. Not you."

Ginny frowned. "But—"

"Until I know for certain that call won't set off

some ticking bomb in your mind, you don't hear it, okay?''

She paled. "Of course. I don't know what I was thinking.''

Sully laid a hand on her back, then pulled her close beneath the shelter of his arm.

"That's why I'm here,'' he said.

Ginny's eyes brimmed. "Yes, but how long will *I* be here?''

There was nothing the men could say to give her comfort. Her shoulders slumped as she turned and walked away.

"Her attitude isn't so hot,'' Dan said.

Sully glared. "Yours wouldn't be, either, if a week ago some nut had tried to gut *you* like a fish.''

"Sorry,'' Dan said, holding up his hands in a gesture of surrender. "I didn't mean to step on any toes...or hearts.''

Sully's glare deepened as Dan grinned.

"Don't you have someplace else to be?'' Sully asked.

Dan glanced at his watch. "Yes, actually, I do. FYI, besides yourself, there are three men on guard, none of whom will be intrusive. They're staying in the guest house out back and have their own set of orders. Unless you need something specific, you will have little to no contact with them. By the way, two of them, Franklin and Webster Chee, grew up local to the area. They're Navajos, and brothers to boot—two of the best agents the Bureau has. The other man, Kevin Holloway, is good, too. I've worked with him on several cases.

Sully nodded. "I know the drill."

"Yeah, I know. But don't take on too much by yourself. You just got out of the hospital, too, remember? If there's any heavy work to do, ask for help."

Sully grinned. "Yes, Mother."

Dan grinned back. "Fine, if that's the way you want to play, then give Mommy a kiss goodbye. I've got to leave."

This time it was Sully who held up his hands in surrender.

"You win, Howard. You're too ugly to kiss."

"Yeah, but I'm faithful," Dan said.

"Tell that to your wife. I'm not interested."

Dan waved goodbye. "I'll be in touch."

Sully watched the helicopter ascend and then disappear into the sun. He turned, instantly moving into agent mode as he began his own tour of the house, checking out strong points and taking note of the areas where security might be breached.

It wasn't until he walked outside to the walled backyard that he found Ginny again. She was sitting by a small in-ground pool, dangling her feet into the water.

"Why don't you go for a swim?" he said. "It would probably feel good after that long flight."

"No suit," she said.

"Come with me," he said, and took her by the hand. She followed, leaving wet footprints on the dark red tiles as they moved through the house.

Inside the first bedroom down the hall, he pointed to an armoire.

"I was snooping earlier. Look inside. Maybe one of those will fit."

Ginny opened the doors to find an assortment of both men's and women's bathing attire.

"I suppose I'm not the first to pack and run," she said, alluding to the fact that many other people must have been secluded here.

"Find one for me, too," Sully said. "I'm going to make us something cold to drink."

Ginny smiled as she turned and began digging through the shelves and drawers. Maybe this wouldn't be so bad after all.

Sully was rooting through the well-stocked pantry for something to snack on when Ginny came into the kitchen. Her shoulder-length hair was in a high ponytail, and the only suit that came close to fitting her had been a black two-piece. It was modest, as two-piece suits went—more like a bra and panties than a bikini. But even so, it was what the lack of fabric revealed that she couldn't deny. Again she wished for more flesh to fill out the suit, and if it had been anyone but Sully, she wouldn't have had the guts to put it on.

"I laid some trunks on the bed that might fit you," she said. "What do we have to drink?"

He smiled and turned, a package of pretzels in his hand. The smile froze and then died. He'd seen the bruises on her face and arms many times, but this was the first time he'd seen the ones on her body. Even though they were fading, they were a vivid reminder of what she'd endured.

"I will regret not killing that man for the rest of my life," he said softly.

Ginny flushed and crossed her arms across her midriff in self-defense.

"Don't do that," he said, and pulled her arms away from her body.

"I just—"

He cupped her face in his hands. She stood motionless, watching the changing expressions on his face. She saw his pupils dilate and then his nostrils flare, and she knew he was going to kiss her. It seemed as if they'd been waiting for this moment ever since the night he'd knocked on her door and come in from the rain.

"Sully..."

"Shhh," he whispered, and rubbed his thumbs gently across the cuts on her lips. "I don't want to hurt you."

"I'm tough, remember?" *Besides, you're already going to hurt me when you leave.*

He inhaled slowly and lowered his head. Her lips were soft and yielding. Tunneling his fingers through her hair, he pulled her closer, tasting the hesitation and then acceptance of a question that had yet to be voiced—a question he wasn't sure he could ask.

Sullivan was the first to break away. He groaned beneath his breath and then touched her forehead with his own, feeling the heat of her breath upon his chest.

"Forgive me, Ginny. I stepped out of line."

Two small creases appeared between her eyebrows as she studied the expression on his face, then she shook her head and walked away.

Sully started to call her back, but he didn't know what to say. Hell yes, he wanted to make love to her. Worse than he'd ever wanted anything before. But he'd gotten careless once, and it had nearly cost Ginny her life. He stood at the kitchen door until he was certain she was safely in the water. One of the men on guard stepped around the corner of the house long enough for Sully to know he was there. Satisfied for the moment that she was safe, he hurried to change.

Ginny had tried to swim a lap but found it too much of an effort and had opted for hanging on to the side of the pool and just letting the water lap around her body. The water was lovely in the almost unbearable heat, but the longer she lay there, the more aware of her surroundings she became.

It was the quiet that got to her. No cars. No planes. No sirens. Not even the sound of other people's voices. Just the water lapping against the side of the pool and the occasional hum of the central air-conditioning unit as it kicked on.

"Ginny, come out of the water for a moment."

She looked up. Sully was standing near her head, dangling a small plastic bottle in the air. From this angle, he looked about ten feet tall, with bulges in all the right places.

"Sunscreen," he said.

She felt her arms. They were already hot.

"Oh. Right." She lifted a hand, and he pulled her out of the water.

"Ouch, the concrete is hot," she muttered, as she began to dance from foot to foot.

Sully tossed down a towel. "Stand on that," he said.

Gratefully, she stepped on the terry-cloth, thankful for the barrier.

"This won't take long," Sully said. "I'm going to undo the back of this top so I can put it on your shoulders."

She nodded and grabbed the front of the bra with both hands as the back came undone. And then his hands, slick with lotion, were cupping her shoulders and rubbing her.

It was reflex that made her tense, but Sully felt it. He stopped instantly.

"Damn. Ginny, I'm sorry. I didn't think. Maybe you'd rather do this yourself than cope with the feel of a man's hands on you."

She shook her head. "No. Don't be silly. It was just a reflex. The lotion was cold, that's all."

She was lying, and he knew it, but it made him all the more careful of letting his thoughts get out of hand.

"I'll be quick," he said. "Tilt your head down a minute, will you? I need to get some on the back of your neck."

She did as he asked, absorbing the feel of his fingers against her skin, stroking, rubbing, over and over. The image of Carney Auger straddling her body suddenly popped into her mind, but before she could panic, his features began to morph into Sully's. Suddenly the gut-wrenching fear was gone, too, replaced by the feel of Sully's body between her legs. She knew without ever having experienced it that he would make love as superbly as he did everything else. With total focus on her, mindful of nothing but bringing her pleasure.

She moaned.

Sully stopped. "Am I hurting you, honey?"

"No. It just feels good."

Jesus. "Okay, I think that's good enough," he said. "You do your legs." He handed her the bottle and then dove headfirst into the pool, thankful to be hidden within the tepid water. He needed to put a barrier between him and Ginny, and it was the only thing at hand.

Ginny fastened the top of her suit and then quickly rubbed the sunscreen on her legs. When she straightened, Sully was in front of her, chest deep in the water and waiting.

"Are you ready to get back in?" he asked.

"Yes."

"Need some help?"

"I can manage," she said, and then had to deal with the spurt of disappointment as he swam away.

Dinner that evening was almost as strained as that night back at the cabin when they'd been at each other's throats. Only now Sully could look back and know what had been at the root of their dissension.

Attraction. Yes.

Lust. Hell, yes.

But there was more, at least for him. The moment he'd seen her face in the picture at her apartment, she'd become more than Georgia's friend—more than an intended victim. She'd become real. And then, when he'd crawled between the sheets of her bed and laid his head on the pillow she'd slept on the night before, it had been like crawling into her skin. He'd gotten too close, too fast, and it was too late to take it back. Sully was falling in love, and the timing couldn't have been worse.

Ginny tried not to stare at Sully, but his casual grace was impossible to ignore. Dressed in a white polo shirt and pale blue slacks, he looked like he'd stepped out of the pages of a men's fashion catalogue. That Hollywood look was unexpected, especially after the jeans and T-shirts he'd worn at the cabin. She wondered if he'd had those clothes all along, or if they were something he'd scrounged up on the premises. Even the small patch of hair they'd had to shave to stitch up his scalp was starting to grow back. It blended quite well with the somewhat spiky hairstyle he seemed to favor.

"Is your hamburger not done enough?" he asked, noting that she'd taken all of three bites.

Ginny blinked and then looked down at her plate.

"Oh...no...actually, it's quite good."

Suddenly starving, she picked it up with both hands and took a big bite.

Sully shook his head and then took a second helping of potato salad. It wasn't as tasty as his mother's, but knowing Ginny's talent for cooking, anything that came already prepared was fine.

"You sunburned a little this afternoon," Sully said, pointing to her nose.

She nodded as she swallowed.

"I doubt if it will peel, though," he added. "It's only a little pink."

Ginny laid her hamburger down and then dabbed her mouth with her paper napkin. This tiptoeing around each other was getting on her nerves, and it had to stop.

"Sully, stop it."

Startled, he swallowed, his bite only half-chewed.

"Stop what?"

"This...this...small talk. For God's sake, surely we've been through enough together to get past that."

Sully laid down his fork and leaned back in his chair. "So the small talk is out, huh?"

"Yes, please," she said, and absently brushed a crumb off her only dress, thinking to herself that she would have to find a dry cleaner soon or run completely out of clean clothes, before remembering the washer and dryer she'd seen earlier.

"Then what do we discuss? Surely not the incident that put us both in the hospital. And surely you're not in the mood for me to drag you over the coals again about Montgomery Academy?"

"Well, no, not exactly."

"Then short of trading stories about our childhoods, which we pretty much covered at the cabin, that leaves sex and board games, and I'm pretty sure we're out of Monopoly."

Ginny gulped, but she couldn't let him get by with this. Not again.

"What do guys talk about when they're hanging out?" she asked.

"Sports, work, girls and sex."

She narrowed her eyes in disgust.

"You're not serious?"

Sully grinned. "No, but it got a rise out of you, didn't it?"

She glared for all of a second and then began to grin.

"You're impossible, aren't you?"

His smile stopped. His voice lowered. "Honey, I'm so easy, it would make your sweet head spin."

Ginny had a vision of bare sweating bodies before she stood abruptly.

"Where are you going?" Sully asked.

"To get some air."

"But it's hotter outside than it is in here."

"Don't bet on it," Ginny muttered, and walked out of the dining room, leaving him to make what he chose of her remark.

Sully started to follow her and then stopped. He'd done it again. Pushed when he should have stayed put. Angrily, he started gathering up their dishes and carrying them into the kitchen. He would wash them later. Even if she didn't want company, he wasn't letting her out of his sight.

12

Ginny thought she was alone. One minute she was standing beside the pool, listening to the water lapping at the sides, and the next thing, Sully's voice was at her ear.

"Come inside with me."

She turned, looking up at him in the moonlight and wishing she could read his mind.

"Please," Sully added.

She sighed and then surprised them both by walking into his arms and laying her head against his chest.

"I don't know how to play this game," Ginny said. "We crossed a line that I didn't see until it was too late to go back. Truth is, I'm not sure I would have stopped even then."

It was instinct that made him hold her, but it was shock that kept him silent. She was baring her soul, and he couldn't find the guts to answer.

"It's not hero-worship, either," she added, looking up at him in the shadows. "Although you've twice proven yourself to be mine."

He shook his head, willing himself to be still, but

God help him, he wanted to make love to her there in the moonlight worse than he'd ever wanted anything in his life.

"You care about me, Sully. I know that. But what I don't know is how much. Is it duty that turns you into my knight in shining armor, or is this nothing more than lust?"

"Hell," he muttered, wanting to shake her. But he kept remembering the bruises. "This is just like a woman. Always needing to analyze everything."

"Maybe, and maybe it's just the reporter in me. Needing to know all the facts before I proceed."

He didn't answer, and the pain of his rejection broke her heart, but she would be damned before she'd let him know.

"Sorry," she said. "I guess I'm out of bounds here, but don't worry. I'm not going to dissolve into some crying, screaming fit because some man doesn't want me."

She pushed herself out of his arms and then suddenly shivered.

"You know what, Sully? You were wrong. About the weather, I mean. It *is* cooler out here than it is inside. And I'm tired. Really tired. I'm going to go to bed now, and when we wake up in the morning, this is going to be nothing more than a bad dream."

He heard tears in her voice, and they were his undoing. Right or wrong, he'd reached the limit of his endurance.

"Wait."

The urgency in his voice made her stop, but she couldn't bring herself to turn and face him.

"What?" she muttered.

"You think I don't want you? Lady, I lie awake nights thinking of all the ways I want to make love to you. I dream of being so deep inside you that it hurts to pull out, and of watching your eyes lose focus right before you come. And it's not duty, and it's not lust. I don't know what to call it, but I'll spend the rest of my life with your face in my mind." He touched the back of her head, fisting a handful of her dark, silky hair and then letting it go. "You want truth? I'll give you truth. I'm afraid to touch you. I'm scared sick that if I do, you'll flash back to what happened between you and Carney Auger, that if I take you in my arms, the only man you'll see is him."

Ginny turned, shock in her voice. "Oh, Sully, no. Never that. Never with you. I slept in your arms, remember? You held me in the hospital, and when I woke up that next morning, it was with deep regret that things weren't different. Many times I had thought of what that would be like—to wake up beside you, I mean. I'd fully expected we would have made love that...that night. And afterward... I didn't want to be battered and ugly and half out of my mind."

Her words slid through his mind like a knife, cutting through defenses he didn't know he had. Without thinking, he pulled her to him, and when her arms slipped around his waist, he knew he was gone.

"Ginny, you're so beautiful. What you survived was ugly—not you."

She looked up at him there, his features barely evident in the dark desert night. As she stood there, it dawned on her that she didn't need to see him to know the truth. It was in the tone of his voice and the tenderness of his touch.

She sighed and then dropped her chin, resting her forehead against his chest.

"So...?"

Sully had to smile. Ginny was like a dog with a bone.

"So I'm admitting there's something real between us. Is that what you wanted to hear?"

"Yes."

"Is there anything else I can do for you?" he muttered. "Like slitting my own throat before I make a bigger ass of myself?"

She didn't answer. Instead, they stood for a moment, staring intently at each other's faces.

"There's a part of me that's afraid to let go and trust you all the way. Oh...I know you'll take care of me physically without fail, but it's my heart that's in danger, and right now, I need to believe that you're telling me the truth."

"Damn it, Ginny, I don't know what else to—"

"Wait," she begged, and put a silencing finger

against his lips. "What I'm trying to say is...if this is only an illusion—if you're just telling me what you think I needed to hear—I don't want to know."

Hurt and angry, Sully struggled with the urge to walk away, but there was a part of him that almost understood. She'd already lost so much. And she was still in danger. It wasn't the time to give away the only thing she had left of her own—her heart.

"I'm going to ask you again," he said. "Come back inside."

"Yes, I think it's time."

Moonlight lay across the floor in broken pieces as Sully undressed her. Ginny knew in her mind what was about to transpire, but it seemed as if she were watching herself from a distance. Nothing seemed real. Her dress lay like a puddle of ink upon the floor, the dark, navy blue color lost among the shadows. Sully's breath was warm against her face as he reached around her back and unfastened her bra. The coolness of the air-conditioned room hardened her nipples, bringing them to instant attention, as if begging to be touched.

So he did.

She inhaled sharply as his tongue encircled a pouting peak. When he moved to the other one and caught it in his teeth, she pulled him closer, wanting more of the pleasure and the pain. But he didn't linger there. It wasn't time. As she was struggling to catch her breath, his hands slid around her back and then beneath her panties, cupping her hips and then stripping her bare.

Again his head dipped as he sought out the lobe of her ear, drawing it into his mouth, laving the tip with his tongue, then letting her go. The cool air hit the place where the warmth of his mouth had been, and she shivered. Then he picked her up and laid her down in the middle of his bed, moving on to the next step of the seduction.

She watched him, almost objectively, as he began to undress. Piece by piece, he removed his clothing, revealing a broad chest and flat belly, then long, muscled legs. Even before he took off his briefs, she could tell he was aroused, and yet when he was totally nude, she was stunned by his size.

He heard her gasp and looked down.

"I won't hurt you."

"It isn't that."

"Are you afraid? All you have to do is say no and I'm gone."

"No...not of that. Not what you mean."

"Then what?" Sully asked.

"I want this—so much. I want it to matter to you as much as it does me."

"Why do I sense there's a 'but'?"

"Don't take this wrong."

He sighed. "Ginny, I'm about as defenseless as a

man can be. Say what you have to say. You'll see my reaction, good or bad.''

"This first time... I don't know how I'll be. But I need it to take away the bad memories. Can you do that for me? Can you forgive me if I hesitate—if I flinch or start to cry? Will you make love to me anyway? I need to close my eyes and see something besides that man's face above me.''

His hands were shaking as he lay down beside her. *Please, God, don't let me do anything wrong.* When he brushed his hand across the flat of her belly, she flinched.

"Sully, I—"

"Shhh. Don't talk. Just feel. If it helps, close your eyes, baby. And whatever you do, for God's sake, remember it's me.''

Tears rolled from the corners of her eyes onto her pillow. He rose up on one elbow and kissed them away. Then he began a journey across Ginny that neither one would ever forget.

He crawled to the end of the bed and sat down, then took one of her feet into his hands and began to rub. Gently he stroked the delicate arch, then moved toward the back of her heel and across her ankle, kneading away all her stress.

Her toes began to tingle, and she began to relax. When he took the second foot into his lap, she was ready, anticipating the aches he was willing to rub away. Somewhere within the time when he moved up to her legs, she knew it was going to be okay. This total acceptance of his hands on her body had not been easy, and yet it was there. He was moving up the length of her legs now with those magical hands, up the backs of her calves, then her thighs. Always stroking, sometimes pressing his thumbs into hard, knotted muscles, mixing a breathless sort of pain with the bone-melting pleasure. When his thumbs rested at the juncture of her thighs, she knew the focus of his journey. The urge to part her legs for him was startling. But to her shock, he only brushed across the spot with the backs of his hands and then moved up to her belly.

Lightly now, ever conscious of the bruises, his hands skimmed across the surface of her skin, until she felt like a guitar string that had been tuned too tight. When he palmed her breasts and then rolled the nubs between his fingers, her hips arched up from the bed in reflex. She began to moan, clutching at his arms and then his hands.

"Not yet, baby. Not yet," she heard him whisper.

Reluctantly, she dug her fingers into the mattress instead.

Sully was almost at the end of his own endurance, and yet he couldn't—wouldn't—take his pleasure until he knew it would be hers, too. Her breath was hot against his face as he lowered his head, capturing her mouth with his own, swallowing her short, gasping moans. When she dug her fingers through his hair and caught his lower lip between her teeth, he knew it was time.

He moved swiftly, straddling her legs, yet ever careful not to let his weight down upon her. His hands were on her thighs again, moving up, then up some more. Thick, dark curls tangled around his fingers as he felt for the core of her. This was where pleasure began and ended. This would tell the tale.

"Ginny, open your eyes."

As her eyelids came up, he began to rub. Whatever panic she might have felt at seeing him above her was lost in the pleasure that she felt. He heard her sigh, then moan, and still he rubbed—around and around in a perpetual motion of ecstasy. When she opened her legs farther, he moved deeper, and when she inadvertently arched off the bed, he knew he was home.

He looked up at her face. Her eyes were closed again, and she was lost to herself and at the mercy of his hands. Almost out of his mind with the need to be in her, he had to move now before it was too late.

"Baby..."

It was the plea in his voice that brought her back from where she'd been. She opened her eyes just as he shifted position. She had a moment's impression of him coming down and then inside her, filling her, pushing into her deeply.

"Look at me. Look at me."

The urgency in his voice was unmistakable. She looked, and for a second, time seemed to stand still.

Her body was quivering on the brink of an orgasm with no end. His face was dark, his muscles jerking as he held himself above her, unwilling to burden her with his weight until she knew that it was him. But she could feel him deep inside her, pulsing, pushing, and dear God, she needed more. Without words, she encircled his neck and pulled him down to meet her.

It was all that he needed to know.

He thrust himself the rest of the way in, and when she arched up to meet him, he began to move.

She came within seconds as a gut-wrenching moan slipped out from between her teeth, and he could feel the constriction of her muscles as the ripples fanned throughout. She was hot and wet, and he went out of his mind.

The digital clock registered a little after four in the morning when Ginny woke. She needed to go to the bathroom, but unwinding herself from Sully's arms without waking him was going to be impossible.

"Sully, I need to get up."

He was awake instantly. "Are you all right?"

"Yes. I just need to go to the bathroom."

"Okay."

He unwound himself and then watched the reflection of the fading moonlight upon her body as she walked across the floor. Once she was gone, he rolled over on his belly and closed his eyes, but the knowledge that had accompanied him into sleep was still

there. He was in love with her—pure and simple—
and it had nothing to do with sex. Oh sure, that had
been something out of a teenager's dream. But he'd
never made love *and* been in love before, and the
combination had been something close to nuclear. His
protective instincts were in overdrive, competing with
his libido for dominance. He didn't know whether to
put her on a pedestal or drag her off the damned thing
and use it for a pillow while they made mad, crazy
love.

When he heard her coming back to bed, he rolled
onto his side and opened his arms. She came willingly, laying her head on his arm and using his chest
as a resting place for her arm. Within seconds she was
fast asleep. He lay there without moving as his heart
swelled inside his chest.

So this was what love felt like. Damn. If it was so
good, then why was he so scared?

The wind had come up after dark, a portent of a
change in the weather. Lucy hoped it would rain. Her
flowers were drooping out in their beds, and the grass
was beginning to turn. She made a mental note to find
the sprinkler tomorrow and set it in place. It wouldn't
do for Emile to come home to imperfection.

She sat at her desk, absently answering the bits and
pieces of personal mail she had received the past
week, but the joy she usually got from such tasks
wasn't there. She kept thinking of Phillip. He'd

changed so much over the past two years. Once he'd been so amenable, willing to help her without question. This ugly side of him was more than troubling. There had even been times when she had actually been afraid. She scoffed to herself, then shook her head. How foolish. Imagine, being frightened of your very own child. It was ludicrous.

She glanced at the clock as she put the stamp on the last letter. It was time. Phillip would be asleep by now. She'd watched him taking a sleeping pill when she'd turned down his bed. Normally she would have questioned him as to the wisdom of something that drastic, but it seemed to fall in with her plans. Her steps were light as she hurried down the hallway with the tape recorder clutched to her chest. Oh, Emile would be proud of her if he knew the initiative she was taking. And it would work. It had to. Nothing must interfere with the rise of her husband's star, not even the troubles of their only son.

She held her breath as she peeked into the room. Phillip was lying on his side with his back to the door. The steady rise and fall of his shoulder, along with the occasional snore, was evidence enough for her to proceed. Slipping off her shoes at the door, she proceeded barefoot across the room, then knelt beside his bed and carefully pushed the tape recorder beneath the bed skirt. The sound had already been adjusted, yet she would wait long enough to make certain it wasn't something that would awaken him. The tape was, after all, designed to appeal to the subliminal mind.

She stood then, looking down at her boy and wondering if he would ever become a man. She yearned for a daughter-in-law, someone she could confide in, another woman who would share her love of homemaking, someone who would give her the grandchildren she so desperately craved. But Phillip would have to be more than he was at this moment before that could ever happen. He had yet to hold a permanent job. Supporting a family at this point was out of the question. The fact that he made no attempts to pursue the opposite sex was lost upon her. Still, when the right woman came along, she was certain everything would work out.

Shaking off her worries, she pressed Play and then stood.

You will listen to the sound of my voice and my voice only. You will free your mind of everything. All thoughts are wiped clean, like chalk from a blackboard. You are standing at the foot of a long, ascending staircase, and at the top, there is a beautiful light. You will follow my voice up the stairs, and we will go together into the light. You with me. Me with you.

Lucy shivered. After all these years, the one thing about Emile that had not changed with age was his voice. That beautiful, compelling, magnificent voice. Giving Phillip one last look to make sure he was still asleep, she tiptoed from the room and then picked up her shoes. Just before she closed the door, she turned and blew him a kiss.

"Sleep well, my love," she said softly. "Mother is taking care of everything."

Dan Howard tossed aside the file he'd been handed moments earlier and stifled a curse as he strode to the window.

"I can't believe there's nothing on there we can use."

The lab tech shrugged. "Sorry, sir, but we did our best. There are no hidden messages, no whispered words, nothing except what you hear."

"A goddamned doorbell that someone is laying on and the distant sound of thunder. I might as well have added a little whistling to the tape. At least we'd have something entertaining to hear."

"Sorry, sir. If there's nothing else...?"

He left the sentence dangling, waiting to be dismissed, which Howard promptly did.

Once Dan was alone in the room, he thought about where they were on the case. Basically back to square one. They had no new leads and six dead women. He needed to call Sully. Maybe the world had opened up while he was sleeping and dropped the answer to this mess in their laps.

He strode back to his desk, rifling through his Rolodex until he found the right number, then made the call. It wasn't until he looked at his watch that he realized he might be calling too early. But what the hell. Time and crime waited for no one.

When the phone began to ring, Ginny came awake with a jerk, her heart pounding, her mind fumbling to orient herself to where she was. Expecting Sully to answer it from somewhere else in the house, it took a moment for her to realize she could hear water running. She glanced toward the bathroom. He must be taking a shower.

"Sully!" she yelled, but got no reply.

The phone rang again, and then again. She jumped out of bed and ran to the bathroom door.

"Sully! Telephone!"

The water stopped. Seconds later he came out on the run, leaving a water trail behind him as he went.

"Hello?"

"Sully, it's me, Dan."

Sully mouthed an okay to Ginny and then motioned for her to hand him a towel. She disappeared into the bathroom with a smile on her face.

"What's up?" Sully asked.

"The tape was a bust."

"Are you sure?"

"The lab couldn't identify one single thing that would give us a lead."

"Damn it."

"Look, at the risk of totally pissing you off and

putting Ginny at risk, I'd like for her to listen to the tape.''

''I don't know,'' Sully said, glancing toward Ginny, who was coming out of the bathroom with a couple of towels.

''What's wrong?'' Ginny asked.

''Just a minute,'' Sully told Dan, and then covered the mouthpiece with his hand. ''Dan says the tape was a bust. The lab couldn't find anything on there that would help us.''

The smile on Ginny's face went south. So much had been riding on that lead, including her life.

''Are they sure?'' she asked.

Sully shrugged. ''They don't think it's anything, but he wants you to hear it anyway.''

Ginny stood with her head down, absently studying the trail of wet footprints Sully had left behind.

''Look, honey, you don't have to. In fact, I'd much rather you—''

''Tell him to bring it.''

Now that she'd taken the decision out of his hands, Sully was the one who felt panic. It had been much easier when he'd just said no. But it was her life that was on hold, and Dan had said there wasn't really anything to hear. He didn't have it in him to say no.

''You sure?''

She nodded.

Sully sighed and turned back to the phone. ''Dan,

she says bring it. She'll listen. But I'm warning you now, if this goes bad..."

"I've got it handled," Dan said. "I'll be there this afternoon."

"Yeah, all right. Oh...hey, Dan?"

"Yes?"

"Since you're coming, how about packing a couple bottles of champagne and some Godiva chocolates."

Ginny's eyes lit in appreciation.

"What the hell do we have to warrant that kind of celebration?"

"I didn't say it had anything to do with you," Sully said. "Just do it, okay?"

Dan chuckled. "Oh. Her. Don't tell me the mighty Sullivan has fallen?"

"None of your business," Sully snapped. "Just do as I asked."

"Okay, okay, keep your shorts on. Or...maybe not," he added, breaking into a chuckle.

Sully hung up the phone and was about to turn around when something warm and soft brushed the backside of his leg. God almighty, Ginny was drying him off. He stood in total silence, reveling in the feel of her hands on his body until she put the towel between his legs. He turned, a growl of anticipation purring deep in his throat, and took the towel out of her hands and tossed it on the floor.

"You want to be on top or on the bottom?"

"Both," she said, and surprised him with a laugh.

He pushed her backward onto the mattress and without so much as a kiss to pass for foreplay, slid between her legs and thrust himself inside. The water on his body was all the lubricant they needed, and after they began the dance, he would have sworn it turned to steam.

13

Two hours had passed since Dan Howard's call, and Sully knew he was going to have to get out of bed and get dressed. The last thing he wanted was to field the taunts about falling for the woman he was supposed to be guarding. It was as old a joke within the Bureau as the corny ones about the traveling salesman and the farmer's daughter. Besides that, what he felt for Ginny didn't belong within the atmosphere of locker room talk. He was in love and teetering between obsessed and just plain possessive.

Ginny was in the bathroom now. He could hear the water running in the shower, and the thought of joining her was almost too tempting to ignore. But he bypassed the urge by getting out of the bed and going across the hall to his room, then digging through his limited supply of clothing for something clean to wear.

As he reached in the drawer where his clean shirts were kept, he felt something hard beneath the stack. Shifting the shirts aside, he saw the back of a book, and it wasn't until he picked it up and turned it over that he realized what it was. Dan Howard's men must have slipped it between the shirts when they'd packed up all their gear, and when he'd unpacked in a hurry the other night, he hadn't seen it. He couldn't believe that he'd forgotten about it again.

"Well, hell," he muttered. "Blame it on the hole Auger tried to put in my head."

Ginny had yet to see it, and there was always the chance that it would trigger a memory they could use. Dressing quickly, he hurried across the hall into her room with the book in hand.

Ginny's hair was wet and clinging to the back of her neck as she pulled a clean T-shirt over her head.

"My hair dryer doesn't work anymore. Do you have one?"

He noticed a tremble in her lips but thought little of it as he answered.

"Yeah, hang on a minute, honey. I'll be right back."

He was halfway across the hall when it hit him. Auger had tried to tie her up with the cord from her dryer. God only knows what had gone through her mind when she'd picked the damned thing up.

He came back with his, ready to take that look off her face.

"Sit down here near this outlet and I'll dry your hair for you while you look through Georgia's yearbook."

"Oh my gosh," Ginny said. "I'd forgotten all about it."

"Yeah, so had I," he said, and rubbed the scar on his head. "It's no wonder, right?"

She nodded, trying not to think about the blood on Sully's face and the weight of Auger's body as he pinned her to the floor.

"Is this too hot?" Sully asked, as he turned the dryer toward her head.

"A little. Try the medium setting, okay?"

"You got it, babe. Now put your feet up and take yourself a stroll down memory lane. And if you see something that might help on the case, give a holler. We need a break in the very worst way. I marked the pages with your class picture and then the gifted class down below."

"Okay."

As she allowed herself the pleasure of concentrating on Sully's hands combing through her hair and separating the strands so the warm air could circulate better, the bad thoughts began to dissipate.

"If you ever decide to give up your day job, you'd make a good stylist," she said.

"I wouldn't do this for anyone but you."

"Too macho?" she taunted.

"Yes."

"At least you're honest," she said, then grinned to herself as she turned to the pages he'd marked.

As she did, her mind slid back to that first day of

school and how afraid she had been—until Georgia. Georgia, with pigtails and freckles, was all giggles and light, bouncing from the swings to the slide like a butterfly too flighty to linger. Oh, the times they'd had. It didn't seem possible that she was gone, that all of them were gone—except herself. She sighed. Looking at those little smiling faces, so unaware of what lay in store, seemed obscene. It was like looking at ghosts.

Sully turned off the dryer and leaned down beside her. "You okay?"

She nodded.

He knew this was difficult for her, but it had to be done.

"Anything ring a bell?"

"Not really. I never did see Frances after the school burned down. The others, I saw off and on. Some of their parents stayed in the same area where we grew up." Ginny traced the faces in the photograph with the tip of her finger. "We were so young."

Sully squatted down beside her. "I remember noticing something different about this picture when I first saw it in Georgia's things."

"Like what?"

"Well...see these other group shots? There's a teacher or a sponsor in every one. But not in yours. Why is that?"

Ginny frowned. "I don't know."

"It probably doesn't mean anything. Maybe he or

she was sick that day and they just didn't want to photograph the sub. But you'd think the name would have been listed, anyway, wouldn't you?''

Ginny's frown deepened as she sifted through the pages. ''I wonder why there's no mention of his name?''

''His?''

Ginny blinked and then looked up. ''I don't know why I said that. It just came.''

''You said before that you didn't remember who the teacher was, but you'd recognize him, wouldn't you, if you saw him in here?''

''I don't know. It was my first year of school, re- member? And I was so timid. If it hadn't been for Georgia, I probably wouldn't have said a word all year.''

''You? Timid?''

She grinned. ''I grew out of it.''

''Look through it anyway, from top to bottom. If you see someone familiar, let me know. I'm going to put on a pot of coffee. Dan should be here any time now, and if I know him, it's the first thing he'll ask for when he hits the door.''

''Okay,'' Ginny said.

''Keep looking. I'll be right back.''

Ginny started at the front of the book and began to study the faces of every teacher. Some she remem- bered vividly, others were only names that she'd heard. Mrs. Milam had been her first-grade teacher, and she quickly picked her out of the lot. By the time she got to the end, she was convinced that whoever had taught that class was not in this book.

"What did you find?" Sully asked, as he came back into the room.

"Nothing. Whoever he was, he's not there."

"You keep saying he."

She hesitated and then nodded. "Yes, for some reason that seems right. But I don't get a face or a name, only a sense of an overpowering presence."

Sully frowned. That was an odd choice of words to associate with a teacher.

"What does Dan think?" Ginny asked.

Sully grinned. "He's going to have my head, for one thing. I haven't showed him the book."

"But why?"

"I didn't have it when everything first happened. My initial conversation was with the director and mainly about the other women. I gave them all the information I had at the time from Pagillia. Georgia was dead, and I was so stunned." He paced the floor, remembering. "Stunned doesn't even come close. I felt guilt for not being there when she needed me, and I was so damned mad that they believed she'd committed suicide. I know...knew...Georgia like a sister, and that's the last thing she ever would have done." He shoved his hands through his hair, spiking the short, straight ends even more. "Then it became a race with time, trying to find you before someone else did. After I got the yearbook from the convent, I tossed it into my luggage and forgot about it. By the time I found you, I had other things on my mind. After Carney Auger...well...I didn't have much on my mind at all, except you. Not very professional for a Fed, is it?''

She smiled. "I'm not complaining."

"No, but Dan will."

"But I've seen the book, and nothing I saw relates to the case. Other than the fact that there's no teacher for that class, of course."

"Yes, but if Dan can locate any of the teachers who were there, they might be able to tell us something that you can't."

"Oh. I hadn't thought of that." Then Ginny quickly leafed through the book, searching for a page she'd seen before. "Here," she said, pointing to a picture near the front. "That's Mr. Fontaine. He was the principal...actually, more like a headmaster. He was so nice. If anyone would remember the teacher, I'd think it would be him. He founded the school and did all the hiring and firing."

Sully looked at Ginny with new respect. "Good job, honey. You might just have bailed me out of hot water with Dan."

"My pleasure," Ginny said. "I'll take my pay later in kisses."

Sully growled beneath his breath and started to reach for her when someone knocked at the door.

"I'll get it," Sully said. "It's probably one of the guards." Sure enough, when he opened the door, Franklin Chee nodded, then stepped inside. Dressed in an oversize shirt that was hanging loose on the outside of his jeans, he could have passed for a young man on vacation.

"What's up?" Sully asked.

"Just got a call from the boss. Said he's going to be a little bit late. Something about forgetting the Godivas?"

Sully laughed. "Okay, thanks." Then he motioned for Ginny to come over. "Ginny, this is Franklin Chee. He and his brother, Webster, grew up in the area. The other agent is Kevin Holloway, who you saw yesterday while you were swimming."

Ginny smiled and held out her hand. The man's dark eyes flashed as he returned the gesture.

"Thank you so much for being here," Ginny said. "When this nightmare started, I thought I'd be dealing with it alone. You don't know how much your presence means to me."

Franklin Chee nodded, taking great care not to stare at the healing cuts and bruises still evident on her face.

"It is our job, but this time it is also our pleasure," he said quietly.

"Would you please pass my appreciation on to your brother and your friend?"

"Yes, miss." Then he turned to Sully. "Is there anything you need?"

"A miracle?"

This time Franklin grinned. "I'm good, Sullivan, but not that good. The Navajo are remarkable people, but we have yet to walk on water."

Ginny grinned as Sully laughed aloud. For the moment, she almost felt lighthearted. If she didn't focus too much on the problem at hand, she could pretend this was a friend who'd just come for a visit. But then he turned to leave, and as he did, she caught a glimpse of his gun beneath his shirt. Just as suddenly, the game was over.

Sully closed the door. When he turned around, Ginny was gone.

"Ginny?"

"In the kitchen."

He followed her there. "So, we've got a reprieve. Dan's on his way, but his arrival isn't as imminent as I'd imagined." He glanced at his watch. It was already after one. "Are you hungry, honey? If you are, say the word."

"These men put their lives on the line every day, don't they, Sully?"

He leaned against the cabinets and folded his arms across his chest, studying the seriousness on her face.

"Yes, but it was a choice we made when we entered the program. It's not a lot different from being a cop. We just patrol a larger area."

"I guess. But it doesn't stop me from feeling guilty that you're here because of me."

"No, that's where you're wrong. We're here because someone caused six women to die. We don't know how, but we still know it's true."

Her shoulders slumped. "I guess the most difficult part for me in all of this is that I can't be in the middle of the hunt. I'm a reporter. I'm used to digging for the facts, not hiding from them."

"Extraordinary situations call for extraordinary measures. You're a target, Ginny. If you want to live, you stay out of sight."

"I hate this."

"Yeah, so do I. But there's a part of me that recognizes a distasteful truth. If none of this had happened, I would never have known you, and I can't imagine not having you in my life. I've learned one thing about this job over the years, and that is if you want to survive, you have to stay objective. I can't be objective about you. I'm too close to the fire, so to speak." He smiled and then pulled her into his arms, soothing the tension in her body by rubbing her back. "We'll find out who's making the calls, and when we do, we'll have our man. Until then, you're here."

"Okay."

"Okay. Now, how about some lunch? Dan will probably show up about the time we're done. He can eat leftovers while we tell him about the yearbook. Maybe it'll put him in a good mood."

"Are you hungry, too?" Ginny asked.

"Yes, but not for food...for you." He bit the edge of her lower lip and then gently traced the bite with the tip of his tongue.

"Sully, I—"

He shook his head and then held her close to his heart, fighting a fear that he could not keep her safe.

"How about ham sandwiches?" he asked.

Ginny sighed.

"I'll put radishes in them, if you like."

She buried her nose against his chest.

"You're never going to let me hear the end of that, are you?"

Sully grinned. "Just because you're a woman, it doesn't automatically follow that you can cook. Now, do you want that sandwich or not?"

"Yes, but I can make them for us."

Sully hesitated and then shrugged. She couldn't ruin a ham sandwich. "Sure, why not? I'll take mustard on mine, okay?"

"Want some cheese?"

"Yeah, sure. Add some cheese. Bread, ham, mustard, cheese."

"Calm down," Ginny muttered. "I will not sabotage your sandwich."

"Thank you," Sully said.

He was being silly on purpose, and she knew it. "You're welcome," she said and then grinned. "Now go away and let me do something domestic."

"I'll just be in the living room, watching TV."

"Whatever," Ginny said, as she began pulling the makings of their lunch from the fridge.

Sully eyed her nervously one last time and then left, reminding himself that he loved her, therefore he would eat anything her two little hands made. Even if it killed him.

It wasn't until Ginny had all the makings laid out on the table and was ready to assemble the sandwiches that she realized they were going to appear quite ordinary. And if so, how could she impress Sully with her kitchen expertise?

Totally ignoring the fact that she had no expertise to display, she began rummaging through the drawers and shelves, looking for something to give the meal a flair. She reminded herself that Sully had asked for a specific combination, therefore he should have it. However, nothing was said about the way in which it should be presented, and when she stumbled onto the box of cookie cutters, her creative genius began to tick.

Sully was absently flipping channels while listening for Dan Howard's arrival when Ginny called to him from the kitchen.

"Sully?"

"Yeah?"

"Lunch is ready."

Tossing the remote aside, he strolled into the kitchen.

"I'm starved," he said. "Hope you made a—" His gaze fell on the plate of sandwiches, and although he tried to hide his shock, he could tell by the look on her face that he hadn't done a very good job. "They're rabbits."

Ginny struggled with the urge to hit him as she poured iced tea into their glasses.

"No. They're ham and cheese sandwiches in the *shape* of rabbits."

"Yeah, right. That's what I meant."

"So, aren't you going to sit down?" Ginny asked.

"After you," he said, and seated her first, which earned him one small point in his favor. But when he dropped into his chair and then picked up his fork to poke at the rabbit on top of the pile, Ginny stifled a snort.

"They're dead. Trust me."

Sully glared. "Don't get all defensive with me, Virginia. I haven't said a damned word against your food."

"You are so conventional," she muttered, and put two rabbits on her plate, then added a handful of carrot sticks and a couple of stuffed green olives for garnish.

Sully felt safe in going for the vegetables. At least they were in recognizable form.

"I didn't know you liked olives," he said, as he popped a couple into his mouth.

"I don't," Ginny said, and then bit off one of the rabbit's ears.

Sully stared at the food on her plate, knowing when he asked that it was going to be the wrong thing to do, but the man in him needed to know anyway, if for no other reason than future reference.

"So, if you don't like the olives, why did you put some on your plate?"

Ginny rolled her eyes, as if it was the stupidest question she'd ever heard.

"Because they look pretty, that's why. Garnishes are an important part of food presentation."

"Oh. Yeah. Right."

"Good grief," Ginny mumbled and bit off another ear. "What a dumb question."

Sully stuffed a whole carrot stick in his mouth so he wouldn't be expected to do anything but chew. But his stomach was growling, and the smell of deli ham and cheese was too enticing to ignore. He glanced toward the window, making sure that no one saw what he was about to do, and then scooted three of the rabbits onto his plate. He demolished the first in two bites, and to his surprise, it was good.

"Really good, Ginny."

Resisting the urge to smirk, she nodded. "Thank you."

"I think I saw some dip on the top shelf of the fridge. Want some to go with the carrot sticks?"

"Sure. That would be good."

Now that he was moving onto firmer ground again, Sully bounded up from his chair and almost swaggered to the fridge. He was getting this woman stuff down pretty good. Whatever it was, praise it. Whatever she did weird, ignore it. Whenever she cried, hug her. And then the biggie. If she's mad, don't ask why, just apologize anyway. It'll save a lot of time later on.

He reached for the container of ranch dip and started back to the table, admiring the tender curve at the nape of her neck when he heard the familiar sound of an approaching chopper.

"That must be Dan," Ginny said, and jumped up from the table. "I'll get another plate."

He glanced nervously at the table. *Oh hell. I'll never hear the end of this.* "He's probably not hungry," Sully said. "Are you finished? I'll help you clean up."

Ginny took the dip and pushed him out of the kitchen.

"No, I'm not finished. We've just begun. Now go get your friend and tell him to hurry. The bread's drying out."

"Can't have that," Sully muttered, as he stomped toward the door. "Damn it all, how did I let this happen?"

Dan came in the door without knocking.

"I come bearing gifts," he said, handing over the champagne and a large gold-foiled box of the best

Godiva chocolates, and he'd added a flourish of his own, a dozen red, long-stemmed roses. "Thought she deserved a little petting, right, buddy?"

"Thanks," Sully said. "I owe you."

"Actually, you do. A couple of hundred bucks should cover most of it."

"You'll get your money," Sully said, and then hesitated.

The last thing he wanted was for Ginny's feelings to get hurt. He needed to warn Dan what he was about to eat so he wouldn't say the wrong thing. But he waited too long. Ginny was already here.

"Hey, beautiful!" Dan said. "Did you miss me?"

Ginny grinned. "You liked this place so much you just couldn't stay away, right?"

"For you," Sully said quickly and thrust the flowers at her, hoping it would delay the inevitable. To his delight, Ginny's smile lit up the room.

"Oh, Sully... I can't remember the last time anyone gave me flowers."

Since he was doing so well, he thought he'd go for the gold and handed her the chocolates, too.

"Oh my gosh," Ginny groaned. "Godiva! I am in heaven."

"I'll hang on to the champagne, since your hands are full." Then he gave Dan a cool look. "Besides, I'm not sharing this with him."

Ginny hesitated, then followed her instincts and quickly kissed Sully on the cheek.

"Thank you so much," she said softly. "I'd better put these in water." Her smile was particularly vivid as she turned to Dan. "We just started lunch. Come join us."

"Great!" Dan said. "I'm starved." He took her by the arm as they left the room.

Defeated, Sully followed them. "What the hell. They're only rabbits."

"I need to wash up before I eat," Dan said.

"Bathroom is down the hall," Ginny offered.

"No need. I'll just wash right here at the sink."

He quickly soaped and rinsed and reached for the hand towel as he turned around.

"What's for lunch?" he asked, as he moved toward the table.

"Just ham and cheese sandwiches," Ginny said. "Have a seat."

Dan scooted a chair up to his place and then cast a curious eye around the table.

"Where are the—"

The sharp blow to his shin was not only startling, it came damn near to bringing tears to his eyes.

"What in hell did—"

Sully handed him the platter. "Take a couple," he said, slowly enunciating every word.

The look that passed between them was brief, but once Dan saw the sandwiches, it didn't take him long to get the hint. Straightfaced, he unloaded three of the hammy hares onto his plate and then dutifully piled on a handful of carrot sticks and a half-dozen olives, although he would have preferred plain old chips. With a wink at Ginny, he took a big bite and then rolled his eyes in exaggerated ecstasy.

"Ummmnnn. I don't know when I last had rabbit."

Ginny threw an olive at his head and rolled her eyes in disgust.

He grinned around a mouthful and then started to chew. A few moments later, he looked up.

"These are actually really good."

"I know," Ginny said.

"Then can I ask you a question. And I'm not being facetious, okay? I really want to know."

Ginny sighed. "Ask away."

"Why rabbits?"

Sully leaned forward, too, glad that Dan had asked what he'd been dying to know himself.

"Because they're cute," she said.

Both men looked at Ginny, then at each other. To their credit, neither one cracked a smile.

"Well, sure," Dan said. "That they are." And to prove he was serious, he danced one through the air all the way to his mouth.

14

Lunch was long since over, and Sully had confessed about the yearbook. To his relief, Dan seemed to take it in stride and was now going through it, rapidly taking down names and making notes beside each one while Ginny answered the occasional question.

"This is good. Really good," Dan said, and then gave Sully a casual glance. "Glad you decided to share."

Sully sighed. He'd expected that and more.

Ginny frowned at Dan and decided to change the subject.

"Will it be difficult to find these teachers? I know Mr. Fontaine retired after the fire. I've heard Mother tell the story many times."

"They can be found," Sully said. "It's hard to hide from Uncle Sam."

"But what if you find him and he doesn't remember? By now he should be in his eighties, maybe older. That was more than twenty years ago, and he seemed really old to me then."

"I don't know," Dan said. "We'll just have to take

it one step at a time.'' Then he added, ''But you've helped a lot. This gives us a new angle at which to proceed. We'd tried earlier to find a listing of the teachers, but everything was destroyed in that fire.''

''You can thank Georgia for this, not us,'' Sully said. ''She's the one who put all this together.'' He looked away suddenly, his voice softening. ''It's just a damned shame it didn't help save her life.''

Ginny laid her head on Sully's shoulder and slipped her hand in his.

''If you'd asked her, Sully, she would have said her life was already saved.''

The simple truth of Ginny's words was a balm to his soul. He slipped his arm around Ginny and gave her a quick hug.

Dan stood abruptly.

''I need to check in. Be back in a few.''

He strode out of the room, leaving Sullivan and Ginny alone.

''He's going to spend the night,'' Sully said.

Ginny shrugged. ''There are two spare bedrooms.''

Sully brushed his mouth across her lips. ''You don't care if he knows that we're together?''

''No.'' Then her eyes narrowed thoughtfully. ''Is fraternization between agent and witness frowned upon? You won't get in trouble or anything like that, will you?''

Sully shrugged. ''No, and besides that, it's not my case, it's Dan's. I'm here because I asked to be, not because I was assigned. Therefore, my business is my business. I was mostly thinking of you.''

"I'm twenty-eight, almost twenty-nine. I am a thoroughly modern woman in every sense of the word. I do not need or want anybody's permission to have sex, or for that matter...to fall in love.''

Sully was speechless. It was the first time she'd said the *L* word, and he didn't have time to respond. Dan was already back.

"I almost forgot this,'' Dan said, and tossed it in Sully's lap.

"Is this the tape?''

Dan nodded.

Ginny grabbed Sully's arm. "I want to hear it.'' When he hesitated, she added, "Please. You're both here. I can't possibly do anything to myself. Besides, Dan says the lab got absolutely nothing useful from it, remember?''

"Yes, I remember,'' Sully muttered, fingering the small plastic case. "But for the record, I'm not happy about this.''

"Unhappiness noted,'' Ginny said. "Did you bring the player?''

Dan handed it to Sully, as well. Sully loaded the cassette, then hesitated, his finger above Play.

"I want to hear this first,'' he said.

"Fine with me,'' Ginny said. "I'll just be sitting here, waiting for you two to finish running my life.''

Ignoring her sarcasm, Sully moved into the hallway, unaware that the domed ceiling was a natural conductor of sound. He glanced at Ginny again, decided she was a safe enough distance away, and then pressed the button.

The first thing he heard was the thunder, distant, but distinct. Then the chimes began, deep tone upon deep tone, then clearer and higher, as if moving up a scale. The series repeated itself three times before the tape went blank.

"Doesn't make much sense, does it?" Sully said. "Just some thunder and a funky doorbell that nobody answers."

"I know, that's what's so damned frustrating," Dan said. "So let her hear it, okay? Maybe it'll mean something. Maybe it won't. I don't see how it could hurt."

"Yes, all right, but I—" Sully glanced across the room and forgot when he'd been saying. There was something about the way Ginny was sitting that didn't seem right.

"Ginny?"

Her eyes were closed, her chin was resting on her chest, and there was a kind of tension in her posture, as if she was waiting.

"Oh hell," Sully muttered, thrusting the tape recorder at Dan and bolting across the room. He went down on his knees and looked into Ginny's face. "Dan! Get over here. *Now!*"

Sully grabbed her by both arms. When had this

happened? Even more—what in hell had they just done?

"Ginny!" He shook her just a little, and she slumped forward on his chest.

Dan grabbed his shoulder. "What's wrong?"

"You tell me!" Sully shouted, and yanked her to her feet. "Ginny! Ginny! Wake up! For the love of God, wake up!"

Ginny's head rolled on her neck like a limp rag doll. Sully shook her again, then put a hand on either side of her face and began to yell.

"Ginny! Ginny! Wake up!"

To his everlasting relief, her eyelids fluttered, but when they finally opened, his relief was short-lived. Her expression was empty.

"Sweet Jesus," he whispered. He'd never been so scared in his life. And then his survival instincts took over, and his fear slid into second gear. "Virginia! Look at me, damn it! Open your eyes! It's over. Whatever happened to you is over! Do you hear me?"

She blinked once, then twice, and Sully knew the moment reality surfaced because he saw it in her eyes.

"Sully?"

"Ah, God," he muttered, and wrapped her tight within his arms. His hands were shaking, his heart was thundering in his chest. They'd fooled around with something they didn't understand and almost lost her without knowing why. "I'm sorry, I'm sorry. I swear to God, honey, we didn't know."

"Know what?" Ginny asked. "When are you going to let me hear the tape?"

Dan whistled between his teeth and then slowly shook his head.

"I think you just did."

Ginny was starting to get scared. "What happened? What did I do?"

"The acoustics," Sully said, suddenly eyeing the high domed ceiling. "Son of a bitch, I didn't think about the acoustics. She must have heard everything we did."

"Yeah, but what did we hear?" Dan asked.

"What did I do?" Ginny asked, her voice rising higher with every word. "Will somebody just answer me that one question before I scream?"

"You went out like a light," Sully said. "It meant nothing to us. Just a recording of some distant thunder and then someone ringing a doorbell over and over."

Something hovered at the back of Ginny's mind, but it was too indistinct to identify.

"Thunder always makes me—"

"Sleepy," Sully finished. "That's right. You've said that before." He looked at Dan. "Thunderstorms almost put her in a—"

"Trance," Ginny said, for the first time wondering if that lifelong trait of lethargy might not be natural after all.

"Do it again," Ginny said.

"Hell no," Sully said.

"You brought me out of it before. You can do it again. Besides, what if that was a fluke? Did you see what happened? Were you watching me?"

Neither man could answer.

"That's what I thought. Neither one of you can be sure that it was the tape. Play it again. Right now. Right here in front of me so there's no mistake."

"Then get the others in here, too," Sully said. "I want all the witnesses we can get. Someone might notice something that we don't."

"Good idea," Dan said, and headed for the door.

Sully wanted to argue, but this was a side of Ginny he hadn't seen before. She was in charge, and she was focused on doing this her way.

He frowned and then smoothed a wayward hair off her face.

"Just so you know..."

"I know. Opposition duly noted."

He frowned, but before he could comment further, Dan was back with the men. Obviously he had explained the situation to them before they'd come in, because none of the trio seemed surprised by the request.

"All right," Sully said. "I want you to pay close attention to Ginny's behavior. Something in this tape put her out like a light. When this is over, I want some opinions. Short of flying her to one of our specialists, which I have yet to rule out—"

Ginny put her hand on his arm. "Sully...play the tape."

He wanted to yank it out of the recorder and set the thing on fire, but that wouldn't solve a thing. Somewhere the perpetrator was waiting for them to lower their guard, and when they did, Ginny would become another of his victims.

He looked at her once—at the determination in her eyes—and then nodded. When she sat back in the chair, he pressed the play button and then turned up the volume.

Thunder sounded, then rippled through her skin, like echoes off distant mountains. Her eyes widened; her mouth went slack.

Sully held his breath as on the tape the sound of chimes superimposed itself above the storm—resonating deeply and then moving up the scale in clear and precise tones.

Her eyes went flat. Her head rolled on her neck, and then her chin dropped toward her chest.

Sully grunted as if he'd just been punched in the gut.

Even though the chimes repeated twice more, Ginny had no other reaction. It was as if she was waiting. But for what?

Sully turned off the tape and then looked at the men. They were as stunned as he. He laid the recorder aside and had started to reach for Ginny when Franklin Chee suddenly grabbed his arm, holding him back.

Let me, he mouthed silently, and then squatted down in front of her, studying her face without touching her.

"Ginny...can you hear me?"

When she nodded, Sully felt as if he'd been sucker-punched.

"It's time for you to wake up now. I'm going to count backward from ten, and when I say *'Now'* you're going to open your eyes and you will feel fine. Are you ready?"

She sighed, then nodded again.

"Ten. Nine. Eight. Seven. You're feeling lighter, more alert. You can hear the sound of my voice even better than before. Six. Five. Four. It's almost morning, and you're ready to get up. You will be happy and refreshed when you open your eyes, and you will not be afraid. Three. Two. One. Now!"

Ginny looked up, saw the Navajo agent on his knees and grinned.

"Is this a proposal?"

Franklin Chee smiled as he stood.

"I think Agent Dean would have my head for even thinking it," he said, and then turned and faced the other men.

"How did you do that?" Sully asked.

"Sometime during her life she has been given a post-hypnotic suggestion that was never removed."

"But I didn't hear any words on the tape," Dan said.

"It doesn't have to be words. It can be anything, even a series of sounds. Whatever she's been conditioned to respond to is the thing that will put her quickly under. After that, it's simply a matter of waiting for instructions. It's a fairly common method, like a parlor trick professional hypnotists might use at a party."

"How did you know to do that?" Sully asked.

Franklin shrugged. "I read a book."

"I'm thinking there's more to you than meets the eye," Dan said. "Maybe I need to read your file a little closer."

"Guys..."

They stopped talking among themselves and looked at Ginny.

"Forgive me if I'm interrupting this discussion, but did I do it again?"

"Oh yeah," Sully said.

"What did I do...exactly?" she asked.

Franklin answered in a way she would understand.

"You just closed your eyes as you'd been taught and waited for the voice."

"What voice?"

"The voice of the man who did this to you."

Ginny suddenly felt sick, wondering what else he might have done to seven little girls in a state of unconsciousness.

"Okay," Dan said. "Thanks for your help, men." He clapped Chee on the shoulder as he walked them to the door. "Especially you, Franklin. You're a man of many talents."

Franklin nodded, then cast a teasing eye at his brother and grinned.

"Webster does a pretty good imitation of John Wayne, if anybody's interested."

The solemn comment made everyone laugh, which was what Franklin Chee had intended. He looked back once at Ginny and then walked out the door with the others behind him.

Dan shoved his hands through his hair in quick frustration and then reached in his pocket for his phone.

"What are you going to do next?" Sully asked.

"Find Edward Fontaine and hope to hell he can remember who taught that gifted class."

Orlando, Florida

Edward Fontaine picked his way down the steps of his little cottage, pausing long enough to scoot a beetle out of his path with his cane before continuing on. A young boy on a tricycle came wheeling around the corner with his mother not far behind, moving at a jog.

"Hello, Martin, how are you this fine morning?" Edward called.

The little boy beamed and yelled back, "I can ride this really fast. Watch me go."

Edward watched, trying to remember if he'd ever been that young or that mobile.

"Good morning, Mr. Fontaine," the young mother said, giving him a brief wave as she continued her daily run.

"Good morning to you, too, Patricia. Martin seems in fine form this morning."

She nodded and disappeared beyond the clump of palm trees on the corner.

Edward lifted his head and exhaled deeply. Yes, it was a fine morning indeed. And for a man of his years, he was blessed to be here at all.

The smile was still on his face as he crossed the street, continuing on his daily walk to the beach. He loved the ocean and the solace of the warm, daily sun. The sun was good for his arthritis, as were these walks.

The pier that he favored was almost empty this morning. Just the way he liked it. He would walk all the way to the end, just as he did every day when it wasn't raining, and then on his way back he would stop at the little coffee shop on the corner and have a coffee and a doughnut. His doctor told him not to indulge in too many sweets, but he chose not to listen. He was already eighty-three. He would rather have a doughnut for breakfast and be happy than live to be a miserable one hundred with all his teeth.

A seagull swooped across the pier a few feet in

front of him, and he frowned and waved his cane in the air.

"Get back, you winged beggar. I'm coming through." Then he laughed aloud at his own foolishness.

He gave only the most casual of glances to a couple having their breakfast while tossing bits and pieces of it on the pier to watch the gulls come swooping in.

Tourists, he thought to himself. The rest of us know better.

The ocean breeze lifted the tufts of white hair still clinging to his scalp, ruffling the ends until they stood up from behind his ears like sheer, snowy feathers. Only a few more steps and he would be at the end of the pier. He could taste that doughnut now. Maybe he would have a plain cake one today. He always chose a raspberry filled, but maybe today he would be different.

He reached the end of the pier and punctuated the goal with a thump of his cane, then stood for a moment, staring out into the blue of the Atlantic. There was a sail on the horizon, and a clutch of seabirds overhead shrieked their disapproval of his presence.

"Excuse me. Are you Edward Fontaine?"

He turned. "Yes. I'm sorry… I don't think I've had the pleasure."

"Actually, you have. I'm sorry, but it's all for the best."

"Sorry? What have you to be—"

It didn't take much more than a push. He went backward easily, so surprised he forgot to yell. And when the water closed over his face, his last thought was that after all his years on this earth, he should have learned how to swim.

Emile Karnoff paid the cabdriver and had picked up his suitcase and started toward the front door when it suddenly opened.

"Emile! You're home! What a wonderful surprise!"

Emile put down his suitcase and enfolded his little wife in a warm embrace.

"It's good to be back," he said, and closed his eyes as he kissed the top of her head. Her dress was the color of lilacs, his favorite flower, and she smelled like lemon and thyme. He smiled. She'd been in her garden. It was times like this that made him wonder why he ever left home.

"Come inside," Lucy said. "Have you eaten? Phillip will be so excited. Only last night we were lamenting how long you'd been gone."

She chose to omit the fact that Phillip had been in one of his moods and angry about his father's absence, rather than sad. But she wasn't as worried as she might once have been. She'd been playing the tapes for him every night and was convinced that she had the situation well under control.

Emile opted not to comment on the fact that Phillip

was here, rather than at a job. It wasn't the time to confront Lucy, or his son. This was a time for home-coming, not retribution.

"I had some peanuts and a soft drink on the plane," Emile said. "But I would love nothing better than a cup of your tea and some of your homemade nut bread. Please tell me you have some."

The breeze ruffled Lucy's silvery curls as she clapped her hands in delight.

"Of course I do," she said. "And it's your favorite. Cranberry nut."

Emile picked up his suitcase and then slipped his other arm over her shoulder.

"You are my Wonder Woman. You know that, don't you?"

Lucy beamed. She knew. And the fact that he acknowledged it was *her* special prize.

Phillip stood at the head of the staircase, listening to his parents chatter as they came inside the door. It was always the same with him, somewhere on the periphery of their universe, waiting to be noticed.

Hey, wimpy boy...aren't you going to go down and hug your daddy's neck?

"Shut up," Phillip whispered.

His expression darkened as laughter echoed in his head. As his parents moved from the hallway into the den, he doubled up his fists and spun away. Nothing ever changed. Why had he thought this time would be different?

If you want things different, you know what you can do.

"I don't hear you," Phillip said in a whiney, sing-song voice, just like a little child would do.

Yes, you do, Baby boy. You hear, and one of these days you're going to obey.

He slammed the door shut behind him as he strode over to his dresser. Leaning forward, he braced both hands on the dresser top and stared at himself in the large square mirror.

"Obey? Where the hell do you get obey?" Phillip sneered. "You think I don't have enough people telling me what to do already? You think I'm so stupid that I'd give myself over to even one more will? If you do, then you've got another think coming. I'm getting tired of this. Do you hear me? I won't put up with this crap anymore. You leave me the hell alone or I'll end it all, right now."

Shaking with anger, he stood before the mirror, waiting for another taunt—for that one more dig that would make the rest of the day another hell. Strangely, the voice was silent.

A slow smile split the scowl he was wearing. His eyes began to glitter, and a muscle in his jaw began to jerk. He straightened, his shoulders thrust back in a gesture of defiance, and for the first time in more years than he could remember, he felt like he was the one in charge.

As he went to greet his father, there was so much

going on inside his brain, it never occurred to him that he'd stopped the voice by threatening to end his own existence.

Downstairs, Emile basked in the glory of Lucy's love and care. Except for small, unimportant details that would certainly work themselves out, his life was just about perfect.

"Darling," Emile said. "Sit with me. Tell me what you've been doing while I was away."

Lucy slipped gracefully into a chair, crossing her legs at the ankles and folding her hands in her lap as she'd been taught as a child.

"My days are so unimportant compared to yours. Please, tell me about your trip. Was the consultation a success?"

Emile beamed. Another chance to speak of his work with the person who loved him most.

"Yes, that it was," he said. "The woman was improving daily as I left. I gave one of the young doctors training in my techniques so that her healing would continue." Then he changed the subject, but only a bit. "Oh, Lucy, sweetheart, you should see Ireland! It is the most wonderful place. Quaint villages, the green, rolling hills with hidden valleys down below. Sheep dotting the pastures in the distance like tiny white balls of fluff. And the air! Ah...it's as the world must have been a hundred...no, two hundred years ago. Clean...pure. Oh! I must not forget the people. They are amazing—so kind—so friendly. Quite a lot of people walk about the countryside, many bicycle, not bothered by the danger of being mugged. You would absolutely love it there.''

Lucy nodded dutifully, although privately she would have disagreed. She didn't want to walk or ride a bicycle anywhere. As for country living, she'd had her fill of that growing up on her father's Kansas dairy farm. She'd dreamed of a more genteel life for so many years, and now that she had it, she wasn't going to give it up for anyone or anything—not even Emile, bless his heart.

She sighed, then smiled and nodded as he continued to wax eloquent regarding Dublin itself. She wasn't stupid, although she suspected from time to time that he wasn't so sure. He was laying groundwork, dropping hints. But she wasn't living in a foreign country, not even a charming one, and that was that. And when she saw Phillip coming into the room, she was glad that he'd come. A change of subject was certainly in order.

"Father! Welcome home!"

A momentary frown furrowed across Emile's forehead. He did not like to be interrupted. Surely Phillip could see that he'd been talking.

"Phillip. You're looking well.''

"That's because I haven't been sick,'' he snapped, and gave his father a dutiful peck on the cheek.

The snappish tone in his son's voice surprised him. The boy was usually quite meek.

Lucy twisted the fabric of her skirt and started to giggle nervously. *Lord, please don't let this be one of Phillip's bad days.*

"Phillip has a few surprises of his own to share," she said, then lifted her face to the other man in her life, blessing him with a smile. "Tell him, dear. Tell your father what you've been doing."

Phillip frowned. He would rather have kept this part of his life to himself...at least for a while. But, as always, Mother had interfered. He almost wished he hadn't confided in her, but then dismissed the thought. If he didn't have her as backup, he would have no one.

"Yes, Phillip. Do tell me what you're doing with yourself now."

It was the condescension in his father's voice that tipped the scales.

"I decided to put my English degree to use. I'm writing a book."

To say Emile was surprised would have been putting it mildly. But it was a pleasant surprise. And as he looked at his son, it occurred to him that that was a job for which Phillip might actually be suited.

"Why...that's wonderful," he said, and actually stood and shook his son's hand. "And since I think I understand the creative genius enough to empathize, I won't intrude upon your work by asking you what it's about. I'm sure you'll tell us in your own time."

Phillip wanted to cry. All these years he'd struggled

to please his father—to do something that would earn just this type of response—to see approval light his father's eyes.

"Yes. You're right. I'm in the very first stages of a rough draft, but it's coming along."

Emile smiled and then did something he hadn't done in more than twenty-five years. He put his arms around his son and patted him on the back.

You've done it now. Now you're going to have to actually write the book or you'll be right back in the crapper with the old man.

But the smile on Phillip's face had turned to laughter, and the sound was almost loud enough to smother the taunt inside his head.

15

Ginny moaned in her sleep, then rolled over. Sully was awake within seconds, his heart pounding as he watched her turn away from him. He lay without moving until he was certain she was all right, and then quietly slipped out of bed, pulling on a pair of gym shorts as he left the room.

The rust-colored tiles were cool beneath his feet as he moved into the hall. The faint but constant sound of Dan's snores drifted up the hallway as he headed toward the front of the house. Truth was, he was antsy. Sleep had been almost impossible to come by. Even after making love to Ginny until she'd brought him to a climax that rocked the teeth in the back of his head, he still hadn't been able to relax. He knew why.

He couldn't get rid of that image—how her eyes had lost focus and then her head had just dropped. He kept thinking of Georgia, and of those five other women. That had happened to them, too. Only they'd gotten some horrible message that had led them to their doom.

Sully wanted to weep. My God...the tragedy of it all. And for what? What the hell had that man done to them that he didn't want told? And why now? Why wait all these years to start pulling the plugs? Was he afraid of suppressed memories? Was that it? Had he put his hands on their tiny bodies and robbed them of their innocence?

He shuddered. There was something else that had occurred to Sully that he had yet to voice. What if the teacher of that class had been Fontaine himself? It stood to reason. Otherwise, it seemed that the teacher would have been given separate recognition in the school pictures.

He opened the refrigerator door and pulled out a Coke. He would have preferred a beer—a good, cold one right out of the bottle—but not now. Not when everything that mattered revolved around keeping Ginny alive.

After deactivating the security alarm, he opened the patio door and walked outside, thought about dropping his shorts and taking a dip in the pool and then discarded the idea. It had been years since he'd swum in the nude. It brought back memories of his childhood—of jumping off the creek bank into the Arkansas River near his home outside Little Rock. He and his brother had been like otters, swimming through the hot Arkansas days. The thought made him homesick. It had been months since he'd talked to Joe. That was stupid. If nothing else, this case had reminded him how very short life could be. He would call him when this was over, if for no other reason than just to say hi. And his mom. Still alive, but not in the ways that counted. She didn't know anyone anymore. Thank God Dad hadn't lived to see that happen.

He stared at the water and sat down in the lawn chair instead. As he sat, he heard the crunch of feet on gravel.

Franklin Chee was standing at the side of the house. It would seem it was his turn for night duty.

"Want a Coke?" Sully said. "There's plenty inside."

Franklin shook his head. "Caffeine."

Sully lifted the can in a toasting gesture. "Here's to quiet nights and solving cases."

"A good choice of words," Franklin said.

Sully took a second drink and then set the can down beside his chair and leaned forward, his elbows resting on his knees.

"Tell me about Ginny."

"What do you mean?"

"Tell me how that works...the hypnotic suggestion thing. Can it be fixed?"

"Certainly. I could try a variation of it myself, but this is a rather unique case. We have no way of knowing exactly what he did, or how involved the suggestion is. By that, I mean how deeply imbedded it is in her mind. I could wind up doing more harm than good."

"Then how do we fix her?"

Franklin shrugged, as if the answer was simple. "Find the man. Make him take it away."

"Jesus," Sully muttered. "You can't be serious. We're looking for a man who's turned off the faucet on six innocent women, and you expect him to make this thing right? There's got to be another way."

"Probably," Franklin said. "But I'm not qualified. You have to look for answers where you can find them."

Sully grinned. "Is that some mystic runaround to keep from saying you haven't got a clue?"

"Yes."

Sully laughed. The sound caught and carried, moving out past the pool into the desert beyond. In the distance, a coyote stopped in his pursuit of a rat and slunk off into the night, while inside the house, the sound penetrated Ginny's sleep. She rolled over in bed and realized she was alone.

Uneasy without Sully's presence, she was halfway out the door when she remembered that Dan was here. Quickly slipping on her nightgown and robe, she moved into the hallway, following the sound of his voice. When she saw he was not alone, she stopped inside the door and moved into the shadows, and as she did, unintentionally heard her name.

They were talking about the case and what had happened to her this afternoon. And why not? It was what they did for a living, but she couldn't stifle a small sense of betrayal. She tried to remind herself that it wasn't as if they were talking about her behind her back. She *was* the reason they were even here. They *had* to talk about her. Wondering if there was something they were keeping from her, she moved closer to the door to listen.

"Dan's leaving in the morning, right?" Franklin asked.

Sully nodded. "He faxed that teacher list in to the Bureau before he went to bed. Said the director would put some people on it...try to run down some leads."

Franklin was silent as Sully finished his Coke, but Sully could tell he had something on his mind.

"What are you thinking?" Sully finally asked.

"They say that you cannot coerce a person to do something under hypnosis that they would not do if they were awake."

Sully stiffened. "What are you saying? That those women wanted to die? That's bull, because Georgia Dudley wasn't like that."

"I'm just saying that's what I was taught. And I was also thinking that it would take something very powerful to override the human instinct for survival."

The word *powerful* echoed in Sully's head. Where had he heard that used before? Oh, hell. It was the word Ginny had used to describe the feeling she'd had about the man who'd been their teacher. Powerful. She said she'd had an impression of a large, powerful man.

"She's in a lot of danger, isn't she?" Sully said.

Franklin hesitated and then looked over Sully's shoulder into the house beyond.

"Yes."

"Got any suggestions?" Sully asked.

"Don't let her out of your sight."

The words were still ringing in Sully's ears as Franklin moved back into guard mode and disappeared around the side of the house.

Ginny was shaking. The words had been faint, but she'd heard them just the same. Danger. It wasn't as if the concept was new. She'd known it from the moment she'd learned that Georgia was dead. But hearing it said aloud seemed to give it new life. She looked out into the night to the man beside the pool. He had come to mean so much to her, and in such a short time. It wasn't just because he'd come to save her. She had learned to listen for his footsteps, to appreciate his wit. He made her furious, and he made her laugh, and he could make her come apart in his arms. She was so in love with him that she couldn't think straight. If she was still alive when this was all over, she was going to make him realize he couldn't live without her.

Then she sighed. One thing was for certain. If she didn't do as they said, the chances of that happening were very slim.

Defeated in every fiber of her being, she went back

to the bedroom, shed her clothes and crawled back into bed.

A short while later she heard the patio door open, then close. Heard the beep of the security system as it was reset. A few moments later Sully came into the room. The mattress gave as he slipped back in beside her, and when he snaked an arm around her waist and tugged her against his body, she started to cry.

Quietly.

Allowing nothing but tears to escape.

"Okay, guys, here's the drill," Dan said, as he readied to leave again. "I'm flying straight to D.C. and getting some clean clothes, and then I'm heading to Florida. The info I got from headquarters this morning tells us that at least four of the teachers on that list have retired to that area. I'll know more when I get there."

"Is Edward Fontaine there?"

"He wasn't on the list I received," Dan said. "But we'll find him soon. It's pretty easy to track down people who draw Social Security checks."

"What if he's dead?" Ginny asked.

"Then we'll ask someone else," Sully said. "Don't worry. Dan's good at his job."

Ginny leaned against Sully's chest, savoring the feel of his arms around her, holding her close.

"You'll keep us informed?" she asked.

"Yes, ma'am. You can count on that," Dan said,

and then pointed a finger at Sully. "You keep an eye on her, Dean. Can't lose someone like her. Who knows when I'll be wanting some more of those ham and cheese rabbits."

Ginny rolled her eyes. "Go find the bad guy and quit picking on my cooking skills."

Dan laughed and then waved as he boarded the chopper. Sully pulled Ginny back to the porch, shielding her from the blast of rocks and sand as the chopper lifted off. They watched until it was nothing but a speck. Ginny shrugged out of Sully's arms and turned around.

"Where are you going?" he asked.

"Crazy," she muttered. "Want to come?"

Sully laughed and swooped her off her feet as he carried her into the house and shut the door.

"How far do you think we'll have to go?" he asked, as he swung her around.

Ginny grinned in spite of herself and then thumped him lightly on the arm.

"All the way to the bedroom. After that, I'll leave the travel plans to you."

Sully grinned. "You're all a man could ever want and then some. Won't talk on the phone. Drives me crazy in bed. Course, there is that one small flaw...but hell, it's easy to overlook, considering everything else you have to offer."

She knew she was being set up and still felt compelled to ask.

"Exactly what are you getting at...besides me, of course?"

"Well, honey, I hate to tell you this, but did you know you snore?"

She'd been expecting a crack about her cooking. This took her by surprise.

"Put me down this instant. I don't snore."

"Oh...but you do. However, it's all right. It's not really noticeable until you snort. But I can get used to it."

"Get used to it? There's nothing to get used to. I don't snore. I would know."

Sully didn't crack a smile. "How? You're asleep when it happens."

Her cheeks began to burn, and she knew she was blushing. Damn this man four ways to Sunday.

"I don't snore," she muttered. "But if I did, a gentleman wouldn't mention it."

Sully grinned as he dumped her on the bed and then straddled her legs and began pulling her T-shirt over her head. Before she could think, he had her bra on the floor and her breasts in his hands.

"Now, baby, tell the truth, aren't you glad I'm not a gentleman?"

He didn't give her a chance to answer.

Lucy took a handful of shirts from the dresser drawer and laid them in the suitcase, carefully smoothing at the fabric, although they were still neatly wrapped from their trip to the cleaners.

"I wish you didn't have to go again so soon," she said. "You've only been home a couple of days."

"I know, sweetheart, but it's my work."

She pasted a bright smile on her face as she turned. "Of course, and I wouldn't have it any other way for you. I was being selfish. Forgive me?"

Emile smiled as he put his wallet in his jacket.

"There's nothing to forgive." Then he looked around the room, making sure he'd left nothing behind.

"Do you have your tickets?" Lucy asked.

"In my briefcase."

"Did you get extra cash from the ATM this morning when you went out?"

"No. I forgot."

"Then wait here. I'll go downstairs to my desk. I keep a little mad money there, you know."

"You don't need to do that," Emile said. "I can use the ATM at the airport."

"I don't mind," Lucy said. "It won't take a minute. Why don't you go tell Phillip goodbye while I'm gone?"

"Yes. Good idea," he said, and followed her out of the room, turning left down the hall as she went to the right.

Frowning at the style and volume of the music being played inside, he knocked twice and then called out.

"Phillip! It's me. Do you have a minute?"

The door swung inward, and for an instant Emile thought he was looking at a stranger.

"Yeah. What do you want?"

Emile stared. "The music. It's so loud."

"That's the way I like it."

Emile raised his voice a couple of octaves just to be able to hear the sound of his own words.

"Phillip, is everything all right?"

A cocky grin changed the angles of Phillip's face. "Oh yeah, Pops, everything's ducky."

Taken aback by Phillip's sarcasm, Emile's first instinct was to demand an apology, but something told him to hold his tongue.

"I'm leaving for the airport. I came to say goodbye."

A short bark of laughter preceded another snide remark.

"What else is new? So goodbye. Adios. Sayonara. Hasta la vista, baby."

The hairs rose on the back of Emile neck. Dear God, who—no, what—was this manner of man? He reached for Phillip's arm, but his son spun out of the way and danced across the floor toward the stereo that was going full blast.

"Phillip! We have to talk! You must—"

Lucy grabbed him by the arm, pulled him out into

the hall and quickly shut the door. Her eyes were wide, almost frightened in appearance, and she had a nervous giggle in her voice he'd never heard before.

"Emile, here's some cash...almost two hundred dollars. You must hurry or you're going to miss your plane."

"Phillip. There's something wrong with him."

"Oh no, dear, you must be mistaken. Here, put this cash into your wallet so you won't lose it."

"But I'm telling you, he isn't—"

"It's all right," Lucy said. "He's just tired. He was up all night working on his book. Probably letting off a little steam, don't you think?"

"No...it was more than that." He took her by the arms. "You're not listening to me. It was like looking at a stranger."

"Then you must stay home more, my dear, if you don't recognize your own son."

She kissed him quickly to soften the sting of criticism and then took him by the hand and began dragging him down the hall.

"Now come along. The cab will be here any moment."

Emile went, but reluctantly, and even as he was getting into the cab, he couldn't turn loose of the thought that he was leaving a monster alone in the house with his wife.

"Hey, mister...what the hell are you tryin' to prove? This is my beat, and if there's any recyclable stuff in there, it's mine.''

Phillip blinked. There was a very large street person poking him with a stick. He started to laugh at the incongruity of the situation and then realized where he was leaning over a Dumpster. He yanked his hands out quickly, as if he'd stuck them in fire. They were covered in filth. As he looked closer, he realized some of the filth was dried blood. He started to shake.

She was nothing but trash. I just put her where she belonged.

Phillip jerked and then started to moan.

''Oh my God, oh my God, what have you done?''

Does it matter? Does anything matter anymore?

He was afraid to look, but he had to know. He grabbed the edge of the Dumpster and peered in. To his everlasting relief, there was nothing but garbage.

Not in there, stupid. Don't worry. She'll never be found.

Suddenly he doubled over and threw up.

The old tramp covered his nose and started to back up.

''Dang it all, mister. Look what you went and done to my alley. I ain't gonna wade through all that puke for a couple of cans. I'm outta here.''

Phillip was gasping for breath when he finally straightened. With a frantic last look, he stumbled backward a few steps, then spun around and started to run, only to realize as he reached the streets that he didn't know where he was. He needed to get home. He needed to clean himself up and try to forget this had happened.

He patted the pockets of his pants, breathing a quick sigh of relief as he felt the ring of keys beneath the fabric. His car. Where had he parked his car? He started walking.

The other way, stupid. You can't do anything right.

Pivoting sharply, he began walking with long, jerky strides. His fear and frustration carried him three and a half blocks before he realized it was going to be okay. His car! He'd found his car. He bolted out into the street without thinking. The strident blare of a car horn brought him up short, and he jumped back to the curb only seconds away from disaster.

"Watch where you're going!" the driver shouted, and flipped Phillip off as he sped down the street.

Phillip took a deep breath and this time looked both ways before he bounded across the street. Moments later he slid behind the steering wheel and then quickly locked the doors. The car was littered with an empty whiskey bottle as well as condom wrappers.

"At least I'm not going to die of AIDS," Phillip muttered, and then started the car and drove away.

By the time he reached home, he had most of his panic under control. He couldn't let this go on. Something had to be done.

As he pulled in the drive, he noticed that his mother's car was gone. Good. That would give him time to clean up. Make up some sort of excuse as to why he'd been gone—maybe he could say he'd been doing research for his book. Yes. That was it. That would work. He jumped out on the run, desperate to wash away the filth from his body, and as he did, he wondered how long he'd been gone this time. Curious, he picked up the morning paper as he hurried inside, then breathed a quick sigh of relief. One night. So he hadn't come home last night. No big deal. He was a man, not a child. He shouldn't have to check in.

By the time he got to his room, he was running. He opened the door and then stopped in midstride. The room had been trashed. His clothes were in shreds, and his computer was in pieces all over the floor.

"No...not the book," he moaned, and got down on his knees.

You don't do anything without me. I'm the one who's in charge.

"You bastard. You stinking, rotten bastard," Phillip shrieked, and began hitting himself in the head. "I warned you to leave me alone."

Lucy's heart skipped a beat as she pulled into the driveway. Phillip was home. Leaving the sacks of groceries on the back seat of the car, she dashed into the house. Even before she reached the foot of the stairs, she could hear Phillip's screams echoing throughout the house. As she took the first step, a part of her mind was relieved by the fact that it was the cleaning lady's day off. She didn't want her to see this happening. Moments later, she reached the head of the stairs and starting running down the hall, only to hear shattering glass, followed by a wild, primordial shriek that made her stumble.

Clasping a hand to her breast, she stifled the urge to turn and run the other way. This was her son. He needed her, no matter what. Yet the sight that greeted her almost stopped her heart.

"No! Oh no, Phillip! What on earth have you done?"

He turned on her, his chest heaving, his clothes hanging in shreds.

"I've got to stop him before it's too late."

He pushed past her and ran into the hall.

"Stop who?" she cried, as she followed the path of his anger. She couldn't catch up. He was already down the stairs and bolting into the dining room.

"Phillip! Stop this instant and talk to me!"

He didn't respond. Terrified, she took the stairs two at a time and would have fallen had she not been clutching the balustrade with both hands. By the time she got to the dining room, the contents of the sideboard drawer were scattered on the floor.

"Phillip, darling, what on earth have you—"

He was holding a knife.

Oh God. Oh no. I need Emile here. This has gone all wrong.

Then she reminded herself that Emile wasn't here. He was never here when she needed him. So she took a deep breath and held out her hand.

"Darling, hand Mother the knife. It's very sharp, and you don't want to get hurt."

Phillip started to laugh. "But that's where you're wrong," he said, and pushed the point of the knife at his throat. "I want this over. It has to end now."

He pushed the knife deep enough into his flesh that a drop of blood suddenly slid down the surface of the blade.

"No!" Lucy screamed, and dropped down on her knees. "Please, Phillip, darling. Whatever is wrong, we can fix it. Just tell me now and I'll make it all better. I swear."

Tears rolled, washing parallel paths through the filth on his face.

"You can't fix this, Mother. But I can. It's been coming to me for weeks now. Each morning when I wake up, there's a certainty in my mind that was never there before."

She gasped. The tape. These last few weeks he'd been listening to Emile's tape.

"But it was supposed to help you," she whispered.

"What? What the hell are you talking about?" Phillip raged. "No! Don't tell me! Whatever it is, I don't need to know. I am the one in control."

Don't do it!

The panic in the voice was nothing short of an adrenaline rush.

"Now you beg!" Phillip shrieked, and began waving the knife around in the air.

Lucy shrank backward into the corner, certain she was going to die.

"I love you, son. Please stop. Please, before it's too late," she begged.

Listen to her, you idiot. She loves you. Do you want to make your mother cry?

"Not really," Phillip said, and then giggled. "But she won't be crying half as loud as you."

He thrust the knife into his throat, instantly piercing the jugular vein. A pumping spray of blood began dotting the sideboard, the table, the floor, even spattering on Lucy's face. Phillip's smile faded almost as quickly as the life in his eyes. He went down on his knees and then fell forward, driving the knife all the way through to the other side of his neck.

Lucy touched the dampness on her face, her eyes wide with shock. When she saw the fresh blood on her fingertips, she began screaming in long, gasping sobs. The woman next door heard the shrieks, became concerned and called the police. By nightfall, Lucy Karnoff's world was in shambles. Too hysterical to make any sense, she'd been hospitalized and sedated while the authorities tried desperately to locate the man of the house.

In Santa Fe, Emile was basking in the glory of yet another victory. Being the guest of honor at the New Mexico State Medical Convention was like something out of a dream. His appointment book was filling by the hour as he promised himself to one facility after another. He'd already set aside the problems he'd sensed brewing at home. It was a case of sacrificing the few for the good of the many, and there were so many people he needed to teach in order for his life-saving technique to continue. It was his legacy to the world.

16

Ginny was poised at the edge of the diving board, waiting for Sully to swim out of range before she dived in. But he stopped about halfway out and turned, treading water and motioning for her to come in.

"Get back!" she yelled. "You're too close."

"No, I'm not."

Webster Chee was leaning against the side of the house. The gun and shoulder holster he was wearing stood out in stark contrast to his white short-sleeved shirt. Kevin Holloway was coming out of the house carrying two cans of Coke. He was wearing shorts and an unbuttoned cotton shirt, but Ginny knew he also had a gun beneath his shirt. Ginny supposed Franklin Chee was asleep. She was getting used to being the object of so much attention, but the guards seemed an incongruous accessory to the holiday atmosphere around the pool.

"Come on, Ginny. Don't chicken out on me now," Sully jeered.

"I don't chicken," she said, and then took a deep

breath, but instead of diving neatly, she bounced as high as she could and then cannon-balled right where Sully was waiting. She saw the startled look on his face just before she went under and knew that she'd scored a big hit. Seconds later, she felt hands at her back. Sully was pulling her up. She surfaced laughing.

"So you thought that was funny, did you?"

The growl in his voice was fake, and she laughed again as she wrapped her arms around his neck and let him carry them both to solid ground.

Kevin Holloway handed her a towel as Sully set her on the side of the pool.

"She got you good, Sully."

He grinned wryly. Holloway was the youngest man there and was, he suspected, more than slightly infatuated with Ginny's charms. But that was as far as it went. Holloway was a by-the-book man, just like his two partners.

"Yeah, she did that," Sully said, and hefted himself out of the pool. "If you guys want to swim a bit to cool off, I'd be glad to stand watch for you."

"Thanks, but no. Orders are orders. Besides, I took a quick dip last night before I went to bed," Kevin said, then looked at Webster. "I'm going to check the perimeter."

Webster nodded, then took a slow sip of his Coke while Ginny slid into the lounge chair, lay back and closed her eyes.

Sully was drying his hair when his cell phone rang.

Ginny pulled a towel over her face to shield it from the sun as he reached across her stomach to the table where it was lying.

"Sullivan."

"It's me," Dan said. "I've got news, and it isn't good."

Sully stilled. Suddenly the fun of the day seemed silly, as if they'd forgotten why they were there.

"What's wrong?"

"We found Fontaine."

"And?"

"And he's dead."

"Shit."

"That's not all."

Sully's chin jutted as he unconsciously braced himself for a blow.

"He hasn't been dead all that long," Dan said. "It seems he went for a morning walk a week or so ago, just like he's done for the past twenty years, only this time he fell off a pier. And get this, the pier has a five-foot-high railing around it."

"Not the best diving board in the world," Sully muttered. "I don't suppose there were any witnesses?"

"Hell no, and funny you should mention diving," Dan said. "People said the old man had never learned to swim."

The hairs rose on the backs of Sully's arms.

"Are you thinking what I'm thinking?" Sully asked.

"Yes, only we checked his house. Everything was in perfect order. The phone was on the hook, and there were witnesses who saw him on the way to the pier. He stopped and talked to them, just as he did every morning, so he wasn't in any kind of a trance. If he died because of those women, then he had a little help."

"Have you located any of the other teachers?"

"All but two. One's deceased, and the other has Alzheimer's. The ones we've talked to remember a guy who came once a week for the hour in which the class was held, but no one remembers his name or what he looked like. They said he always left when the class was over."

"Great. That's just great," Sully said, and started pacing.

Ginny took the towel off her face and sat up.

"What? What is it?"

Sully was too deep into the conversation he was having to answer.

"Isn't there anyone else? Like a janitor...or some of the cooks from the lunchroom? It can't end here, damn it! Someone has to remember something!"

Dan sighed. "We're working on it, Sully. If you'll check the book, you'll see that there weren't any pictures of the staff. We're re-interviewing a couple of the teachers today who might be able to help us with some names in that direction, but it's a long shot. According to their stories, most of those people were close to retirement age then, and it's been twenty years. The chances of them still being alive are not on our side. When I know something, you'll know something, okay?''

"It has to be okay, doesn't it?" Sully said, and disconnected.

Ginny stood. She could tell by the set of Sully's shoulders that she needed to be standing when he told her the news.

"It isn't good, is it?" she asked.

He shook his head. "No, baby, it's not."

"They couldn't find Mr. Fontaine?"

"He was dead."

"Oh, that's too bad," she said. "Well, he must have been pretty old. I guess it was to be expected."

"That's not what I mean," Sully said. "They fished him out of the ocean about a week and a half ago. Seems he forgot he couldn't swim and took a dive over a five-foot railing on the pier."

Ginny clapped a hand over her mouth to keep from screaming.

The world was coming undone. When Sully took her in his arms, she began to cry.

"He's killing everyone, isn't he? He'll find me, Sully, and when he does, I'll be helpless."

"I won't let that happen," he said. "Remember what I promised?"

She shuddered.

"Look at me, Ginny."

A wave of calm swept through her body. Those were the same words he'd used the night they'd first made love. *Look at me, Ginny.* And she'd looked and seen the eyes of love.

"I see you," she said.

"What did I promise you?"

"That you wouldn't let me die."

"That's right, and don't you forget it."

"Okay."

He rubbed his hands up and down the sides of her arms and then kissed her gently.

"Honey, you've had too much sun. Why don't we call it quits for now and come back out after sundown?"

She nodded, picked up her towel and walked into the house.

The moment she was out of sight, Sully headed for Webster. The men needed to know what had happened and to be on the alert. There was no way of knowing how long they could keep her location a secret.

The evening meal had been a sober affair. Ginny had picked at her food, and every bite Sully put in his mouth burned his gut. Idle chitchat seemed superfluous, but discussing the issue at hand was too painful. Finally Ginny carried her plate to the sink and scraped the contents down the garbage disposal.

"I'm sorry," she said. "It was good, but I just wasn't hungry."

"It's all right, honey. We've had some hard news today. It was a setback, but it's not the end of the world. Why don't you watch a little TV? Find something good, and I'll come watch it with you as soon as I clean off the table."

"No. I'll help you. When it's done, we'll both go watch some TV."

"It's a deal."

He emptied his plate down the garbage disposal, while Ginny cleaned off the table. Then he loaded the dishwasher as Ginny put some of their clothes into the washing machine. It was a very domestic moment for a woman on the run for her life.

A short while later they were side by side on the sofa. Ginny was skimming through a magazine she'd already read two times while Sully channel surfed the TV.

"What time is it?" he asked. "I left my watch on the bedroom dresser."

She leaned forward to read the dial on the clock across the room.

"It's about ten o'clock. Let's watch the news, okay? I've been so focused on what's happening to me I have no idea what's been going on in the world."

Sully aimed the remote. The screen blipped, and then the familiar logo of a national syndicated network appeared.

"Just in time," he said.

Ginny tossed the magazine aside and then pulled her feet up off the floor to sit cross-legged on the sofa. Sully grinned to himself, marveling at how someone as tall and lithe as Ginny could wind herself up into such a small ball.

"And now for the national news. Recently crowned Nobel-Prize-winning doctor Emile Karnoff is in Santa Fe this week, speaking at a state medical conference. His revolutionary technique of using hypnosis as a healing tool is being shared with his younger colleagues, much to the dismay of some die-hard practitioners. Dr. Karnoff recently returned from Ireland, where he was instrumental in reversing the terminal prognosis of a young mother dying of cancer."

As they flashed a picture of Emile Karnoff coming out of a hotel, waving at the cameras and then getting into a cab, something went off in Ginny's mind. She leaned forward, her elbows on her knees, her chin resting in the palms of her hands.

Sully noticed her interest, and it occurred to him what Ginny's life had been like before all this happened.

"You know, we've never talked about your career. I'll bet you've met some really interesting people over the years. Who was your favorite person to interview?''

"Sully, I—''

The story shifted from the archived film clip to a sound bite of Karnoff's address to the medical community.

"Turn it up!'' Ginny said.

The tone of her voice was a little startling, but Sully reached for the remote without comment. As he aimed it toward the screen, the deep, resonant voice of Emile Karnoff filled the room.

"*...lifelong pursuit of the human spirit as well as the mind. As you know, we use but a tiny portion of the marvelous brain that God has given us. It only made sense to me that we were capable of so much—*''

"I know him. *I know him.*''

Sully looked at her, and as he did, a shiver ran up his spine. Not only was the childish singsong manner in which Ginny had spoken almost creepy, but she was sitting with her eyes closed, listening to the man talk.

Oh hell. "Ginny?''

"Do you hear the power?''

He stared at her, his mind turning in a dozen directions at once.

"What do you mean?''

"In his voice. Do you hear it? I know him.''

"Well, sure you know him. He's been on television

quite a bit in the last few months. It isn't every day that an American wins a Nobel Prize.''

She was rocking back and forth now, her eyes still closed, and there was an almost imperceptible tremor in her hands.

''I know him.''

Panic struck. Sully bolted up from the sofa and ran into the kitchen, where he'd left the walkie-talkie. As he pressed the button to talk, a short burst of static erupted from the mike; a warning for someone to listen.

''Franklin! This is Sully. I need you in here now.''

By the time he got back into the living room, Franklin Chee was coming in the front door, his weapon drawn.

Sully shook his head and motioned toward Ginny. Franklin replaced his weapon as he moved to Ginny's side. She was rocking to and fro in a childlike repetitive motion, her eyes closed, her hands folded in her lap.

''When did this happen?'' Chee asked.

''Just now.''

''Do you know what triggered it?''

Sully pointed to the screen. The last images of Emile Karnoff were fading as the newscaster moved on to other stories.

''Who was he?'' Franklin asked.

''Emile Karnoff, the doctor who—''

''Won the Nobel Prize for using hypnosis to cure

disease,'' Franklin said, finishing Sully's sentence for him.

They looked at each other and then again at Ginny. Franklin laid his hand on Ginny's knee.

''Ginny?''

''Yes, teacher?''

At the sound of her own voice, she jerked and then opened her eyes.

''Franklin. For a moment, I thought you were someone else.''

''Christ almighty,'' Sully murmured, as the implications of what she'd said began to sink in. All this time they'd been looking for an educator. But what if...?

''Ginny, where did you go just now?'' Franklin asked.

Ginny swayed where she sat and then looked at Sully for guidance, her eyes a bit dazed and unfocused.

''Did we go somewhere?''

Sully groaned. ''Damn it, Franklin, tell me I'm wrong in thinking what I'm thinking.''

Franklin shrugged. ''I can't do that. I don't know what you saw or why Ginny slipped away, but I know where you're going with it. Are you going to call Dan or shall I?''

Ginny covered her face with her hands.

Sully was at her side within seconds.

"It's all right, baby. I was right here all the time. Nothing happened to you."

Angrily, she pushed him away. "Nothing? You call losing touch with reality nothing?"

Franklin got to his feet. "I am going to call Dan."

"Use the phone in the kitchen if you want," Sully said.

Franklin patted his pocket. "I have mine. I will be back."

He walked out of the house, leaving Ginny and Sully alone.

"Why did this happen?" Ginny muttered. "What happened? You didn't play the tape, so what was it that—"

"You don't remember?"

"No," she said, and jumped to her feet, unable to sit still any longer. "We were watching the news, for God's sake, and then…" She frowned and then stared at the floor, mentally replaying the sequence of events. "And then…they had a piece about…" She looked up. "About the Nobel-Prize-winning doctor, right?"

He nodded.

"What else do you remember?"

She started to pace, mentally ticking off the images still lingering in her head.

"There was a film clip…and we were talking about…about…" She frowned. "I don't remember anything more until Franklin spoke to me. What did I do? What did I hear?"

"A man's voice. You kept telling me you knew him, but you weren't looking at him, honey. You were listening to the sound of his voice."

"Then what?"

"You called him teacher."

Her legs buckled. Sully caught her before she fell. Her head lolled against his arm as he carried her to the bed. When he set her down on the spread, she covered her face and began to cry. Not loudly, just soft, helpless sobs that nearly broke his heart.

"Honey? Talk to me. Come on now. You're tougher than this. I saw what you can do. Don't give up on me now."

"I am coming apart, aren't I, Sully? First the tape, now something as simple as the sound of a voice. What next? How will I ever cope again? I wouldn't dare drive a car for fear of blanking out at some inconsequential sound. I can't do my job if I'm afraid to answer a phone. I don't know what to think, and half the time I don't even want to remember. We were babies, Sully. Six years old. What did he do to us? My God...what did he do?"

Sully lay down beside her and pulled her close against his strength.

"I don't know, but we'll find out. And you will be all right. And it will be over. And I will be with you every step of the way."

She turned her face against his chest and finally let herself grieve—not just for herself, but for Georgia, and Emily, Jo-Jo and Lynn, for a woman named Frances and a young teacher named Allison. She cried because she was the only one left who could.

A short while later the phone rang. Sully slipped his arm from beneath Ginny's neck and then answered.

"Sullivan," he said, speaking quietly.

"I got Chee's message. We need to talk."

"Hang on a minute," Sully said. "Ginny's asleep. I'm going into another room."

With a last glance to make sure she was still resting, Sully headed for the living room.

"Okay, start talking," Sully said.

"First things first. How is she?"

"She's coming undone," Sully said, and then shoved a hand through his hair in frustration. "It's killing me just sitting here, not being able to do anything. I want to find the bastard who's doing this and break his sick neck."

"What do you think about her reaction to the piece on Karnoff?" Dan asked.

"Hell if I know, but you should have seen her. And when Franklin came in and woke her up, just before she came out of it, she called him teacher." His voice rose angrily as he slammed the flat of his hand against the wall. "Teacher! All this time we were looking for a regular teacher. What if we were wrong? What if that was just a name he told them to call him to make it okay for him to do what he was doing?"

"What do you think he *was* doing?" Dan said.

"I don't know," Sully snapped. "But it's eating Ginny alive. Get some sound bites of Karnoff from some of the television stations and bring them with you. We've got to make sure this isn't a fluke. But I swear to God, if she reacts this way again, I want a background check done on the son of a bitch. I want to know where he was in 1979. I want to know what he was doing and who he was doing it to, right down to how many times he made love to his wife."

"Is that all?" Dan drawled.

"Sorry. It's your case, but she's my—"

He stopped. What was she, exactly, besides the woman he loved?

"You didn't finish what you were saying," Dan said. "Don't know how, or don't want to?"

"Let's just say that I'm not looking forward to a future without her in it."

"Enough said. I'll be there in a few hours. I've got to set the wheels in motion on Karnoff and get some film on him, too."

Dan disconnected, and Sully tossed the phone on the sofa and walked outside. As late as it was, it should have been dark, but with the full moon reflecting off the light desert sand, the air seemed caught between daylight and dusk. In the distance, he could just make out one of the Chee brothers sitting on an outcropping of rock. A tiny lizard scooted across the gravel in front of him and disappeared between a pair of round squatty cactus, a huge contrast to the stately

Saguaro scattered about the area. Compared to the lush green mountains and deep running creeks where he'd grown up, it was like looking at the surface of the moon.

He thought better when he walked, so he stuffed his hands in his pockets and began a trek toward the back of the property.

It was almost too improbable to contemplate, but stranger things had happened in this world. Could Emile Karnoff, the current darling of the medical world and the man most likely to be the news magazines' man of the year, be involved in something this sinister? If they went exclusively by Ginny's reactions, then his guilt seemed evident. But there were so many things to consider. Phone records to trace. Trips that might coincide with the deaths of Georgia or Edward Fontaine. That part of the case he would have to leave up to Dan. All he could do was make sure that Ginny stayed in one piece, both physically and mentally, until someone was charged with the crimes. After that...

He stopped, staring across the pool and into the desert beyond. What about after that? Would Ginny be so sick of it all that she would want to be rid of everything connected to this case, including him? Or would her feelings still hold true? He could only hope. All he knew was that when she'd collapsed in his arms earlier today, he'd never been so scared in his life. In those few seconds, he'd wanted to take her and run and never look back. If she would have him, he would spend the rest of his life with her and consider himself blessed. But until the mystery was solved and the guilty brought to justice, what he wanted would have to wait.

Emile was preparing a drink before dinner when someone knocked at his hotel door. He set the glass down and went to answer it, smoothing his hair as he went. The hotel manager and a police officer were standing outside his door.

"Dr. Karnoff? Emile Karnoff of Bainbridge, Connecticut?"

Puzzled by the officer's presence, he smiled nervously at the manager and then nodded to the cop.

"Yes, I'm Emile Karnoff."

"Dr. Karnoff, may we come inside for a moment?"

Emile's heart gave a little skip and then settled back into rhythm. It couldn't be bad news, but rather something to do with a needy patient.

"Certainly. I was about to have a drink before going down to dinner. Would you join me?"

"No, sir," the officer said. "But thank you, just the same."

The manager shook his head in denial, but stood back. It was obvious to Emile that he'd come only as an accompaniment to the policeman.

"Officer, how may I help you?"

"Sir, I'm sorry to have to inform you that your son, Phillip, is dead, and your wife, Lucy, is in a hospital under sedation."

Emile blanched. For a moment he thought he'd misunderstood, but the sympathy on both men's faces told him otherwise.

"Dead? Dear God, how? Was there an accident? Was Lucy injured as well?"

"All I know is that the Bainbridge police asked us to find you and give you this information. I can say that your son did not have an accident. We were told it was suicide. Your wife witnessed it, and that's why she's under doctor's care at this time. However, we were not led to believe she was injured in any way."

"No." Emile staggered. "Not suicide. I can't believe it. There was no warning, no—"

He suddenly flashed on Phillip in his room, ranting and laughing and flaunting his sarcasm and disregard for courtesy. Emile covered his face. He'd known then that something was horribly wrong, and he'd turned his back and walked away.

"If I had paid more attention. Oh God...helping everyone but my family. What kind of man have I become?"

"Dr. Karnoff, I think you'd better sit down," the manager said, and helped him to a chair. "Sir, on behalf of everyone here at the hotel, please accept our sympathies. If there is anything I can do...anything at all, you have only to ask."

Emile shook his head, like a dog coming out of the water, and started fumbling with his tie, then the creases in his pants, as if neatness was the most important thing in his life.

"Home. I'll have to go home. I need to call the airport and cancel my appointments here. And Lucy...dear Lucy. That a mother should have to witness such a horrible thing..."

Tears rolled down his cheeks.

"Dr. Karnoff, if you have an itinerary, I will see to calling all your people here. And if you would allow me, I will make arrangements to get you on the first plane out of Santa Fe."

Emile nodded. "Yes. Yes, I would appreciate it very much." Remembering his manners, he stood abruptly and shook hands with the officer, as well as the manager of the hotel.

"Gentlemen...I must pack now."

The officer departed, leaving the manager to wait for Emile to furnish the itinerary.

A short while later Emile found himself alone. Now there was no one between him and that which he knew to be the truth. He'd seen something dangerous in Phillip and let Lucy's will prevail because he hadn't wanted to be bothered. Now the death of his son and the sanity of his wife would be on his head.

He went to the closet to begin packing his clothes. Halfway through the process, he began to shake. Within minutes, he was in the bathroom, on his knees, vomiting until there was nothing left in his belly but guilt.

17

Dan Howard's arrival at the safe house coincided with Emile Karnoff's exit from Santa Fe. Only a half hour later either way and they would have crossed paths in the air without knowing it.

He knocked once and then entered. Although it was a hundred and two outside in the shade, Ginny was sitting in a chair, wrapped up in an afghan, still shivering from shock.

After she'd awakening this morning, she had been antsy, jumping at every movement and refusing to have the radio or the television on anywhere in the house. Every time Sully walked out of a room, she was tense until he came back. She was nothing more than a time bomb, waiting to detonate.

"Come in," Sully said.

Dan strode into the living room. Franklin Chee was right behind him. Holloway and Webster Chee were somewhere on the perimeter, making sure no uninvited guests tried to crash the party.

Dan nodded to Sully, then gave Ginny a hard stare. Sully was right. She *was* coming undone. He could see it in her eyes, and in the tension around her mouth. There was a brittleness about her that hadn't been there before.

"Hey, Julia Child, am I too late for supper?" he asked, trying to tease a smile out of her.

She pulled the afghan a little closer around her shoulders.

"Too late? We're all too late," she muttered, and looked past him out into the yard, as if she was expecting someone else.

Sully frowned and shook his head. Dan nodded. He got the message. Chitchat was definitely out.

"Did you get the tape?" Sully asked.

Dan handed it over. Sully slipped it in the VCR, but he didn't turn it on.

"Ginny, remember what we talked about?"

"Yes."

"Are you ready to watch? It's a bunch of film clips of Karnoff, right, Dan?"

"About fifteen minutes worth," he said. "I didn't figure we'd need more, although I can get them if needed."

"If it's anything like before, you won't need more than fifteen seconds," Sully said.

Dan pivoted, his eyes narrowing sharply as he gave Ginny a hard look.

"That fast?" he muttered.

"Oh yeah," Sully said.

Franklin Chee moved to within a foot or so of

where Ginny was sitting and then squatted down on his heels and gave her a wink.

She looked at him and then blinked. Her reactions were so slow, it was almost as if she'd been drugged.

"What? Waiting to see if my head starts to spin?"

Franklin grinned. "Yes. But don't throw up on me, okay? I have a weak stomach."

The incongruity of a hard-nosed Fed who had an aversion to puking was too funny to ignore.

She grinned and then shook her head. "You're good at making people feel better, aren't you?"

"Yeah. They call me Doctor Killdeer out on the rez. Get it? Kildaire? Killdeer?"

The play on the name was even sillier, and this time she managed a laugh. Then she sighed and tossed back the afghan, as if readying to do battle.

"Sully?"

"Right here, honey."

"Don't lose me, okay?"

Sully's gut knotted. "I won't."

She looked around the room at the men standing there and then nodded.

"Okay. I'm ready. Turn on the VCR."

The first clip was from the news conference that had been held after Karnoff had been notified as recipient of the Nobel Prize. He stood to the right of the podium, a tall and distinguished gentleman in his late sixties. At his side were a small, elegantly dressed woman and a young, thirty-something man who appeared to be a somewhat faded version of the man himself. Not quite as tall. Not quite as assertive. And obviously not comfortable with being in the public eye.

Ginny stared at the trio, trying to put that face to a man from her past, but it wouldn't come. He looked like any number of distinguished older men she'd seen in her life. She looked at Dan and Sully and shrugged, as if to say, "So?"

And then the sound bite came on.

"Ladies and gentlemen, it is official. Dr. Emile Peter Karnoff has just been awarded the Nobel Prize for Medicine, for his strides in using hypnosis as a basis for physical healing. Dr. Karnoff, on behalf of the American public, may I be the first to congratulate you on your amazing accomplishments."

Emile moved to the podium, smiled at his wife and son, and then nodded to the dozens of reporters on the scene below.

He cleared his throat.

She held her breath.

"Today is a great day for me and for my family..."

The air slid out of her lungs, as if she'd been dealt a blow in the middle.

"...who have sacrificed much that I might follow my visions. I have been given a great honor, but none so great as..."

Her eyelids were heavy...so heavy. His voice was pulling her under.

"...the knowledge that my discoveries will live on long after I'm gone."

The timbre of his voice rose and fell with the rhythm of her heart. In learned abeyance, she let it wash over her, warm, compelling, yielding to the inevitability of sensory persuasion.

Sully hit Pause, his gut still in knots. The more they played with her mind, the more dangerous he felt it became. He didn't give a damn what Ginny or anyone else said, this was never happening again.

"You see," he said. "She's out."

Dan waved a hand in front of her face. She didn't flinch. Her eyelids were down; her body seemed to be hovering in a state of suspension; not asleep—just waiting for someone to come turn on the lights in her head.

Dan touched her arm. "Ginny?"

She took a slow breath.

Sully nodded at Franklin, who quickly moved in to help bring her back.

"Ginny, listen to the sound of my voice. You can hear me clearly from where you are. Isn't that right?"

She nodded.

"I'm going to count backward from five. When I say 'Now,' you will wake and feel good and refreshed, and you will remember everything that we've said. Are you ready?"

"Yes."

Her voice sounded hollow. Franklin took her by the hand.

"I'm with you. You feel my hand. You hear my voice. I'm going to start counting, and when I say 'Now,' you will wake. Five. Four. Three. Two. One. Now!"

Ginny took a deep breath and looked up. She was smiling.

"It happened again, didn't it? He has something to do with what's happening, doesn't he, Dan?"

It was difficult for Dan to deny the obvious, although he had to be cautious, considering the high visibility of the man who had suddenly become their prime suspect.

"It looks as if the possibility exists," he said. "I'll know more in a few hours."

"What are we waiting for?" Ginny asked. "What do we need to link him to the other women's deaths?"

Sully sat down on the arm of the chair in which she was sitting and put his hand on the back of her head.

"For starters, honey, we have to have some concrete evidence linking him to the case, like phone records that show he called the women who died, or proof that he was in those cities during the time of the incidents...things like that."

"And what if you don't find them? It's quite obvious the man is brilliant. I don't think he'd be stupid enough to leave evidence that would link him to a crime like this.''

None of them had anything to say. It wasn't good enough for Ginny.

"I'm giving you people two days to dig through his life, and if nothing comes up you can use, I'm out of here.''

Sully jumped to his feet. "What the hell do you mean, out of here?''

She stood, her hands on her hips, her eyes blazing. "I'm sick and tired of being the victim. I'm tired of hiding. I'm tired of being a target. The way I see it, I come out of the closet, whoever's out there comes calling, and it's up to you guys to keep me breathing. How's that for a plan?''

"It sucks," Sully snapped.

"So does this," Ginny countered.

"It's not a good idea," Franklin Chee said.

"Chee's right," Dan added.

"I didn't say it was a good one, but it's what's going to happen.''

Then her voice shook, and they realized how much it was costing her to put on a brave face. After that, they were putty in her hands.

"So, guys...are you going to be my pillows if I fall?''

Sully looked at her and then sighed. "You know I'm there.''

"Webster and I are getting tired of all this heat.

We'll be packed and waiting when you're ready to leave.''

Dan sat down with a thump and then dug at a spot on the floor with the toe of his shoe.

"I'll put Holloway on point. He's like a bird dog anyway, always sniffing the air for trouble, and I'll bring up the rear. I've got a couple of extra guys we can pull in if need be. But don't start packing just yet. Maybe we'll get lucky. Maybe he's laid a paper trail so wide and long that you'll never have to show your face.''

"Thank you,'' Ginny said.

Chee nodded and left to inform the other men what had occurred, while Dan took out his cell phone and moved into another room to make some calls.

"Are you mad at me?'' Ginny asked.

Sully shoved his hands in the pockets of his jeans. "No.''

"Well, something's wrong, and I need you to be on my side.''

"I'm on your side. I'm also trying to get up the guts to tell you something, but I'm pretty sure this isn't a good time.''

"The only guarantee we have in life is now.''

"I know that,'' Sully said.

"It's your call,'' she said, and started to leave the room.

"Okay.''

She stopped and then turned. "Okay, what?''

"I'm going to tell you."

She put her hands on her hips and restrained the urge to tap her toe in nervous frustration. Waiting was not one of her strong points.

Sully took a deep breath, aware that what he was going to say would change everything between them. Whether it was for better or for worse had yet to be seen.

"Sully..."

"I'm getting there, damn it," he muttered.

"There's nothing you can possibly say that is worse than what's already happened."

"I'm not saying it's worse," he said.

She threw up her hands in a gesture of defeat.

"Then what, for God's sake?"

"I'm in love with you. Don't give a damn that you can't cook. Don't care that you're argumentative as all get-out. Don't even mind that you take up more than half the bed. And I don't want to lose you when this is over."

Ginny was speechless. All this time she'd known that their chemistry was just about perfect, and she had known and accepted that her feelings for him were stronger than his for her. But this blew every theory she had of Sullivan Dean. She started to grin.

"You're serious, aren't you?"

He swiped a sweaty hand across his face and wished he had a stiff drink.

"Oh yeah."

"You're in love with me? As in, take thee Ginny to be my—"

"Virginia. I like that name, and you're going to have to answer to it, at least when we get married."

Her smile widened. "Married."

"Yeah. Would you?"

"Yeah. If you asked."

He started to smile and then strode across the room and swung her off her feet.

"Baby, I'm desperate here. I've got a brother I like and a mother who doesn't remember her own name, but I have a steady job, benefits and a fairly good retirement plan." He nuzzled the side of her neck with his lips and then nipped the lobe of her left ear, knowing it made her ache in all the right places. "So, if I asked you real nice, would you marry me and make babies with me and scratch the itch I can't reach on my back?"

Ginny laughed out loud just as Dan came back into the room.

"Did I miss something?" he said, grinning at the scene he'd obviously interrupted.

"Nothing that mattered," Ginny said, as Sully set her back on her feet. "But if you miss our wedding, we are not naming any of our children after you."

"The hell you say," he crowed, and then clapped his hands. "This calls for a celebration. Hey, Sully, have you popped the top on that champagne yet?"

"No, but—"

"Fantastic! I'll go get some glasses." He bolted out of the room before Sully could stop him.

Ginny turned, looking up at Sully with all her emotions there for him to see.

"I will love you forever," she said softly.

"Thank you, baby."

"Don't thank me yet," Ginny said. "You have yet to taste one of my pies."

Emile sat at Lucy's bedside, trying to find his perfect little wife in the ragged old woman on the bed. Her hair was in tangles, her eyes red-rimmed and constantly brimming with tears; even when she slept, tears still seeped from under her eyelids. He'd been here at the hospital for almost twenty-four hours and had been unable to get a response from her. She just kept muttering something about tapes, which was an odd subject to focus on considering they had yet to put their son in his grave.

Emile leaned his forehead against the mattress, so weary in body and spirit he didn't think he could go on. Mr. Important, that was him. Taking care of everybody's health and business but his own family's—putting his ego and his glory above their care.

Lucy rolled her head from side to side on the pillow and began plucking at the sheets with her fingernails, as if she were trying to pick something up. He covered her hand with his own and gave it a pat.

"Lucy, dear, it's Emile. I'm here. You don't have to bear the burden alone."

"...strong and focused...under the bed...Mother's good boy..."

Emile covered his face with his hands.

"Dr. Karnoff?"

Emile looked up. Lucy's doctor had come in.

"Dr. Rader?"

"Yes. I'm sorry to meet you under these conditions, but I have long been an admirer of your work."

Emile bowed his head slightly. It seemed so unimportant now.

"It's a shame that your techniques do not work on mental trauma," Rader said. "I can only imagine how frustrating this is for you...being able to help so many and yet helpless in this type of situation."

Emile's expression gave away nothing of what he was feeling, although he could easily have choked the air out of the doctor's mouth for rattling on so blithely about such a tragedy.

"When can I take Lucy home?" Emile said.

"Well, you see how she is. She can't take care of herself at this point and—"

"She needs to come home. I will hire nurses around the clock if need be."

"Have you been home yourself? I was told it's in a terrible condition."

Emile's argument froze on his lips. He hadn't considered that aspect. In his mind, he'd pictured the rooms as they always were, clean and smelling of lemon-scented oils, with fresh flowers from Lucy's garden in every room.

"We have a woman who comes in to clean. If given time, there is nothing that cannot be overcome. Will you release her to me?"

Dr. Rader nodded. "In this situation, I bow to your superior wisdom regarding your wife's care. You know her best. Maybe familiar surroundings will bring her out of this shock."

That and no more mind-altering drugs. But Emile didn't voice his opinion of that. Instead, he extended his hand.

"I thank you for taking care of my Lucy."

"Certainly, and again, my sincerest condolences on the loss of your son."

"I will go home now," Emile said, "but I'll be back tomorrow to check her out."

"I'll leave the orders," Rader said, and left to finish his rounds.

Emile turned to his wife once more, and then leaned down and kissed her gently on the side of her face.

"I'm going to leave now, dear. But I'll be back tomorrow and take you home."

"...under the bed...under the bed..."

He sighed and then patted her hand. "Yes, I'll look under the bed."

To his surprise, she seemed to settle, and as he took

a cab home, he reminded himself to look under the bed, just in case.

The cab ride seemed endless, but the closer he got to their home, the more tense he felt. What if the doctor was right? What if the house was in shambles?

"First things first," he muttered.

"Did you say something, mister?" the cabdriver asked.

"Just talking to myself."

Five minutes later, they pulled into the driveway. Emile tossed some money on the front seat of the cab as he got out.

"I'll get my own luggage," he said.

"Have a nice day," the cabdriver said, and drove away.

Emile stood outside the front door for a good five minutes, unable to bring himself to go in. It was the next-door neighbor's curiosity that drove him inside. He wasn't in the mood to talk to anyone.

He got as far as the entryway, carefully locking the door behind him, then stood without moving, afraid to advance—afraid of what he might find.

The house felt empty, as if all the life had gone out when Lucy was taken away. Even the grandfather clock was silent. He moved then, opening the case and resetting the hands before giving the pendulums a delicate swing. Immediately the familiar tick, tick, ticking gave impetus for him to proceed.

There was a black mark on the floor, probably from

the heel of someone's shoe. He could only imagine how many people had been within these walls right after everything had happened. In a way, he felt violated, like a man who had caught his wife cheating— as if that which was his had suddenly been had by all.

As he moved toward the stairs, it occurred to him that he didn't know where his son had died. He just assumed it had been in his room, because he was rarely anywhere else. But when he glanced into the dining room and saw the stains on the floor and the chalk outline of where the body had been, he stumbled. Catching himself before he fell, he staggered to the doorway and then braced himself against the wall.

"Phillip. My poor, poor Phillip. What torment you must have been in."

He turned away quickly and almost ran up the stairs, thinking of their bedroom as a refuge from the horror of the sight. But when he gained the top of the stairs, he realized that the chaos must have begun up here. Broken furniture was out in the hall, and a clump of dead flowers lay in the midst of broken glass and spilled water. He moved like a man in a trance toward the open doorway of Phillip's room.

Even though he'd expected destruction, he never could have imagined anything on this level. He stood for a moment, trying to imagine the fury that could drive a man to these ends, but he couldn't wrap his mind around that kind of emotion. Too weary to contemplate the amount of time and money it was going to take to make everything right, he turned to leave when something under the bed caught his eye.

In that instant, he remembered his promise to Lucy. She had kept talking about something under the bed. Maybe this was what she meant. Picking his way through the chaos, he reached the bed, then got down on his knees. With a little effort, he pulled the thing out and then grunted with disappointment. It was only a tape recorder. Nothing of consequence.

He pulled himself up and then tossed it onto the bed. As he did, the little lid popped open, revealing the tape within. He stared, telling himself that his eyes were surely deceiving him, but the dark black lettering on the pristine white label was impossible to miss.

Subliminal Messaging—1980—Studies at Yarmouth Lab.

He yanked it out of the recorder and turned it over in his hand. He hadn't been mistaken. It *was* one of his tapes. How had it gotten in here? It was part of a failed study that had tried to prove that the fear of dying was the trigger that might unleash the human body to fight its own diseases.

It hadn't gone anywhere, and Emile had been frustrated and surprised by the anger it had brought out in patients who were struggling with depression. He started across the hall to his room when something occurred to him. How had Lucy known the tape was there? Surely it wasn't something she'd seen during Phillip's breakdown. He stopped, looking down at the tape once again. What if she'd given it to Phillip, thinking to help his depression and instead furnished the metaphorical bullet that ended his life?

"Please, God, not this," Emile whispered, and then fell down on his bed, prostrate under the weight of his guilt and despair.

It was ten minutes after one in the morning when Dan came out of his room on the run. Sully heard him and rolled out of bed. Something was going down. He just didn't know what. He grabbed a pair of gym shorts and started down the hall. He found Dan in the kitchen, making himself a snack.

"What's wrong?" Sully said, rubbing sleep out of his eyes.

"Sorry, did my phone wake you?"

"No, you did, when you lumbered down the hall like a cross-eyed moose."

Dan grinned. "I'm celebrating," he said.

"You drank the last glass of champagne."

"Bologna's fine," he said, as he smeared mayonnaise on some bread.

"Talk to me," Sully said. "What's worth bologna in the middle of the night?"

"Phone records, but not from Karnoff's house. From a cell phone registered in his name. He's not as smart as he thought."

Sully gawked. "Are you saying they match up?"

"Every damned one of them, including a call to

Ginny's number at her apartment. Probably one of those hang-ups on her answering machine."

Sully dropped into the nearest chair.

"I can't believe it."

"Neither could I, but the records don't lie. We've got enough to get a search warrant. I'm going to enjoy taking Karnoff's world apart."

"Did you make me one?"

They turned. Ginny was standing in the door wearing nothing more than Sully's T-shirt and a smile.

"Didn't mean to wake you," Sully said, and pulled her down onto his lap. "But since you're up, you can hear the good news. We got lucky, honey. Karnoff's cell phone records match calls to every one of the numbers connected to the dead women."

"Oh my God! I can't believe he would be that stupid."

"Maybe he's not in touch with the real world," Dan said. "He's what I would call a nerd, even if he is a genius. Maybe his progress with digital technology isn't up to par with his healing techniques? Who knows? Anyway, I'll be leaving in a couple of hours and will be in Connecticut first thing in the morning. I want to serve this search warrant personally."

"Let me go with you."

Sully tightened his hold on her. "No way."

"How can he hurt me?" she asked. "There will be officers all over the place, right? And if he's got a shred of humanity left in him, maybe he'll remove the curse he left in my brain before they hang him from the nearest tree.''

''I don't think it's a good idea,'' Dan said. ''Maybe later I can work out a visit to him.''

''I don't want to see the man after he's in prison. His only bargaining chip for leniency might be doing this good deed for the victim who got away.''

Both Sully and Dan knew she was on to something with the mention of bargaining power. But neither wanted to be the one who okayed something that might blow up in their faces.

Frustrated, she made Sully look at her. ''Do you want the mother of your children to take a flying leap off some bridge one day because the wrong song came on the radio?''

The color bled from his face. ''You play hardball all the way, don't you, babe?''

''It's my life, Sully. Allow me the dignity of living it.''

Within the hour, they were packed and gone.

18

The FBI helicopter landed outside of Bainbridge, Connecticut, just after 10:00 a.m., having made a stop in D.C. beforehand. Their plans had been delayed after learning what had happened within the Karnoff household, but only slightly. Dan had been warned by his surveillance team that the Karnoff home was in turmoil, that a cleaning crew had been on the scene since daybreak, and that Karnoff himself had left for the hospital, ostensibly to retrieve his wife, sometime after 9:00 a.m, so there was no one home to receive the search warrant.

After the anticipation of facing down the man who'd wreaked such havoc on so many lives, it was an anticlimax for Ginny. Now they sat in a van across the street, waiting for the man to return. Ginny couldn't help but think about the woman who was coming home from the hospital. She'd just lost her son, and now she was going to lose her husband, as well.

Sully and Dan were head to head in the front seat of the van, quietly discussing the pros and cons of the impending search, while the Chee brothers sat in silence behind Ginny, waiting patiently for events to unfold. She leaned back in her seat and then closed her eyes, suddenly weary all the way to her soul. Two months ago she'd been going through her life without a care in the world, and now, to be in this place, about to confront a killer, was almost more than she could handle. She wanted this to be over.

When she sighed, Sully turned around and looked at her.

"Are you okay? You can still back out of this confrontation thing."

She shook her head.

"All right, but it's your call," he said.

"I know."

He winked at her. She smiled, and then another thought occurred to her.

"Sully?"

"Yeah, honey?"

"It's very sad about their son killing himself, isn't it?"

"From where I sit, it's pretty damned ironic. Karnoff causes six innocent women to commit suicide, and then his son offs himself, too. I hope it haunts him for the rest of his natural life."

"I was thinking more about the mother's burden," she said.

For a few moments the interior of the van was completely silent. Then Sully nodded and turned around to face the street.

Franklin Chee leaned forward. "It is the way of the world," Franklin said. "The mother's burden is always heaviest. From the day she conceives, until the day she is laid in the ground, her love for her children will be her greatest joy and her deepest sorrow."

"That's sad," Ginny said.

"Yes, but you have to face life to enjoy it."

Ginny sat, absorbing the wisdom of those simple words.

"Thank you, Franklin."

He touched her shoulder once, in a gesture of understanding.

"You're welcome."

There was a long moment of silence, and then Franklin added one last thought.

"Anyone want to hear Webster do his imitation of John Wayne?"

Dan burst into laughter, while Sully turned and grinned. Ginny hugged the camaraderie of the group to her heart and knew that when this was over, she would miss them very much.

Lucy Karnoff was still picking at fabric, this time at the fabric of her dress. It was one of Emile's favorites, and he'd thought when he brought it for her to wear home that she would fall back into her role as the dutiful wife. But Lucy's sanity had slipped a little too far out of sync to be fixed by one lilac-colored dress.

"We're almost home," Emile said, and covered her hand with his own so that she would stop pulling at the threads of her skirt.

"...under the bed," she muttered.

"Not anymore, dear," he said softly. "Not anymore."

For a moment a flash of the old Lucy returned as she turned to look at him.

"Not anymore?"

He smiled. "No. Not anymore."

"Not anymore...not anymore...not anymore..."

He sighed. One hurdle had fallen, only for him to find he was approaching another.

"Here we are, sir," the cabdriver said, and pulled up to the front of the house. Then he jumped out and ran around the cab to help the old man with his wife. When Emile handed him a twenty, he pocketed it with a smile. "Thank you, sir, and good health to your wife."

"Yes, thank you," Emile said, as he gathered up her small bag of toiletries and took hold of Lucy's hand. "Come along, dear. Let's get you inside, out of the heat."

"Out of the heat...out of the heat..."

He had the key in the door when he heard the sound of approaching vehicles. Thinking it would be the press, he was anxious to get Lucy inside and away

from the cameras. He was all the way into the entryway and turning to close the door when he realized it
wasn't reporters after all.

"Emile Peter Karnoff?"

He frowned. It was unusual to hear his full name
from the lips of a man he'd never seen.

"Yes?"

"I'm Agent Dan Howard of the Federal Bureau of
Investigation. We have a warrant to search your
house."

The warrant was in his hand, and he was pushed
aside before he had a chance to speak.

"Gentlemen! I must argue this intrusion into my
home at such a tragic time. Why could you possibly
have need to search my house? My son's death was
ruled a suicide. Surely you don't suspect foul play?"

Dan wasn't paying any attention. "Agent Chee,
you and your brother begin upstairs. You know what
we're looking for." He turned to the other agents
who'd been on surveillance watch and sent them into
another wing of the house.

In the midst of the turmoil, something clicked inside Lucy's mind. Company was here. She had duties
to perform. Her thin, wavering voice pierced the
chaos, momentarily stopping everyone where they
stood.

"Emile! Dear! You didn't tell me we were going
to have company." She began waving a hand toward
the library, as if directing traffic. "Everyone, please

adjourn to my husband's study. I'll bring refreshments in a few minutes. You will love my cranberry nut bread. It's one of Emile's favorites.''

Sully couldn't look at Ginny. He knew what she would be thinking. She'd already voiced her concerns regarding this pitiful woman, and it would seem that she'd been right.

"Sir, you need to get your wife and make sure she's somewhere out of the way," Sully said.

"But I must challenge this disgraceful behavior!" Emile cried. "Why are you here? What on earth could we have done to warrant such treatment from the government? Do you know who I am?"

Sully turned then, for the first time staring fully into the old man's face.

"Yeah, we know who you are," he said softly. "You're the man who sent six young women to their deaths."

Emile blanched, put a hand to his chest and staggered backward in disbelief. Oddly enough, it was Lucy who led him to a nearby chair in the entryway.

"Come, dear. You look a bit pale. Why don't you sit down while I go make some tea for our guests?"

Ginny was still in the background, an observer to the unfolding chaos, but when Karnoff unintentionally separated himself from the rest by sitting down, she moved through the doorway, quietly closing the door behind her.

Agents had dispersed to all points of the house,

while Dan and Sully stayed nearby in the hall. It was only a matter of time before they arrested the old man, but they wanted the search under their belts before it happened. Even if they turned up nothing more in the way of evidence from this location, they were convinced that the phone records and Ginny's testimony were condemnation enough to put him away for the rest of his life.

Emile's heart was hammering as if it would burst. He put the flat of his hand against the sound and made himself relax. Closing his eyes, he practiced a mental relaxation technique, focusing his skills on himself.

"Is that the way you did it?"

Emile started at the sound of the voice, and then looked up.

"I'm sorry. Were you speaking to me?" he asked, too sick to be concerned with the fact that Lucy was flitting all over the hall, pretending to pour tea and serve cake.

Ginny stared long and hard into his eyes, her anger overriding any lingering fear. Her voice was low, her behavior calm, but her sense of loathing for this man simmered hot below the surface.

"Why did you do it?"

He took a handkerchief from his jacket pocket and began mopping his face.

"I'm sorry, miss, but you'll have to be more specific. I don't know what you're talking about."

His voice made her weak, but her hate kept her

focused. She wanted him flushed from her senses like the waste that he was.

"We weren't hurting you," she muttered, thinking of a little boy who would grow up without a mother, and of Georgia, who'd had so much to give the world. "You had your way with us when we were children, but that wasn't enough, was it? You needed to destroy the evidence. Were you afraid we'd remember? Was that it?"

"Miss, I don't know what you're talking about!" Emile shouted, then covered his face with his hands. "This is a nightmare!" he cried. "A nightmare with no end! God, please let me wake up!"

Sully spun around and bolted toward the end of the hall. He hadn't seen Ginny come inside, but it was obvious from Karnoff's behavior that she'd confronted him. He grabbed her by the arm, intending to pull her out of harm's way, but she yanked free, her attention completely focused on the old man in the chair.

"Don't," she muttered. "I have to do this."

Lucy followed the sound of her husband's voice and then, like a child, scooted herself into his lap and put her arm behind his neck as she spoke.

"This is my husband," she said. "He's a very important man, you know."

Emile tried to pull her arm from around his neck, but she was clinging to him like a kitten with its claws caught in the drapes.

"I miss him dreadfully when he's gone," she continued, "but I know his work is important to the world. It's my duty to keep his home trouble-free so that he can have a pleasing environment in which to work."

"Yes, ma'am," Sully said, and put his arms on Ginny's shoulders, gently pulling her back against the wall of his chest.

"I can see that you're good at your job."

Lucy beamed as she patted Emile's cheek. "So much to do. So many cobwebs to sweep out. After all these years, so many cobwebs."

"Yes, ma'am. You have a very clean house," Sully said.

Emile laid his forehead against Lucy's breast and closed his eyes, struggling between the urge to laugh and the urge to follow her into madness. This mannerly conversation was ludicrous, considering what was going on beneath the roof of his own home.

"I have a cleaning lady, you know," Lucy said. "But I tend to the important things. She couldn't possibly be trusted to clean out my husband's files. I do that on my own. No one touches my husband's files except me...and him, of course." She giggled.

"Lucy, dear, they don't want to know about the dust in our house," Emile said, wishing to God she would hush.

"Oh, it isn't the dust that's important. I let the cleaning lady tend to the dust. I clean the cobwebs."

Emile looked up at Sully, silently begging for something he couldn't voice. Then he sighed. If this was happening, he needed to know why.

"I know you people think you have a reason for doing this, but as God is my witness, I don't understand. By what right are you here?"

Dan Howard walked up just as the question was asked. He pointed to the paper in Emile Karnoff's pocket.

"That search warrant explains it all, sir. We're here because your phone records show you had contact with every one of our victims on the day of their deaths, except for Sister Mary Teresa at the Sacred Heart Convent. We haven't proved exactly how you contacted her yet, but we know that you're responsible."

Karnoff shook his head. "I'm sorry, but I don't know—"

"Cobwebs," Lucy cried, and clapped her hands. "Emile, you must see the convent some time. The stained glass windows are so very beautiful. All the colors shine true in the sunlight, like the flowers in my garden."

Sully was the first to grasp the relevance of what she'd just said. He lowered his voice, making it seem as if he and Lucy Karnoff were in the room on their own.

"You've been to the convent, have you?"

"Oh yes," Lucy said. "And not too long ago. It

wasn't a long trip, either. About an hour and a half by train. I was home in time to fix dinner for Phillip.'' Her face crumpled for just a moment as she looked at Sully's face. "My son is dead, you know. He bled all over my floor. I tried to fix his head, but I used the wrong tape.'' Her hands began to flutter as her eyes welled with tears. "I need to clean up the blood. We can't eat in the dining room until I clean up the blood.''

As she spoke, both Sully and Dan thought the same thing as they looked at each other. A tape? Had she done something to her own son, as well as the women?

Emile could tell by their expressions that something momentous had happened, but he was so focused on keeping Lucy from dissolving into one of her fits that he didn't bother to ask.

"The floor is clean, my dear. I had the cleaning service over just this morning. Everything is fine. It's all put back just the way you like it.''

She patted Emile's leg, the smile on her face as out of place at the moment as the tears still drying on her cheeks.

"It's clean,'' she announced. "I need to get tea.''

"Wait,'' Dan said. Then he added, "Please. Mrs. Karnoff, can I ask you a question?''

"Why yes, although I'm sure I have nothing important to say. My husband is the star in this family, aren't you, dear?''

Dan persisted, trying to make sense of it all in the midst of her insanity.

"Mrs. Karnoff, do you know who Emily Jackson is?"

Lucy nodded. "Cobwebs."

Sully grunted. *Sweet Jesus.* It was her!

Ginny started to cry, quietly and brokenly. When Sully opened his arms, she turned her face against his chest and let it all go.

Dan persisted. "What about Josephine Henley?"

"Cobwebs."

"And Lynn Goldberg and Frances Waverly and Allison Turner?"

At that point Emile had had enough. "Stop this!" he shouted. "My wife is not saying another word to you until you tell me what's going on."

Lucy frowned. "It's not nice to shout at our guests," she said. "They're only asking about the cobwebs. I took care of them for you. You're an important man. Can't have any cobwebs in our closets. I tried to fix Phillip, too, but I think I used the wrong tape."

Emile looked to Dan for understanding.

"Please. Sir. At the least, I'm owed an explanation."

"Over the past few months, calls have been made from a cell phone registered in your name to six..." He looked at Ginny, then amended the number. "No...seven phone numbers in different parts of the country. Directly after receiving the call, the six women did something completely out of character that resulted in their immediate deaths.''

''Everything's over. Finished. Done. Face your greatest fear, then open your arms and go to God,'' Lucy chirped and then clapped her hands. ''Cobwebs all gone.''

''God. Oh my God,'' Sully whispered. ''Georgia's greatest fear was water. She couldn't swim. The priest said that right before she jumped, she opened her arms, looked up at the sky and smiled.''

Ginny turned, staring at the old woman and unable to correlate the innocence on her face with the horror she had done.

''The families I talked to before I left St. Louis told me that witnesses to the deaths said it looked as if the women were trying to fly,'' Ginny said.

Lucy's recitation had stunned them all, including Emile. Suddenly he was beginning to realize that she'd done something wrong, but he didn't know what, or how.

''Please?'' he begged.

''Dr. Karnoff, do you recognize me?'' Ginny asked. He shook his head. ''No. Should I?''

''My name is Virginia Shapiro.''

A dark scowl spread across Lucy's face. ''Couldn't find that cobweb.''

''And thank the Lord and Georgia for that,'' Sully muttered.

Emile was still staring at Ginny. Finally he shook his head. "No, I'm sorry."

"Do you remember Montgomery Academy? Upstate New York. 1979?"

"Why yes! Of course!"

His answer startled everyone, including Ginny. She'd expected reticence, lies, even denial, but not this.

"You do?"

"Certainly. It was the first place where I began testing my theories on actual people." Then he looked at Ginny again, and as he did, they could see recognition dawn. "Oh my! You're the little girl with asthma."

"No, you're wrong," Ginny said. "I haven't had asthma since I was a—"

Suddenly she got it. He smiled.

"The elation of watching that panic disappear from your eyes, of knowing that you had learned how to stop it before it began to constrict your breathing...ah, you can't know the joy I felt."

Ginny was trying to absorb the fact that the man she'd thought a monster had cured her of a terrible disease when Sully changed the focus of the conversation.

"Do you remember Edward Fontaine?" Sully asked.

"It costs four-hundred-and-seventy-five dollars to fly to Florida," Lucy chirped.

Dan stared at the woman in disbelief. Of course she

was out of her mind. They would never get a convic-
tion, because she was unable to stand trial. She would
spend the rest of her life in a hospital for the criminally insane, and as he thought it, he knew that, in
her fragile condition, she wouldn't last a month. But
as he remembered the people who'd died at her hands,
he decided it might just be thirty days longer than she
deserved.

Unaware of the complete background of Lucy's
deeds, Emile answered Sully's question without concern or guile.

"Of course I remember Fontaine. He was a remarkable man, completely devoted to the children and
their education. That's why he was so amenable to
allowing me into the school. He even dealt with all
the formalities of obtaining permission from the families. I imagine I still have the signed permission
forms somewhere in my file. I'm meticulous about
documenting." Then he looked at Ginny again. "It's
hard to realize how many years have passed. Just look
at you now. A lovely and mature young woman, and
you were such a quiet, sickly child. I wonder if those
other children have fared as well as you? Do you
know?"

"Dr. Karnoff, you've been missing the point,"
Sully said. "Those were the names of the women that
Agent Howard read off...and they're dead. But for
the grace of God and one valiant little nun, Ginny
would be, too."

A sick feeling began to unravel within Emile's belly. Suddenly the accusations and Lucy's odd, nonsensical comments began to tie themselves into neat little knots. He was afraid to ask, and yet he did, knowing it would answer the rest of his questions as to why they were here.

"How?"

"They each received a phone call, at which time they heard a tape of some chimes, prefaced by some thunder in the background. I don't know exactly what they were told, but we know that directly afterward, they committed suicide."

Lucy frowned. "I already told you. Everything's over. Finished. Done. Face your greatest fear and go to God."

Emile jumped up from the chair, in the process almost dumping Lucy on the floor.

"Lucy! What did you do?"

She frowned and brushed her hands together, as if brushing off some dirt.

"I told you. They were cobwebs. I got rid of the cobwebs." Then her face momentarily crumpled. "It didn't work on Phillip. I was trying to fix him, but I think I used the wrong tape."

Emile thought of the tape recorder he'd found under Phillip's bed and knew that somewhere in her meddling, she'd exacerbated whatever had been wrong with their son to the point that he'd slipped over the edge. As he stared at her, it occurred to him that he didn't know—maybe had never known—the woman who was his wife. His voice was shaking as he confronted her.

"You killed those women?"

"They killed themselves," she said matter-of-factly. "You left the button. I pushed it."

"But why?"

Her expression shifted, and for a moment it was like talking to the old Lucy, before everything had gone bad.

"Because the principal forged the permission slips and I knew it. We'd borrowed all that money on our house so you could pay him to let you into his school, and if it all fell through, we would have given him the money for nothing." She seemed angry, as if he had no right to question her. Then she added, "All those years went by and it didn't matter, but then you won the prize, didn't you, dear? After that, I was afraid someone would remember."

Emile made it to the powder room just in time to throw up.

Outside in the hallway, Lucy began running in little circles.

"Emile's ill. Where's the aspirin?"

Dan got on his two-way, calling off all the agents who were still searching the house.

"Come on down," he said. "Bring whatever you've got, although I doubt we're going to need it."

Then he made another call. Lucy Karnoff was going to jail, but not by the regular route.

"It's over," Dan said.

"Not quite," Sully said.

They turned, looking at Emile, who had emerged pale and shaken, mopping his face with a handkerchief.

"Where is my wife?" he asked.

Sully touched his arm. "They're looking after her, sir. I believe she's searching for aspirin."

"What's going to happen to her?" Emile asked.

"She's going to be arrested. She will be evaluated by a panel of psychologists and then probably committed to a hospital for the criminally insane," Dan answered.

"My God!" Emile cried. "I've been in those places. She won't last. She's too fragile. Please, you must have mercy."

"Sir, if we asked the families of those women she killed, how much mercy do you think they would recommend?"

Emile stood silent beneath the condemnation of his wife's actions until he could no longer bear it.

"Dear God...I would give back everything if this would all go away."

"It's too late to give anything back," Sully said, and then took Ginny by the hand. "But it's not too late to take away what you left in Ginny's brain."

Ginny held her breath, afraid to hope. And then the old man sighed and held out his hand.

"If it had not been for the fire, it would have already been done. Come, child, it's time to let go of the past."

She hesitated.

"I'll be there with you," Sully said.

She sighed and then let the old man lead her away, and in her mind, she saw herself at Montgomery Academy, walking hand in hand with Georgia toward the last door on the left.

Epilogue

The Realtor's For Sale sign at the Karnoff residence had been up for months. So far, few lookers had availed themselves of the opportunity for a great buy. It would take time for the gossip and memories of the tragedy that had occurred inside to fade.

Karnoff himself had been besieged by the press to the point that he'd had to get a restraining order preventing anyone from setting foot on his property, and it had not been enough. The neighbors felt sorry for him, but they still whispered, trading gossip and lies. And then one day he was gone. No one had seen a moving van come. No one had seen him leave. An accumulation of newspapers had gathered on the lawn.

The day the For Sale sign went up on the property, it became apparent he was not coming back. In the course of everyday living, his tragedy became old news, and only now and then did someone chance a guess as to where he had gone.

Lucy Karnoff had died in jail on the tenth day of her incarceration, succumbing to a heart attack on the floor of her cell. When Emile buried her beside their son, he laid more than his wife to rest that day. It was his last tie to a burden that had become too great to bear.

"What do you think about this one?" Sully asked, watching the play of emotions on Ginny's face as they walked about the rooms of the vacant D.C. apartment. Outside, the late morning sky was rapidly darkening, but they were so focused on finding a new home before the wedding that they didn't notice.

"It has lots of windows, I like that," she said. "But is it large enough? I don't want to move in after we're married only to discover that we need more room. Besides that, I'm not sure how I feel about raising a baby in an apartment. I had a yard to play in when I was a child."

The mention of marriage and babies made Sully's silly grin appear. He'd been having trouble with it for months, and the closer they came to their wedding day, the sillier it got.

"I still vote for the house in Virginia," Sully said. "The commute is nothing compared to the privacy and space we would have."

Ginny frowned. "I liked it best, too, but I still don't think it's fair for you to have to spend so much time on the road."

He laughed. "Honey, think about what I do for a living. I'm always on the road."

She grinned. "Yes, I guess."

"Then it's settled," he said, and tugged on her coat until she relented and gave him a hug.

"Are you cold?" he asked. "This is unseasonably warm for November, but still, there's a bite to the air."

"I'm fine," Ginny said.

"Then let's go. I know a really great place for chili."

"Do they have cornbread, too?" she asked.

"Oh yeah, big, thick, yellow slabs of the stuff."

"I'm sold," she said, and they walked arm in arm toward the elevator. "Do we have to stop back by the manager's office?"

"No. He said to drop the key in his mailbox on the way out."

She nodded, her mind already moving to the two-story, Cape-Cod-style cottage they'd looked at last week. Sully was right. Virginia wasn't far at all, and she could plant flowers in the yards and—

As they exited the elevator, her thoughts were interrupted by a loud roll of thunder. Sully dropped the apartment key in the manager's mailbox and then turned up the collar of his coat as they started out the door. He couldn't help but watch Ginny's face for lingering signs of Emile Karnoff's handiwork, but he saw nothing to give him cause for concern.

As they began the half-block trek to where he had parked, the first drops of rain began to fall. Ginny laughed and turned her face up to the sky, catching a drop on the end of her tongue.

"Needs salt," she said. "And maybe a little spice."

"You and your cooking expertise," Sully laughed, and then took her by the hand and started running to the car.

They got inside just as the sky unloaded.

"Let me get the heater warmed up before we take off," he said. "I don't want you getting chilled."

"The cornbread and chili will warm me up just fine. All of a sudden I'm starving. Let's go."

Sully's grin was still in place as he pulled out into traffic. A few blocks later they passed a newsstand, and Ginny's gaze instinctively scanned what she could see of the selection through the downpour.

"Do you miss the job?" Sully asked.

She shrugged. "Sometimes." And then she grinned. "I know Harry Redford was sorry to see me go. Especially after the piece I turned in. We scooped the entire nation. It was the biggest coup of his life, and he will love me forever because of it," she said.

"Yeah, but he won't love you as much as I do," Sully said. "As for resuming your career as a journalist, you could pretty much pick any paper around here and they'd hire you on the spot."

"I know."

"I think I hear a 'but' in there. Am I right?"

She nodded. "If you don't mind, I think I'd rather

stay home for a while after we're married. I really want to work on that cooking thing a little more.''

''You're getting better,'' Sully said. ''The spaghetti last night was really good.''

She rolled her eyes. ''Sully, it was out of a can.''

He grinned. ''I know.''

She hit him lightly on the arm and then settled back, comfortable with the idea that for now, this big, wonderful man beside her wanted to be in charge and she wanted to let him.

''I want to have babies right away,'' she said.

''I'm ready, willing and able to do my part,'' he said, eliciting a chuckle from her.

Although they'd talked about it a lot between them, it was the first time Sully had heard her say anything that specific. He pulled to a stop at an intersection and then glanced at her. He thought he could see tears in her eyes. He reached over and took her by the hand, giving it a gentle tug.

''Ginny?''

She sighed.

''If we have a girl, I want to name her—''

''Georgia,'' Sully said, finishing her sentence for her.

Her eyes widened with surprise. ''How did you know that?''

The light turned green and they moved on. It was a moment before Sully answered.

"Sully," Ginny persisted. "I asked you a question."

"Because you told me last night in your sleep."

"I didn't."

"Actually, honey, you did. You woke me up, talking, and at first I thought you were talking to me. Then I realized you were just talking in your sleep. You said, 'When we have a baby, I'll name her after you.' I figured you were dreaming about Georgia."

The tears that had been hovering finally spilled as Ginny turned and stared out the window, looking past the rain into the city beyond.

"I dream about her a lot," she said. "Sometimes she's so real I think I could reach out and touch her."

"Maybe it's just Georgia's way of telling you she's okay."

Ginny looked at him through a blur. "Do you really believe that?"

Although the urge to cry with her was strong within him, he managed to grin instead.

"I don't just believe it, I know it. Besides, if we name our daughter after a nun, just think of the guardian angels she's going to have."

Ginny laughed through her tears.

"Here," Sully said, handing her his handkerchief. "Wipe and blow. We're almost at the restaurant."

Ginny did as she'd been told, then stuffed the handkerchief in her coat pocket. As she watched the wipers swiping back and forth across the windshield, it occurred to her that sometimes people needed to cry, just like the earth needed rain. Both were renewing affirmations that life still went on.

A half a world away, on a small dirt road in the countryside of Ireland, an old man rode his bicycle along the path with nothing more on his mind than getting back to his cottage and making himself a cup of tea. He was in need of a haircut; the white, wispy strands lay upon the collar of his coat like feathers, fluttering lightly in the breeze as he pedaled along. His corduroy pants were a soft dove gray; his shoes were worn at the heels and scuffed at the toes, evidence of how many miles he'd walked through the boulder-strewn hills.

His eyes were constantly on the land, looking with the curiosity of a child at all that lay before him. As he came around a corner, he saw two children in the road ahead. One, a little girl of no more than six or seven, was sitting on the ground weeping, while a larger boy, most likely her brother, was kneeling at her side. A small red wagon was lying in the dirt.

He pedaled up to them and then parked his bike.

"What have we here?" he said gently, as he got out his handkerchief and knelt at the little girl's feet.

"She fell out of the wagon, she did," the boy said, the lilt of the Celt deep in his voice.

"It's bleedin', it is," the little girl said, and then sniffled again on a sob.

"Yes, I can see that," he said, and handed the boy his handkerchief. "You can tie this around her knee until you get home."

"Yes, sir, thank you, sir," the little boy said, and proceeded to make a clumsy bandage around his little sister's knee.

The old man rocked back on his heels and started to stand, then looked at the tear tracks on her cheek and stopped.

He hesitated but a moment, and then touched the little girl's cheek.

"Would you like for me to show you a way to take away the pain?"

She snuffled and then looked to her brother. He nodded an okay.

"Yes, please," she said. "'Tis a hurtin' somethin' fierce."

"I know…but you'll have to close your eyes."

As she did, he touched the top of her head, leaving the pressure of his hand light but firm so she could feel, as well as hear, his presence.

And then it began.

"Listen to the sound of my voice…."